Countdown to Justice

CORDELL PARVIN

ISBN 978-1-7372234-0-5 (paperback)
ISBN 978-1-7372234-1-2 (eBook)

Printed in the United States of America

CHAPTER 1

Gabriela Sanchez

It's never easy to represent a lawyer in a criminal investigation. It is especially difficult when the lawyer doesn't listen to advice, keeps secrets, and is notorious for negotiating a $2 billion contract described by media as the worst deal in the state's history.

On the Friday before Christmas, I walked into George Gonzalez Elementary School to eat lunch and mentor Angela Dupree, a fourth grade student I had mentored since the beginning of the school year. It was Angela's last day of class before the holiday break, and the school had invited parents to join their children for lunch and then take them home. Angela's parents couldn't leave work, so I planned to take Angela back to the office with me and then drive Angela home.

One of my partners once had asked why I wasted my time mentoring students. I told him it was my way of keeping a young girl's dream alive. Growing up in the Rio Grande Valley, I had watched poor Mexican-American boys and girls quit dreaming about their future by the time they were in middle school.

I grew up as one of the most fortunate kids. My father was a lawyer, and my mother was a teacher. They pushed me to excel in school and even though many of my father's clients could not afford to pay him, being in the middle-class made us among the most affluent in the Valley.

Several of my friends worked in the fields picking crops with their parents and missed school while they were picking crops. The white students in our school made fun of my friends who struggled to speak English. I vowed that when I became successful, I would never forget the Mexican-American children and I would help them make it in America.

When I checked in at the elementary school's front office, my name tag with the photo from my driver's license was waiting for me. I sat on a bench across from the main office and watched lines of students walking by on their way to the cafeteria. As they passed in single file, I spotted Angela, who ran over and gave me a hug.

We walked together to the cafeteria and sat one of the tables on the stage designated for children and their parents or their mentors. Most mentor days I stopped at Chick-Fil-A, Angela's favorite restaurant and picked up meals for the two of us. But today the school served the holiday meal, so we stood in line for the sliced turkey, dressing, and mashed potatoes.

At most of our lunch meals, I started the conversation and asked questions to get Angela to share what was on her mind.

"What are your plans for your holiday break?"

Angela shrugged her shoulders.

"Will anyone come to visit?"

She shrugged her shoulders again and shook her head. "I don't think so."

I doubted Angela's parents had made any plans, so her silence was no surprise. Finally, Angela pointed at my iPad. Back during the second week of mentoring, I had clicked on: 'Are You Smarter than a 5th Grader?' on my iPad, and Angela had wanted to play each week. This day she was all smiles as she correctly answered the least difficult Math and Geography questions.

At 12:30, the teachers stood and asked the children to clean up their tables. Angela and I cleaned our table, then exited the cafeteria and went to my car, where I handed Angela a box wrapped in Christmas tree wrapping paper. Inside the box was a handwritten note: 'Angela, I love you and I believe in you because you try hard to learn in school. I am blessed to be your mentor and watch you grow each day.'

"Now, I want you to save this until Christmas morning. Can you do that?"

I knew my gifts would be among the few Angela would open on Christmas morning.

She smiled and looked up at me with those beautiful brown eyes sparkling. "Yes, Ms. Sanchez. Thank you." She grabbed me by the waist and dropped the packages. I reached out to catch it and missed.

Angela's face turned red and I saw tears on her cheeks.

"Angela, it's okay. Nothing broke."

I started my car. Before I could back out of my parking space, my telephone started vibrating. I saw a text message from Lucia.

"Allen O'Grady, Roberson Grant partner wants u 2 represent 1 of their lawyers. Call him."

I texted back: "Call O'Grady. Tell him I will call him in 20 minutes."

When we arrived at my office, I took Angela to Lucia's desk.

"Please look after Angela while I return Allen O'Grady's call.

Angela smiled when Lucia brought out the Uno cards and started dealing.

I stepped into my office, closed the door and called Allen O'Grady, and he explained that Roberson Grant had received a grand jury subpoena to produce client files and the Assistant U. S. Attorney had told him that one of the firm's lawyers would be served a subpoena to testify before the grand jury on January 2nd.

I asked the name of the lawyer and he told me her name was Gina Rossi. When I asked what he could tell me about her, he hesitated. Then he told me Gina was the daughter of the famed Dallas trial lawyer, Leo Baretti.

I put Gina Rossi in Google and did a search. Her law firm bio came up first. I clicked and saw a full-length photo of an olive-skinned, brown eyed blond woman. She looked like Jessica Alba with toned muscles.

"She'll remind you of Claire Underwood," O'Grady said.

"Claire Underwood?"

"Yes, Claire Underwood. You must not have watched House of Cards."

"I don't have time to watch television."

"Well, I recommend you read all you can about the Claire Underwood character in House of Cards, because that's what you will be dealing with when you represent Gina Rossi.

O'Grady spent the next ten minutes telling me how I would have a difficult time representing Gina Rossi. He concluded with something for me to remember, "Gina Rossi's soft-spoken and elegant, but don't let that fool you. She'd cut your heart out to advance her agenda, just like Claire Underwood."

I finally asked, "Allen, are you trying to convince me not to represent her?"

"No, I'm giving you the heads up that Gina Rossi is a handful. She uses people and she'll use you."

"What positive thing can you say about her?"

"What she lacks in brilliance as a lawyer, Gina has overcome with her energy, self- confidence, and hard work. She is also the most tenacious and ambitious lawyer you will ever meet."

I smiled and replied, thinking that it is ok for male lawyers to be determined and ambitious, but if a female lawyer has those traits, she's narcissistic.

"Gina used her hard work and determination to get where she is," added O'Grady. "But she also used her good looks. Gina is a beautiful blond after her mother and has her father's olive skin. She's a fitness fanatic. She turns heads when she walks into a room."

I wanted to get an idea of what I would be doing so I asked Green to tell me about the grand jury subpoena. He told me the Special Counsel's office is investigating former Governor Harrington for accepting a bribe from Gina's client, Randall Burke, in return for awarding his company the $2 billion Cross-Town Tollway contract. Green advised me that Gina will refuse to testify.

I wanted to know why, so I asked. Green's reply didn't surprise me.

"Out of loyalty to her client, Randall Burke. She is loyal to her friends, and Randall Burke is her number one client and friend. She will have his back, no matter what the cost to our firm."

"Does she know something damaging to her client and Harrington?"

"She might. I don't know. Maybe you can find out."

I thought for a moment and wasn't sure I wanted to represent Gina. "Allen, I've never represented a woman and I've already had a lifetime supply of representing difficult clients. I'm not sure I want to be in the media spotlight again."

"You won't be back in the spotlight. Gina is simply a witness in a grand jury investigation. I expect your work to be finished on January 2nd. We'll make it worth your while for two weeks of work."

I spent that evening reading every article written about Claire Underwood. She was an interesting character to say the least, but it was hard to picture anyone in real life being like her. I knew better, but I decided to represent Gina Rossi anyway.

CHAPTER 2

Gina Rossi

It's never a good thing when the FBI comes calling on a lawyer about a matter involving her client. It almost always means her client is in trouble, and if so, she may lose her client. It sometimes means the lawyer is also in trouble. In which case, she may lose her client and her career.

I began my run that morning thinking about the good and bad I expected over the Christmas holidays. I looked forward to time with Tony and our son, Mateo, and looked forward to coffee and breakfast on Christmas Day with my father and my brother's family. But I was already dreading our visit to Tony's parents in League City on Christmas afternoon and evening.

It was freezing cold that morning when I was running outside. I held my head high to breathe the fresh air, and I could feel the tingle of cold, icy air rushing in and out of my lungs, and burning on my bottom, thighs, and calves-despite a merino wool running shirt, wind proof running jacket, running tights and wool socks. I turned on my afterburners as I started the last mile of my early morning run in my far north Dallas neighborhood.

I had never been a natural athlete like my mother and my brother. I had seized every opportunity to study the scrapbook Grandma Mary had kept with news articles about my mother, wanting to know everything about her. Carol Ashworth starred both in the classroom and on the tennis courts. I wanted to follow in her footsteps.

My brother, Sam, had inherited my mother's natural ability. He was a top tennis star from the time he was eight years old. He finished first in his high school class and then earned both a finance degree and an MBA from Harvard. He started as an investment banker in New York and was one of the many investment bankers who were under investigation after the 2008 crash. An Assistant U. S. Attorney had interviewed Sam in 2012, but nothing came of the investigation. Within months, Sam, his wife Leah, and their two perfectly behaved children, Samuel, Jr., and Daniele, had moved back to Dallas to get away from Wall Street.

I couldn't match my mom's or Sam's natural talent. I made up for it with sheer determination and grit. My father Leo kicked me in the behind whenever he thought I had not given my best and praised me when I exceeded his expectations.

Last year I trained for months before running my first marathon. Afterward, I posted a photo showing me crossing the finish line with the caption:

> *I didn't win today. In fact, I finished in the second half of the runners. But, I am not discouraged. I will win in the long run because I will work harder through the, blood, sweat and tears and I believe my passion will help me overcome my physical shortcomings. I will be the best I can be. No excuses! I will be better than I was yesterday. It's me vs. me.*

As I ran toward home that morning, I looked back. A teenaged newspaper delivery boy stood staring at me. I grinned. *It must be the running tights. Not bad for a 39-year old.*

An hour later, while backing my BMW out of my garage, my phone rang. It was Randy Burke, my one and only current client. I put my car in park and clicked to answer.

"Rossi, the FBI served me with a subpoena for all documents related to the Cross-Town Tollway contract, the Hill Country Estates partnership and any other documents related to my interactions with Austin Harrington."

"What?"

"You heard me! The Special Counsel's office is investigating whether I bribed Austin Harrington to win the $2 billion contract you negotiated. Heck, Austin has been my best friend since we were ten years old. I've given him lots of things over many years, but I never asked for or expected anything in return from Austin."

"And now he's on the President's list for the next Supreme Court appointment."

While we were talking, my phone vibrated. I put Burke on the speaker and saw a text from my assistant, Sandra:

"Gina, two FBI agents are in the lobby, and they told the receptionist they need to see you."

I typed: "Why?"

"Don't know. Could say you won't be at work today."

I thought about it and typed: "No, be there in 30."

"Randy, the FBI is in my building and wants to see me."

"You know why they want to see you," Burke replied. Don't say anything to them."

Forty-five minutes later, I exited the elevator on the 37th floor reception area.

"Ms. Rossi, these two gentlemen are here to see you."

The two FBI agents stood up and the tall one showed me a subpoena to testify before a federal grand jury on January 2, and bring our firm's files and other documents associated with the firm's work for Burke Construction Company on all the Texas State Department of Transportation, (TxDOT), and Dallas Toll road, design-build, public-private financed projects. TxDOT had awarded those contracts to Burke Construction without bidding, including the $2 billion Cross-Town Tollway project. The subpoena also demanded that I bring any documents, emails and text messages related, or pertaining to the Hill Country Estates partnership and my conversations or interactions with the former Texas Governor, Austin Harrington.

From 2006 to 2010 Austin Harrington was the chief justice of the Texas Supreme Court. In that role he had gained a reputation for being conservative and interpreting the Constitution as written.

In 2010, Harrington left the court and joined one of the largest law firms in Texas. At the time, the media and public assumed he would run for governor, and he did in 2014.

When I looked up, the shorter agent said: "Ms. Rossi, this is a subpoena to testify before the grand jury investigating bid rigging and bribery on Burke Construction Company's design-build and public-private financed projects. You are not a target of the investigation. We would prefer that you meet with us before your scheduled testimony and bring the subpoenaed documents with you. You wouldn't even need a lawyer to accompany you. You know what we want to learn from you. If you cooperate and tell us what we want to know, you would not need to testify."

"What is it you want to know?"

"You know what the investigation is about and what we want you to tell us. You somehow convinced former Governor Harrington to award a $2 billion contract to your client. We want to know what your client or you gave Governor Harrington to win the contract."

I wasn't surprised. Ever since Governor Rogers called the Cross-Town Tollway contract the worst deal in Texas history, and the media bought his story, I figured the FBI would someday show up at my office to serve me with a subpoena to testify before a grand jury. Right then and there, I started plotting how to get out of the testifying against my one and only client.

"The lawyer-client privilege covers everything you demanded. I can't disclose the information covered in your subpoena and I can't tell you anything."

"Ms. Rossi, you'll have to take that up with the judge. We'd prefer that you cooperate and tell us what we want to know."

"You can bet I will. Just because the press and current governor are criticizing the Cross-Town Tollway deal, that doesn't make it illegal."

"Ms. Rossi, we'll see you before your grand jury testimony to discuss the Cross-Town Tollway contract."

When they left, I went into a small conference room and called my father. He was one of the top trial lawyers in Texas and I hoped he would tell me what I needed to do to avoid testifying. When he didn't answer, I left a voicemail telling him I wanted to meet him for lunch on Saturday. Then I called Tony.

After I told him about Burke's subpoena and my subpoena, Tony said, "Ask your father. This is how the government begins these investigations. They start on the outside in the hope Burke will plead guilty to save his company and then they can go after Governor Harrington."

"Burke will never plead guilty."

"Now you know why they want you to testify. They think you either did something, or you know something that will help them get Harrington."

"I won't let them intimidate me. The lawyer-client privilege prohibits me from disclosing my advice and the work I did for Randy Burke and Burke Construction."

"Talk to your father about that. Are you still going to the firm's holiday party?"

"Yes, I promised I would go."

"Don't mention the subpoena to anyone and don't drink any alcohol. You've been sober for several months and you need to stay sober."

Don't tell me what to do. "All right, I won't mention the subpoena, but I can't promise anything about the drinking."

"Damn it, Gina. Don't drink alcohol. You know what will happen. You will embarrass yourself. When you've been drinking, you think you are the life of the party. Worse, you might talk about the investigation."

"Yes, I know, but I can't promise anything. I've had a tough day. How in the world can the government make me testify against my client?"

"We'll talk about that tomorrow morning."

"Tony, the FBI wants to meet with me before my scheduled testimony. The two agents told me in no uncertain terms that if I give them what they want, they won't bother me further and I won't have to testify. I know what they want, but there is no way I will give it to them."

"That's routine, but have you asked your father? He'll know for sure."

"I left a message telling him I want to meet him for lunch tomorrow."

No way will they force me to testify.

CHAPTER 3

―― ⚮ ――

Gina Rossi

I had been planning to attend the Roberson Grant firm's annual holiday party that night, and Tony had planned to attend the Dallas Legal Aid Holiday party. After the events of the day, I was in no holiday party mood, but I had promised David Coleman I would at least make an appearance. I changed into my black cocktail dress, put on my heels and went downstairs to meet my driver, Mario.

Five minutes later we arrived at the entrance to the swanky Royal Hotel in Uptown Dallas.

Mario opened my door and said, "Ms. Rossi, what time do you want to me to pick you up?"

I wasn't sure. I replied, "I plan to only make an appearance. Can I send you a text?"

"Yes, ma'am. I'll stay close by."

When I walked in the room standing tall in my heels, two of my male partners turned their heads. I was so focused on avoiding testifying against my client that I didn't even smile at them.

I had planned on taking Tony's advice and not drink any alcohol. I started the evening holding court with some of our younger women lawyers. They asked for some advice, and I told them to fake it until they make it. They were clearly paying close attention to my every word. So, I felt like I was being interviewed, especially after other young women stood near me and asked questions.

One young associate asked, "Do you have any regrets for not starting a family earlier in your career?"

"No," I replied. "Do you have any regrets for starting your family when you were a young associate?"

If looks would kill...

"How have you dealt with being a mother and a successful lawyer?"

Young women had asked me that question many times. I wasn't sure anyone would ever call me a good mother. I didn't care what anyone else thought.

"I'll never win the mother of the year award, but I strive to be the best all-around. It takes a team; and I am very fortunate. My husband, Tony, works at Legal Aid so he can spend more time with our son. We also have two nannies who are available when I have to travel. It's a team effort."

A red-headed lawyer named Andrea remarked that she didn't want to have nannies raising her children.

"I appreciate your honesty," I told her. "But I doubt that any of you have what it takes to become a partner in our law firm."

The blonde blinked, but, came right back at me. "Why do you say that? You don't even know us."

"I don't know you, but I bet that none of you will sacrifice what it takes for a woman to become a partner in our law firm. Most of you, maybe all of you, came to work here to earn a lot of money for a couple of years to pay off your student loans, and as soon as you do, you'll look for a job with a corporation where you can work 9 to 5."

Several of the young women were frowning at me, but they all knew what I said was true.

"I am not criticizing you for making that choice. I would only criticize you if you think you can become a partner in a large law firm, while leaving work to go to events in your child's school. You are dreaming if you believe our firm is a mother-friendly firm."

I looked straight in the eye of the one young associate I had been told referred to me as the "ambitious bitch." She quickly looked away, knowing she would never become a partner in our law firm.

After I let sink in what I had said, I excused myself and headed for the bar. When I looked back, the group of women had dispersed and were talking to other lawyers.

Despite Tony's warning, I ordered a Cosmopolitan, then a second one. I decided to stop right there before I started feeling woozy.

David Coleman, the firm's most pious son-of-a-bitch, spotted me and asked, "Why are you drinking?"

In David's eyes anyone who drank alcohol was an alcoholic. I wanted to tell him to go fuck himself. But I kept that to myself.

"David, quit judging me."

"You're an alcoholic who gets her jollies flirting with men. It's not professional. You're setting a bad example for the young lawyers." David walked away shaking his head. I caught up and pulled on his arm.

He spun around. "Yes, flirt. You wear tight blouses with no sleeves to show off your toned arms, tight skirts to display your bottom and high heels to show off your legs. You don't do that to impress women."

He was actually right. I do flirt. When I am on a mission, I use my feminine charm, and any other tool. I don't let anything stand in my way. And so far, it had worked very well. I found flirting rather than acting like a tough ass had helped me close many a deal.

"I do my best to be attractive and special, whereas you're boring and judgmental. Stop judging me with your condescending attitude." I said it softly while surveying the room and making sure no one had overheard me.

He pointed a finger at me, started to say something and then turned and walked away. I started after him, and then I stopped. I had nothing to prove to David. It was past midnight, the Friday before Christmas. I decided it was a good time to leave the party. As I walked out of the ballroom, I sent a text to Mario.

"Meet you at the hotel entrance."

He texted. "Around the corner. Be there in 2."

Two minutes later, Mario pulled up in his Lincoln Town Car. The hotel valet held an umbrella over my head and opened the back door and helped me get in the backseat. I told Mario to take me back to the office. While riding, I looked outside Mario's rear car window and noticed that the downtown canyon of Ross Avenue was deserted, its glass and steel towers lashed by gusting winds and horizontal rain. *Mario must be wondering why he's taking me back to the office now.* Mario rounded the corner and glided to a stop in front of the 50-story glass and steel building.

Mario climbed out, dashed around and opened the right door of the Lincoln. Holding an umbrella with one hand, he helped me to my feet. I stumbled a little, and he caught me.

"Can I help you, Ms. Rossi?"

"No, Mario, I've got my balance now."

I started toward the firm office building, holding my umbrella over my head, noticing the ice on the sidewalk. Mario raced toward me. Just as he reached out toward my arm, I slipped, my umbrella went flying. I caught my heel in the sidewalk crack and tumbled forward catching my fall with my palms.

"Damn!" I screamed. It hurt like hell. Mario helped me get up and I almost fell again. I was embarrassed because Mario had never seen me drunk. At least my heel hadn't broken off. That would have been a major tragedy, given how much I had paid for the shoes.

Damn, I said to myself. I couldn't see the ice in time.

I looked at my scuffed hands as Mario took me by the arm, picked up my purse and helped me back on my feet. By the time he rescued my umbrella I was soaked and freezing cold.

I was embarrassed. Mario had once told me I reminded him of the beautiful, stylish women lawyers he had seen on TV. *So much for that image.*

I was shivering. "I'm all right now, Mario. Don't you ever tell anyone you saw me fall," I said.

"Yes, ma'am. Your secret is safe with me." He looked me over. "Are you sure you don't want me to take you home?"

"No, Mario. If I need you, I'll call you."

"Ma'am, you don't have a car here. I'll wait for you here, just in case you need me."

After I left him, I turned back. Mario had picked up his cell phone. *Who was he calling at this hour?*

I pulled my office card out of my purse and held it against the reader to unlock the front office door. As I entered the building, I skidded on the marble floor, still uncertain of my step. *Damn, don't fall on your ass again tonight.*

When I regained my balance, Johnny, the security guard, was laughing. I frowned at him until he stopped. As soon as he looked at my face, he stopped and rushed over to me.

My public image was so crucial. Big prestigious law firms devour and spit out women lawyers who do not come across as brilliant, in complete control, and self-confident. That is why I spent money on designer clothes. That was why I strived to be the most physically fit lawyer in the firm. And, that was why I paid such close attention to my posture and mannerisms.

"You all right, Ms. Rossi?" he asked, offering a hand.

"I'm fine, Johnny. It's just so windy outside. I was practically blown through the doors."

"What are you doing back so late? I thought there you were at your law firm holiday party."

"I was. I just have a few documents to bring home over the holidays."

Johnny shook his head and clicked his tongue. "Working over Christmas. Did you at least have a good time at the party, or did you talk shop the whole time?"

I forced a smile as I signed in. I wasn't in the mood for small-talk. "I talked shop ... over Cosmopolitans. That's as close to fun gets."

"Whew! Those drinks are tricky. Taste like they don't have any alcohol in them until – BANG! – you're passed out on the floor ... or so I hear."

"You're okay, Johnny. The world's all wrong. See you in a few. Keep my visit to yourself."

"Ma'am."

I walked to the elevators. I was still pissed about the FBI visit, but I was planning my next move. I pressed the "up" button. My office was on the 34th floor, one of 12 occupied by Roberson Grant, the fourth largest Texas law firm.

In the elevator, I pondered a question that had been dogging me since the two FBI agents served me with the subpoena. What made the

FBI believe Burke Construction bribed the former Governor, Austin Harrington to win the controversial $2 billion Cross-Town Tollway project? I'm the one who negotiated the contract.

Was it because the Burkes and Harringtons were previously partners in Hill Country Estates? Was it because Burke Construction had submitted the only proposal to build and finance the Cross-Town Tollway project?

Those coincidences were complete bullshit. Austin Harrington was on the President's short list for the next Supreme Court Justice selection. The President had twice nominated conservative judges who, despite all the left's tarnishing, the senate had confirmed. The investigation was politically motivated to take out the President's third selection before he could even nominate him.

When I entered my office, I flipped on the light switch, tossed my briefcase to the floor, and collapsed in my chair. I could barely move. I was tired and could hardly keep my eyes focused.

I heard a noise on my window. The rain had gotten heavier. The sheets of water cascading down the window created a miniature waterfall – through which the lights of downtown Dallas were magnified and distorted.

I was comfortable working late at night when I was exhausted. Over the years I had done some of my most creative thinking in the middle of the night. I started thinking about publicity and suddenly being in the spotlight. I thought about what Mae West had said. "There is no such thing as bad publicity."

I understood because ever since I negotiated the Cross-Town Tollway contract, I had been in the spotlight with a target on my back for taking advantage of the state.

I finally quit thinking and started reviewing my Burke Construction Company files, especially the Cross-Town Tollway project files and the Randall Burke Hill Country Estates partnership files. If necessary, I planned to get rid of anything that would help the government investigation.

I did a search on my computer for the Burke Construction Cross-Town Tollway files.

"What the hell do you think you're doing?"

I jumped from my chair, startled like the boogeyman had entered my office. Standing in the doorway, half bathed in the shadows, was Tony.

"Tony!" I exclaimed startled. "Holy crap, you scared me. What ... how did you get up here?"

"Johnny let me up," said Tony, stepping into the office. He knows I haven't committed any serial killings – not lately, anyway."

"Who's with Mateo?"

Mateo is with Suzy. I paid her double time to stick around."

"How'd you know where to find me?"

"I called Mario to find out where you were," he said, embracing me tightly and giving me a peck on the lips.

He looked over at my computer screen. "Gina, just what the hell are you doing?"

"I'm reviewing my Burke Construction files and the Hill Country Estates files. I have to provide them to the Department of Justice."

"At midnight? This isn't exactly the best time to review files."

He may have been right, but I would never admit it.

" I need to review the Burke files, especially the file on the Dallas Cross-Town Tollway project. And I need to review the Hill Country Estates files to see if there is anything incriminating in those files."

"Gina, you don't want to do anything with those files."

"Tony, I have to study the files to see what I'm missing."

"Gina, you don't want to be studying your client's files after midnight."

"You don't understand me. I have to protect my client."

"That's where you are wrong. I understand you better than you may understand yourself. You're less concerned about protecting your client than you are about protecting your image and career."

"That's a mean thing to say."

"What secrets are in the files?"

I looked at Tony in the eye and said, "There aren't any secrets in the files." Technically that was a true statement.

"It's time for me to drive you home before the rain freezes and makes the roads impassable. It's been a long day. I'll take you home, help you get into bed and we can talk things over in the morning."

I grabbed my coat and hit the lights. No Tony, No. I thought. No more discussion. "Tony, let's just focus on Christmas now. We can talk about this after Christmas."

As we pulled out of the parking garage, Tony stopped beside Mario's Lincoln. I rolled down the window and motioned Mario to roll down his window. I heard a voice on his speakerphone.

"Mario, Tony will take me home. If I don't see you before Christmas, I hope you and your family have a Merry Christmas."

He looked at me and got out of his car. "Ms. Rossi, you left your laptop computer bag in the back seat. You might need it over the weekend."

"Oh, thank you, Mario. I completely forgot it."

"*Feliz Navidad*, Ms. Rossi."

As we drove away, I thought. *I'll never testify!*

CHAPTER 4

—— ⚬ ——

Gina Rossi

What had happened to us? When we were dating and after we were first married, there was sizzle in our relationship. As time went on, though, it seemed I wanted and needed more sizzle and Tony had become less interested. He frequently told me that I was never satisfied.

Our differing views of bedroom activities had become the main argument in our marriage. I almost always made the first move, which was fine with me. Oscar Wilde once famously said, "Everything in the world is about sex except sex. Sex is about power."

That was certainly true in our marriage. Frequently, Tony would respond with eyes almost closed and lips turned downward, as if I had asked for some major favor. In those instances, it just felt like sex with no emotion, no involvement. Rather than put up with that, on this night I just waited till he dozed off, slipped into the other room and made myself come without him. I hoped it would relieve my stress and help me fall asleep that night, but it didn't.

Instead of sleeping, I thought about how I could gain control of this situation. I was Burke Construction's and Randall Burke's lawyer, and I was determined not to testify before the grand jury. *I just tell the prosecutors, and they will excuse me from testifying.*

I looked at the clock. It was three-forty-five. I turned over and thought about the Cross-Town Tollway contract I had negotiated. It was the best legal work I had ever done, and I was damn proud of it. When Governor Rogers complained about the deal, I had gone on TV to defend it.

If Randall Burke bribed Harrington to win the Cross-Town Tollway project, my work didn't mean anything.

Even though I had never practiced criminal law, I didn't need a lawyer. All I needed to do is comply with the subpoena and tell the grand jury I can't answer the questions because of the lawyer-client privilege. That should be enough. My dad would probably say I'm being foolish though, and I must have a lawyer.

That brought me to thinking about my law firm. I would tell Harold Bessemer, the managing partner, and demand the firm provide me with a lawyer.

I wanted to go to sleep, but I was too worked up.

I worried about meeting my father on Saturday. Leo Baretti was famous for his cross-examination of witnesses, and I dreaded him cross-examining me. I could fool almost anyone, but I couldn't fool him. *Better to have Leo Baretti cross-examine me than a federal prosecutor. He would be tougher.*

I looked at the clock again. It was nearly 5 a.m. Then, I closed my eyes one more time, and I must have finally dozed off.

The next thing I knew I was jolted awake. I turned and saw it was 9:30 Saturday morning. Mateo, our dark-haired ten-year-old son, was yanking on my arm. Mateo had been diagnosed with Attention Deficit Hyperactivity Disorder (ADHD) when he was five. He can't sit still and is always busy: I rarely could keep up with him or keep him from getting bored with what we were working on together. Tony claimed Mateo had inherited his high energy, and overactive brain from me.

We never had difficulty getting him out of bed. Like me, Mateo didn't need much sleep. Mateo was usually awake and getting himself dressed when I returned each day from my morning run.

Mateo had rarely seen me in bed at 8:00 a.m., and never at 9:30. *He must think I'm sick.*

He leaped onto the bed with me and hugged me so tight I couldn't breathe. Even though my head ached, I took a breath, hugged back and smiled at him. He started singing "Spiderman, Spiderman, gonna wake up Mom, Spiderman."

He was into superheroes, and Spiderman was his current favorite.

"Mateo, I need some coffee. Could you quiet down and stop using the bed as a trampoline?"

Pointing to the ceiling, he shouted, "There's no need to fear! Spiderman is here!"

As I sat up, my temples were pounding, and my heart was racing. I wanted him to stop jumping up and down on the bed.

"Honey, honey, *please* be quiet. Mommy's just waking up. Where's Daddy?"

"He's in the kitchen making you bed and breakfast."

"You mean he's fixing me breakfast in bed."

"Yeah!"

I finally got Mateo to sit still on the bed. He frowned. I gave him another hug and a kiss on each cheek and smiled.

"Do me a favor, Spiderman. Run and ask Daddy to bring me a cup of coffee."

"Coffee?" Mateo asked, eyebrows raised and mouth wide open. Before I could respond, he shouted, "Coffee dad! Mommy wants coffee right now."

As exhausted from not sleeping, I smiled with joy.

Moments later, Tony appeared wielding a tray loaded with eggs, bacon, and a tall latte. I looked at him and smiled. "Gosh Tony, thank you."

"How're you feeling?"

"I'm tired. I've been plotting how I am getting out of this mess, so I didn't sleep."

"That good, eh?"

I reached for the latte took a sip.

"Mmm. Not bad, but it needs a little more vanilla."

"I'll keep that in mind if I ever become a barista."

I sat up and started eating my breakfast. I wasn't hungry, but I ate every single bite. When I finished, Tony picked up the tray and took it back to the kitchen.

"I am glad you came to pick me up last night, but I needed to review my Burke client files."

Tony sat on the edge of the bed. "Not after midnight. That was not the best time. You shouldn't have had any alcohol."

I decided to lie. I told him I needed to see if there was anything in them that would get Randy Burke or Governor Harrington in trouble. He was shaking his head.

"If Randy Burke bribed the governor to win the two-billion-dollar Cross-Town Tollway project, then they should get in trouble."

Unfortunately, if Randy Burke bribed the governor, then my superstar fame for negotiating the most favorable contract for Burke Construction will be lost. I was the lawyer featured in every major construction industry publication for negotiating the largest highway construction contract in U. S. history. I'm proud of that label and I planned to fight to keep it.

"Gina, did you hear me?"

"What?"

You were daydreaming."

"What did you say?"

"I said you should be concerned about why the government subpoenaed you. They must think you know something that will help their case, and they must believe there's incriminating evidence in your files."

"Bullshit. It's all a political ploy designed to derail Harrington's appointment to the Supreme Court before he is even nominated."

"Do you know something that would incriminate either Burke or Harrington?"

"Damn, Tony. I've told you, Harrington and Burke are lifelong friends. Burke's still close to the governor and the governor's wife. He made major contributions to the governor's campaigns, and the Burkes and the Harringtons were partners in the Hill Country Estates partnership until Harrington became governor. The Harringtons made a lot of money on the Hill Country deal. But, that's all I know."

"It's not a crime to make money and make money with your friends. It would be a crime only if Burke expected Harrington to award him contracts in return. But, the governor is not the one who selects the contractors."

What Tony said was true, but Harrington was deeply involved in the Cross-Town Tollway project. I negotiated the final deal with him in his Austin hotel room and then he appointed the person who selected Burke Construction and its finance partner. I kept that to myself.

"I'm taking Mateo out on a bicycle ride this morning. I better get him ready."

Thank God our conversation was over. "That sounds like fun. I know Mateo will enjoy spending time with you."

When he left the room, I sat there thinking. I'll tell them I can't testify against my client. I am loyal to Randall Burke and it would be unethical. *And they might ask questions I don't want to answer.*

What if a judge orders me to testify? No frigging way a judge would do that to me. I'd lose my one and only client and we'd be in deep financial trouble.

I got up and walked to the shower, thinking about my last argument with Tony.

He was looking at our American Express bill and complaining about how much money I spend.

I just knew he would bring that up. I was angry because I heard the same criticism each month. I replied, "I make ten times more money than you make and I'll spend it as I see fit. " *As soon as I said it, I was sorry.*

Tony walked out of the room shaking his fist. When he returned he said, "I left my law firm because I didn't want day nannies and night nannies raising Mateo. Because he is so hyper, he needed one of us to spend more time with him. You are the one who told me it was ok since you were putting in the long hours."

"I did, and I stand by that. Just don't give me a hard time about spending money. We have saved over $100,000 each year."

He walked out again and had not brought up my spending since.

As I put on my jeans, I was playing out what might happen. If I lose Burke, I'll find another client. But I can't testify, and I can't be indicted, and for the sake of my superstar reputation, I need for the contract I negotiated to stand.

My chest ached. Christmas was a special time for our family. I wished I could spend this Christmas holiday with Tony and Mateo worry free and focused on them, but that was not to be. I had to call my dad and get his advice.

CHAPTER 5

Gina Rossi

After I finished dressing, I called my dad and told him I wanted to take him to lunch and give him a heads up on what was going on with my client, Burke Construction, and potentially me.

"Why can't this wait until after Christmas?" he asked.

"Dad, Randy Burke is a target in the Special Counsel's investigation of the former governor, Austin Harrington, for accepting bribes from Burke."

"You need to get him a white-collar criminal lawyer."

"You didn't let me finish. The FBI came to my office and served a subpoena for me to testify and bring documents to the grand jury on January 2nd. They are investigating all the Burke Construction State DOT deals I negotiated including, the Cross-Town Tollway contract. It can't wait, even one day. I need your advice. I'll buy you a chile relleno for lunch at Garcia's, and we can talk then."

"Okay, meet you there at noon."

My father, Leo Baretti, was a famous Dallas trial lawyer, who billed clients over $1000 per hour. His brothers owned Las Vegas casinos. He'd once told me that even though he made a significant amount of money, his brothers made at least ten times more money because the casinos made money while they were sleeping."

My dad was a seasoned and prominent trial lawyer, but he'd never wanted me to follow in his footsteps. He'd pushed me to become a surgeon. At his insistence, I started college majoring in Pre-Med, and when my grades weren't good enough, I knew I had disappointed him. That disappointment motivated me to prove I could be a top lawyer like him.

I remember after my mother died, my grandmother Mary and my father argued about my future. Grandma Mary told me I should not be so ambitious. I had never heard of the word, so I opened the Merriam-Webster dictionary and discovered ambition meant "an ardent desire for rank, fame, or power." I knew my father wanted me to succeed and become well-known in school and my career. He pushed me to work harder and become the best I could be.

I loved spending time with my father, and I begged him to let me watch him in court. Whenever he stood to question a witness, he stood tall with his head held high as if he were preparing to pounce on the witness. Judges respected Leo Baretti, witnesses and adverse lawyers feared him, and the juries loved him.

When I was at home, I created my own imaginary courtroom, and I was the lawyer whom adverse witnesses feared, judges respected, and jurors loved. I made up my own cases and cross-examinations.

My brother Sam was the star in our house and received most of the attention from my father. He was a natural athlete and a star in the classroom without even making his best effort. My intense desire to please my father motivated me to work hard. When I started practicing law, I wanted to be recognized as the best lawyer in my field, just to win my father's approval and hear him say how proud he was of me. *Two weeks from now will he still be proud of me?*

At noon, Leo Baretti's black Mercedes S-Class Maybach car was already parked at Garcia's restaurant. I walked quickly to my father's favorite booth with two Pacifico Beers already on the table. Beer was the last thing I wanted that day.

"Dad, you'll be drinking two of those. I just want iced tea." I grabbed the Pacifico bottle and pushed it back towards him.

"Okay, what can you tell me about this DOJ investigation?"

"Well, normally I wouldn't ask for your help, but I have no experience with grand jury investigations, and this one is high profile."

"I've helped dozens of grand jury witnesses. I'll be happy to help you."

"I know."

"Why is the government investigating your client?"

"DOJ is investigating Burke Construction and Randall Burke both for bribing former Governor Harrington to win those contracts. They have sent Burke and Harrington target letters and served me with a subpoena to testify before the grand jury."

"Burke Construction is also a target? They must want to put the screws to Randy Burke to get him to plead guilty and testify against Harrington."

"That's a problem. No way Burke will plead guilty."

My dad spent the next fifteen minutes asking me about the details of the Cross-Town Expressway project. I answered his questions as honestly as I could choosing my words carefully. He must have sensed I wasn't telling the whole story. I told him that several years ago, before Harrington was governor, other contractors were interested. Three contractors submitted proposals, but Texas didn't have enough highway funds to build the project. After Harrington was elected, Sam helped me find a finance partner from Australia and Burke and its Australian financial partner submitted the only proposal. TxDOT wanted other proposals, but Governor Harrington strongly suggested that TxDOT award the contract to Burke and Merit Project Finance, the Australian finance partner that Sam had found for me.

He finally asked, "Did Burke bribe Harrington to win the contract?"

"No way."

Why did Harrington participate in the negotiations?"

"Because he wanted the contract to be the center piece of his Texas Roads to Destiny program."

"And why did he negotiate the deal with you, and not with Burke?"

"Because of their lifelong friendship, Burke wanted to avoid any appearance of impropriety. Can you quit cross-examining me now?"

"Not until, I figure out why they issued a subpoena for you to testify. What is it that you know that will aid their investigation?"

"I negotiated the terms of the contract and I was also the lawyer on the Hill Country Estates partnership."

"Austin Harrington and Randy Burke won't testify. I doubt they have left any paper trail. They need you to connect the dots."

"You're right. Plus, Governor Rogers wants a valid reason to nullify the Cross-Town Tollway contract."

As soon as he was elected in November 2018, Governor Rogers started a media campaign designed to get a new deal from Burke. The main-stream media both inside and outside gave Rogers the platform he wanted. CNN provided a whole hour to Governor Rogers, during which he described the Cross-Town Tollway project as "the worst deal in Texas history."

Rogers used that theme to create a social media firestorm. They're on the record for suggesting that if they shame us, over time, we will come back to the table and re-negotiate the deal. When Burke refused, the critics turned to the Justice Department to investigate, and they must have found FBI agents who did not want Harrington on the Supreme Court.

Our waiter brought our chile rellenos and filled my glass with tea. I started eating while my father ignored his food and continued asking questions. "What did you or Burke do to make DOJ believe he'd bribed Governor Harrington?"

"They've been lifelong friends. They and their wives were partners in the Hill Country Estates real estate development project. When Harrington ran for Governor, Burke made the Harringtons rich when he bought their interest. Burke also was a major campaign contributor, and Harrington flew all over the state in Burke's jet during the campaign."

"Did Burke do any of that expecting the governor to award contracts to him in return?"

"I'm not sure."

"Why aren't you sure? Didn't you ask Burke if he let Harrington become a partner in the development deal and made his plane available and made campaign contributions to win a $2 billion contract with no competition?"

"Dad, I never asked Burke. The subject has never come up. Take a moment and eat your chile rellenos before they get cold."

He finally picked up his fork and knife and started eating. When we finished, the waiter came and took our plates and my father continued.

"This sounds remarkably like Whitewater."

"Whitewater?"

"Yes. Don't you remember the Whitewater investigation of Bill and Hillary Clinton? In the end, none of the investigations found the Clintons had done anything wrong, but their Whitewater investment with the McDougals was what started the Special Counsel's investigation."

"Ah, okay. I vaguely remember."

I know what he wants to ask next.

"Well then, what did you offer Harrington in return for Burke getting the contract?"

I looked him in the eye knowing my father was looking for any telltale sign I was lying. "I didn't offer anything. What could I have offered?"

"Gina, quit answering my questions with a question. DOJ must believe you were able to negotiate such a great deal for your client Burke because you or Burke gave something to Harrington."

"Dad, they probably do. Randy Burke contributed to the governor's campaign and the Hill Country Estates partnership investment generated millions of dollars for Harrington."

"Did the Harringtons contribute their share?"

I had no idea. I only knew they wrote a check. "Yes, they wrote a check the day of the closing, and made the monthly payments as far as I know."

"You suspect, or you know?"

I was getting on edge from my dad's cross examination. He knew I wasn't telling him the whole truth and nothing but the truth. I looked him in the eye again. "I suspect. I'm betting that Harrington told William Jenkins, the chairman of the transportation commission that TxDOT should seriously consider the Burke proposal. Burke and his finance partner submitted the only proposal, and the governor believed the project would be a feather in his cap."

"That's odd and damaging, but unless there is some written record that it was awarded the contract in return for something we don't know about, or if Jenkins testifies, then it could be difficult for the government to prove."

"True, but you know why I'm worried. I've turned down dozens of opportunities to represent other major contractors. If I testify against my one big client, I lose everything. If I don't testify against him, DOJ might indict me in retaliation. I need a lawyer to help me find a way to not be the target of the investigation, and not be the lead government witness against Randy Burke."

"Better to lose a client than to lose your career. I bet the DOJ wants Burke to be able to go after Harrington. I'm sure Burke could cut a deal with them. For him, it would only be money."

The waiter brought us the check and my father put down cash on the table. I was ready to leave, but I wanted to make one last point.

"I know Burke and he isn't going to enter into a deal that would sink his boyhood pal's Supreme Court appointment. He'd rather go to trial than do that."

"I'm sure that's true, but it doesn't make any difference. Harrington's Supreme Court appointment is sunk already just by the investigation. The President has had a difficult time getting his first two nominations confirmed by the Senate, and they were squeaky clean. If you plan to refuse to testify, you need the best white-collar lawyer in Dallas. You need Jim Hardy."

"Are you sure? It seems cut and dried to me. Everything I worked on for Burke Construction and Randy Burke is covered by the privilege."

"Gina, listen to me. It's not cut and dried. If you do not want to testify, you need Jim Hardy."

"Dad, I don't need Jim Hardy."

"Damn it, Gina! Jim Hardy's the best criminal defense lawyer in Texas. I've tried cases with Hardy, and he has more experience representing witnesses before grand juries than any lawyer in Texas. I thought I charged high hourly rates, but Jim Hardy charges $1500 an hour and has all the work he wants."

Must be lots of rich white-collar criminals in Texas.

"Dad, all I need for him to do is call the U. S. Attorney's office. Tell the Assistant U. S. Attorney that he is representing me, and that I will not violate the lawyer-client privilege. Seems pretty simple to me for a lawyer charging $1500 an hour."

My father took a deep breath.

"Gina, Gina, if only it were that simple. Just take my word, you need Hardy."

I knew Hardy by reputation, but I had also met him several times when he'd worked on cases with my father. Hardy was one of the most colorful and silver-tongued lawyers Texas had ever known.

Jim Hardy had been on the cover of Texas Monthly and D Magazine. I had seen recent photos of him, and he looked pretty damn impressive for a guy over 60. He was tall, well-built, and handsome with medium length gray hair, hazel eyes. He dressed as if he had just stepped off the cover of GQ magazine. The way he looked in the Texas Monthly magazine sitting at his conference room table, gave me more confidence. *That's what the best trial lawyer in Dallas is supposed to look like.*

"Dad, I'll hire Jim Hardy, but if it is anything beyond a phone call, I can't afford him, and I don't want you to pay my bills. I need the firm to pay his fees. I have to get their permission. I need to talk to Harold Bessemer first."

"Since you are meeting with DOJ on January 2nd, you had better talk to him sooner rather than later. I need to stop by the men's room before we leave."

He got up and walked to the back of the restaurant. I got up and saw two men who had been sitting in the booth behind us. They looked overdressed for a Saturday lunch in a small Mexican restaurant. Had they been listening to our conversation? Were they FBI agents?

When my dad returned to our booth, I quietly pointed to the two well-dressed men and my dad said in a voice loud enough for them to hear, "Gina, I'm glad to hear you have nothing of any value to offer to the grand jury. When the government realizes that, they'll pull your subpoena."

We got up and walked silently towards the door.

When we were outside, my dad said, "Gina, you're stuck right in the middle and you make a great punching bag."

"That's for sure. They would like nothing more than to charge the great-granddaughter of one of the most infamous Galveston mobsters and the daughter of a top Dallas trial lawyer."

"And the niece of two of the top Las Vegas casino owners. Your uncles would not want to be left out of your case."

"Dad, that's not funny."

"It wasn't meant to be. Damn few people know the history of Galveston, much less that your great-grandfather has a significant role in that history."

"Well, they certainly know it around my law firm. I'm constantly reminded that my great-grandfather has his own Wikipedia page and is mentioned prominently on the Galveston Wikipedia page."

"Look, don't take this lightly. You have the prime of your career and life in front of you. You've worked very hard and sacrificed a lot to get to where you are now, and it would be a shame to lose it over what Randy Burke may have done behind your back. He may have taken advantage of you."

"Dad, I'll be okay. Thanks for letting me share this with you."

When we reached his car, my father kissed my cheek and told me he loved me. Then he held my arm and stared into my eyes. I sensed what was coming next.

"Gina, what are you not telling me?"

"What?"

"You heard me. You are holding something back from me."

I looked up at my father, gave him a kiss on the cheek, and turned and walked toward my car.

As I walked to the car, I couldn't get the words to Harry Chapin's Cat's in the Cradle song out of my head. I had grown up just like him. I was so driven to succeed, and I would do almost anything to win or make the best deal for my client. My success had gotten me into the crosshairs of the Justice Department.

I pulled up Harold Bessemer's cell phone number on the screen on my dashboard and pressed down. After three rings, he answered.

"Harold, it's Gina. I need to come by your office and see you first thing on Monday."

"What about?"

"I learned late Friday that Burke Construction and Randy Burke were sent target letters and the Justice Department is going after them. And they served me with a subpoena to testify and to bring my files."

"What? What in the world does DOJ believe Burke Construction has done? It must be something on the Cross-Town Tollway contract."

"That's the one."

"I know you negotiated a great deal for Burke Construction and its partner, but what do they think was illegal about it?"

"They believe Burke got that great deal as a result of bribing the governor. You might recall that the Burkes and the Harringtons went into business together before Harrington was elected governor. They owned Hill Country Estates. Because I personally negotiated the Cross-Town Tollway contract, and I know about Hill Country Estates, at the least they think I know something that could help their case. At the worst, they want to indict me as well."

"Okay, come by my office at 8:00 Monday morning. Since it's Christmas Eve, I don't plan to stay in the office past noon."

"Harold?"

"Yes."

"I am sorry to spoil your holiday weekend with this news."

"Gina, I understand and appreciate your concern. You don't have much time to get ready for what may be the most important meeting in your life. You didn't spoil my weekend."

Harold Bessemer had always supported me, so I appreciated his kindness. He was right, compared with my weekend, his weekend would be a walk in the park.

As I disconnected, dad appeared on my dashboard screen. I quickly answered.

"Gina, I have some bad news."

"Bad news?"

"Yes, I'm sorry. When I called Jim Hardy, he told me he had been hired to represent Governor Harrington."

"Damn, what do I do now?"

"I'll think about it over the weekend. Talk to Bessemer on Monday and make sure the firm is paying your legal expenses."

CHAPTER 6

──── ✑ ────

Tony Rossi

When Gina got home from lunch, I was watching a college bowl game on TV with Mateo. Virginia was playing Stanford. I told her I didn't care who won, but it was a tight game tied with five minutes to play and I wanted to see how it ended.

I didn't look up, but I asked, "What did your father say?"

"Tony, do you want to watch the game or talk about what my dad said?"

"Can you wait about ten more minutes? Mateo wants to see the end of the game."

I saw Gina mouth the words, "Fuck you," and she left the room.

Ten minutes later I turned off the TV and walked into the bedroom. "I'm sorry. Mateo has been hyper since this morning and he was finally sitting still watching the game."

Gina smiled ever so slightly. "Okay."

"What did your dad say?" I asked again.

"He said I should hire Jim Hardy because he's the top Dallas trial lawyer."

"He's the best."

"I know. Unfortunately, it turns out Hardy is already representing Governor Harrington, so he's not available."

"So, who did your father recommend after learning Hardy isn't available?"

"He hasn't recommended any other lawyer yet. I need to fix dinner," Gina said.

"Sit down and rest. I'll grill steaks. I already have them ready to put on the grill."

The rest of the night we didn't talk about my subpoena or testimony. Mateo went to sleep early, and I turned on the evening bowl game while Gina played a game on my iPad.

The Sunday before Christmas was a big day in our household. I knew Gina would try to focus on Mateo this day, but it would be more difficult this year.

Gina and I had met during our second year at the University of Texas law school, trying to untangle our intertwined bike chains at the bike the rack after a Federal Prosecution Seminar we'd both attended. I looked up and saw an olive-skinned blonde law student staring at me. I was immediately taken by her smile, and I told her later she looked like my dream girl. It could have been the tank top and cutoff denim shorts she was wearing.

Even with her blond hair, I knew she was Italian American, like me. Italians are the sixth largest immigrant group in Texas, but we were among the few students of Italian descent in our law school class.

After a few jokes back and forth, Gina had asked if I would be interested in studying together. She told me she needed someone to keep her disciplined and focused. I agreed to study with her, and I quickly discovered she was intelligent and hard-working, full of self-confidence and driven to succeed. I kept her disciplined and focused.

Gina knew no strangers and was at ease meeting people. I was more introverted, so she introduced me to all of her friends. I soon figured out that she was an alpha female. I didn't want to compete with her for grades, class rank, or job offers. I knew she needed to win, and I didn't care that much.

Early on, we discovered that our great-grandfathers had immigrated from Italy to Texas at about the same time but had taken far different paths once they'd arrived. My great-grandparents were among the Italian immigrants who had migrated to League City, between Houston and Galveston, from the small Italian town of Cercenasco, in the province of Turin. Like many others, they had entered America via Ellis Island, New York, then sailed to the Port of Galveston, and moved inland to League City to start farming.

Gina's great-grandparents had also sailed to the Port of Galveston. Her great-grandfather, Alberto, became a business leader-and part of the mob that focused on gambling, prostitution and illegal liquor during the Depression. Many who don't live in Texas are not aware of Galveston history. During the 1920s and '30s, Galveston was known as the "Sin City of the Gulf." Reportedly, a Texas Ranger was once asked why he didn't raid one of the famous private gambling clubs. He replied that he couldn't because he wasn't a member.

During law school, Gina and I were just friends and study partners. She was seeing an Austin lawyer at the time, who taught part-time at the law school.

I tried to play hard to get. One time, Gina called and invited me to go out for dinner. I declined and I heard her gasp in surprise on the phone. I told her I needed to study, which she said was bullshit and that's when I knew she had figured out my ploy.

Gina's uncles, Vince and Joseph, own casinos in Las Vegas. Gina worked on several weekends and during the summer as a flight attendant on their private jet. I knew she was hanging out with rich men and I had been jealous, but I tried to hide that from her.

During our second year in law school, Gina arranged a Las Vegas trip over a long weekend. On Friday after class we flew on Southwest to Las Vegas. After a show at one of her uncles' casinos, we left for another casino where Gina could gamble. I watched her play blackjack. Even with three decks in the shoe, I could see she was able to keep track of the cards. She left the table with at least $1000 in chips. Later, we tried to the craps table, and Gina won another $500 or so.

On our flight home on late Sunday night, Gina talked endlessly about her winnings in blackjack and craps. Over the next several weeks, she spent more time focused on gambling than she spent studying for her exams. I thought she might be addicted to gambling.

After that first trip, Gina returned to Las Vegas at least once a month, and sometimes twice a month. I asked to join her a couple of times and she blew me off. That took me by surprise. I frequently urged her not to go, but she told me she needed the money.

In some ways thankfully and in other ways not, Gina came home each time with thousands of dollars she said she had won. Was she a compulsive gambler? It sure seemed that way.

I finally insisted that she stop going to Las Vegas and focus on her studies. To my surprise, she did-she stopped gambling cold turkey. She told me after that, when she visited Las Vegas she was still working for her uncles as a flight attendant, and she was not gambling. I wasn't sure whether she was telling me the truth because she still came home from each visit with thousands of dollars.

During the last semester as third-year-law students, Gina and I visited Dallas one weekend and I met her father. I was nervous. Leo Baretti was an intimidating figure standing four inches taller than I was, with his deep olive skin and his wavy and well-styled dark hair. He was a heavy drinker, and around Dallas he was known to be a better trial lawyer when he was drunk than his opposition when they were sober.

Leo Baretti had constantly pushed Gina to be the best at anything she tried, including being first in her law school class. She'd once told me that she never felt like she was good enough in her father's eyes.

During our Dallas visit, we ate dinner at a well-known steakhouse with Gina's brother, Sam and his wife, Leah. The hostess and the waitstaff all addressed Sam as Mr. Rossi, and the hostess had seated us at his regular table. During the evening, Sam walked and greeted several patrons at their tables.

Sam looked, and acted like a rich investment banker. He wore a navy-blue pinstripe suit, white shirt with silver cufflinks and a light blue tie. When I complimented him, Sam told me his suit was a Brioni and that his father, Leo Baretti, had introduced him to Brioni. After spending the evening with Sam, I understood why he was a hard act for Gina to follow. He was a lot like his dad.

After dinner I searched online for Brioni business suits. The cheapest one I found was over three thousand dollars. The next day, Leo took me by surprise when he said, "Tony, we need to spiff you up. I'll take you to my hair stylist and the men's clothing store where I buy my clothes and we'll find you a business suit to wear when you are interviewed by law firms."

I liked my long hair, and didn't need a designer business suit, but I looked at Gina and knew from her raised eyebrow that I couldn't refuse.

"Yes, sir. I would enjoy that." I looked again at Gina and she smiled.

Mr. Baretti and I spent the morning together. First, we went to the Ricci hair salon where he introduced me to a beautiful brown eyed stylist named Gaia. The inside of the salon was stylish, and I thought for the moment I was in Tuscany. Gaia started cutting my hair and I noticed the sides became shorter than ever before and the top was slicked back. I looked in the mirror and barely recognized myself.

Mr. Baretti took one look and said, "Now you look like a young lawyer, not a law student."

"Thank you, sir." I replied, while thinking about what my mother would say if she saw the haircut."

Twenty minutes later we entered the Giovanni Men's Store. A man approached us with a big smile.

"Greetings, Mr. Baretti. Who is this young man you have with you?"

"Giovanni, this is Tony Rossi. He is a third-year law student at the University of Texas and he needs a suit for interviews with law firms."

"We can take care of that. What size are you son?"

"42."

Giovanni started pulling suits off the rack. He put the suit jacket from the first one on me and shook his head. "This fits you well, son."

I looked at the label on the sleeve. I saw the price-$1995.

"Giovanni, I can't afford this suit."

"Mr. Rossi, I'll give you a special deal because you are a friend of Mr. Baretti. I will sell it to you for $1295."

"I still can't afford it."

"Do you like the suit?"

"Yes, sir."

"Then, I'll tell you what I'm going to do. I will sell it to you for $1295, and you can pay me $50 a month until you get your first job."

I looked at Leo Baretti and he nodded in approval. I knew I could not pass up that offer.

After the tailor took my measurements, we left the store and went back to Mr. Baretti's home. When we got to his home, Gina opened the door and took one look at me and gave me a big kiss. I was happy the next day when we headed back to Austin.

Although it hadn't been easy for her, Gina had ranked third in our class after our second year of law school. Because of her class rank, she was heavily recruited by the top-notch New York, Los Angeles, and San Francisco law firms. That summer, instead of working as a flight attendant for her uncles, Gina clerked for three large law firms, in a series of 4-week sessions.

She enjoyed her work and the entertainment venues in each city, but I knew she was just using those firms for a summer of fun. Top students were wined and dined, and Gina spent a lot of time with successful lawyers and their clients. The lawyers in each firm wanted her to join their firm. After returning to Austin, she received an offer from each firm. I knew she didn't want to move to California and New York.

Gina had never considered practicing law with her father. She'd once told me that if she started with him, she would always be known as "Leo Baretti's daughter" and would always be under his imposing shadow. She wanted to prove to her father that she could develop her own career and shine without his help.

I wanted to stay in Austin I'd told her so. I loved the "Keep Austin Weird" city. When we graduated from law school, Gina came home to Dallas and joined Roberson Grant and I started with the Keely Gray law firm in Austin.

We continued to stay in touch by email and the occasional phone call, but we didn't see each other for a year. When I had a deposition scheduled in Dallas, I called Gina and we went out for dinner. That's when things started getting serious. I wanted to get married and Gina didn't. That created quite a problem with my mother, Silvia, and it got much worse after I moved to Dallas and Gina and I moved in together- "in sin "- as my mother constantly and caustically referred to our arrangement.

For the next two years my mother prayed for me and did everything within her power to break us apart, including introducing me to a friend's daughter who lived in Dallas. I asked my mother to at least get to know Gina and give her a chance. She kept pressuring me, and finally I told Gina I really wanted to get married. One year later, we were married, and Gina quit going to Las Vegas.

In the lead up to the wedding my mother was still hopeful she could persuade me to leave Gina. She insisted that Gina was a narcissist, and more motived by her career than she was by raising a family. If my mother had her way, I suppose, I would have found a stay-at-home wife and we would have given her many grandchildren.

Before we were married, my mother reminded me that I was not just marrying the girl, I was becoming part of her family. Needless to say, my mother didn't like Gina's Galveston family history.

I was one of seven children and my mother wore the pants in our family. She made most of the decisions, and my dad, Marco, went along with them just to get along and not make waves. So, in some ways, my mom and Gina were both alpha wives, which led to many heated discussions between the two of them.

Not long after we married, my mother started harping on grandchildren. Each time we were with her, which I kept to a minimum, my mom's first question was when we were having children. Gina and I had agreed we would not have children until she became a partner in her law firm, and that never did sit well with my mother.

During one visit, out of the blue my mom said, "I think you should have four or five children."

Gina's jaw dropped like she had been hit by a punch, but she quickly regained her composure. She looked at me, with the steeliest eyes I had ever seen. I knew this was not going to go well.

I started to say something, but before I could get the words out, Gina sat up straight in her chair, stared at my mother, and said, "Silvia, I understand your desire and I know that you are sincere. But, we are a new generation. In our generation, women are leading companies, running for political office and becoming top lawyers in law firms. In our generation, successful women don't have four children. I don't need to have children to be fulfilled in my life. My fulfillment will come from becoming a top Dallas lawyer."

"I agree with Gina," I said hoping to avoid a fight. My mother scowled at me. Then she asked, "How would you feel about working for Legal Aid and helping the poor?" Before Gina could respond, my mother added. "If you worked for legal aid, you could do what you love to do and still have time to be a great mother."

Gina started to stand, intending to leave the table, but I gently pushed on her leg and glanced her way. She glared at me and I waited for what I expected to be hellfire.

"Silvia," she said firmly. "Tony and I have talked about this many times. As much as we both care about you, Tony agrees that I will not give up my dream by taking four or five maternity leaves and feeling guilty each time I'm unable to attend a function at our children's school."

"I was just asking…" my mother started to say.

"No, Silvia, you weren't asking."

My mother lowered her head and scowled again. But that was the first and last time she ever brought up the subject of us having a large family.

But, a few years later when Gina was promoted to partner, we decided to have a baby. Gina's pregnancy included problems and complications. Mateo was born prematurely-seven weeks early. I remember holding him and thinking he was no larger than a basketball.

Mateo stayed in the hospital for three more weeks. Each day I went to the hospital to visit him in the morning and Gina and I went together after work. After one visit, Gina started a conversation about our future.

"I don't want to have any more children."

I was disappointed to hear that.

"Why?" I asked.

"I talked to Dr. Klein and he told me I would be at risk if we tried again."

That was the end of it. I never brought up having another baby again. To my mother's dismay, I was the one who left a big law firm to become a Legal Aid lawyer so that I could be more present in Mateo's life. My career and making lots of money were not as important to me. I enjoyed working less, and Gina enjoyed working more. As a result, it all worked out pretty well, and we were both happy with our decision.

Gina has always been very comfortable working with men. So, I wasn't surprised when she focused on the construction industry for her legal work. She once told me that one of her great joys in her career was having power of powerful men. I understood why that was a joy for her. I didn't understand how she was able to have power of powerful men. I finally asked. She told me acting self-confident all the time especially when she didn't feel that way. I could see that just in the way she entered a room. She also told me that knowing as much as men know about professional and college sports, golf, hunting and fishing enabled her to start up and keep up conversations with men in the construction industry.

In addition to perhaps having a gambling problem, Gina had trouble with alcohol. Like her father, she could never just drink one drink. To her credit, she knew she might have a drinking problem, so she rarely drank any alcohol, especially when she was negotiating a deal. She told me she was at her best when she negotiated deals with men who were drinking alcohol, while she was drinking Pellegrino with a lime.

When I got out of bed on Sunday, I put on my cold weather cycling gear. I still loved cycling, and I was active in a local group that rode 20 to 30 miles bright and early every Sunday. In the kitchen, Gina was making a latte for me to drink before I left.

I quickly downed the latte and I rode my bicycle to our meeting point. Damn, it was cold. For the next hour I rode with my friends and enjoyed my intense weekly workout. We barely spoke since our faces were half covered. When I returned home, Gina had prepared scrambled eggs with cheese and bacon for me.

After breakfast, we went to the 9:15 Mass at Sacred Heart Parish in Plano, just north of Dallas. It was hard to keep Mateo still during Mass because he was excited about what we would be doing the rest of the day.

We came home and changed our clothes again and drove to the ice sculpture at the Gaylord. We go every year. The Gaylord Texan Resort overlooks Lake Grapevine and features seasonal events and acres of indoor gardens. I wanted the Gaylord to ask our family to appear in a TV commercial for this annual event, which includes snow tubing and ice skating along with the ices sculpture festivities. We waited in the long line and finally reached the entrance where each person was handed a parka. Like always, we were freezing in the 10° F room, where 2 million pounds of ice had been hand-carved by a team of Chinese artisans.

Later, Gina and I took Mateo tubing, and he had a blast riding down. Before we left, we went through the Christmas area, awed by the thousands of twinkling lights and ornaments, the tallest rotating Christmas tree we had ever seen, and a life-sized gingerbread house.

In the afternoon, Gina baked Italian Christmas cookies. Mateo helped her in the kitchen. A couple of times when I ventured into the kitchen, I caught Mateo sneaking a finger full of cookie dough. Each time a pan came out of the oven, Mateo wanted to eat several cookies while they were warm. I could tell Gina was enjoying the holiday time with our son.

In the early evening, we went to the Dallas Jingle Bell Run at the Hilton Anatole Hotel. Gina's brother, Sam, his wife Leah, and their two children met us there. It is both a charity event, benefitting the Dallas Mavericks Foundation, and a family-friendly event. Leah and her children and Mateo and I ran in the "fun run" at 6:00, while Gina and Sam looked on. Then Gina and Sam ran in the 5k race at 6:30. She never ran to win it, she just ran to finish ahead of Sam, and on this night she did.

After the race, we took Mateo to Santa's Workshop, with storytelling by Rudolph, and the holiday light shows. Mateo wore himself out in the Bounce House, Santa Slide, Velcro Wall, and an ice-skating rink.

As expected, Mateo fell asleep on the way home, and when we arrived there, I carried him to his bed.

After he fell asleep, we finally had a chance to talk. "You look like you had a good day with Mateo."

"I did. But she quickly changed the subject. "While you were out this morning, I made a list of all the things I have to do before January 2. I've got to hire a lawyer who will persuade the government lawyers that I should not have to testify against my client. My career depends on it."

I didn't say anything, but she was probably right.

CHAPTER 7

Gina Rossi

On Monday at 8 a.m., I walked past Harold Bessemer's trusty assistant, Linda Ramsey, and was ready to knock on his door.

Linda stopped me. "Gina, your favorite partner, Allen O'Grady, is in there with him."

I stopped in my tracks. *Damn.* "Oh my," I replied. Then I smiled. "I can deal with O'Grady. Thanks for the warning."

"Good luck, Gina."

Allen O'Grady was an overweight Irish guy who must have had an acne problem in his teenage years. He was one of the most powerful men in the Roberson Grant law firm. My father once told me that what O'Grady lacked in good looks he made up for in his brilliance as a lawyer and his take-no-prisoners way of doing business. No one wanted to negotiate a deal with Allen O'Grady.

I had started my career in O'Grady's litigation practice group. But I never got along with him. After I'd been there a few years, he lost a major energy contract case to my dad and he took it out on me.

O'Grady took every chance he could to criticize me and diminish me in front of partners in the law firm. He called me a narcissist and labeled me the "firm bitch"- mostly because of my self-confidence, directness, and desire to be treated equally.

That set me off. I started by suggesting it was important for the firm to attract top woman lawyers and keep them. Then pushed further telling O'Grady that Roberson Grant was not fair to its women lawyers, and many of the senior male lawyers were regularly guilty of sexual harassment. Needless to say, he did not take that well. He told me that I was free to leave the firm any time I wanted, and he was sure my father would find a place for me at his firm. I told him I knew that, and I appreciated his reminding me.

O'Grady likely knew there was no way I would join my father's law firm. I was pissed off, but I decided to stay at Roberson Grant and just quit working for Allen O'Grady. On the Monday after my review, I announced I was leaving the litigation practice group to work for David Coleman in the Construction Law practice group. Coleman was a hotshot rainmaker who ran off the lawyers who worked for him faster than any other partner in the firm.

When I told my father that I had left the litigation practice group, he told me he was disappointed, and then he said, "Litigation is contentious. One lawyer wins, and the other lawyer loses. Maybe working as a construction lawyer will be less pressure for you."

I had expected my dad would be disappointed, but what he said to me still hurt. "Dad, you're right and there are several thousands of top litigators in Dallas," I replied. "I can build a career in a niche practice and become a top lawyer representing contractors."

David Coleman was known to be the most smug and sanctimonious lawyer in all of Dallas, but I preferred to work for him to O'Grady. Then, I quickly learned that my fellow associates had grossly underestimated Coleman's sanctimonious, self-righteous, and smug demeanor. He made clear that alcohol was a product of the devil and anyone who drank it was most certainly an alcoholic.

When Burke Construction hired Roberson Grant to handle a case in Denton County, I was given credit for bringing in the client. Allen O'Grady was livid about that and made a big fuss. I didn't really care, because the look my father had given me when he told me how proud he was that his daughter had brought in the largest contractor in Texas. I believe his perception of me as a lawyer had changed that day and I was on cloud nine.

I learned from David Coleman that Allen had lobbied hard against my making partner. After I became a partner, he made several attempts to harpoon my career. So, I now expected Allen to argue against the firm's paying for my lawyer.

I entered Harold Bessemer's office and looked at him and O'Grady as they got up from their seats. Bessemer gave me a reassuring look, but O'Grady once again looked away when I put my hand out to shake his. After 11 years, he still could not look me in the eye. *What a coward.*

"Good morning, Gina," Bessemer said. O'Grady didn't say anything.

"Good morning, Harold," I replied. I stood close to Allen and put my hand on his arm. He finally looked at me. "Good morning, Allen," I said while smiling.

"Gina, Allen received a call from the U. S. Attorney's office on Friday morning. They sent him a copy of the DOJ letter that you emailed to me. They not only issued a subpoena to you, we learned today they plan to subpoena Anna Lang."

Damn "Anna Lang? She's my associate. She doesn't know anything. I'll talk to her as soon as I leave here."

"We prefer you not talk to Anna."

"I understand your feelings, but Anna is not a strong woman. She'll need my guidance and I plan to give it to her."

"We've hired a lawyer for her. Let Anna's lawyer give her the advice."

No F... way.

"I know you are here seeking our agreement to advance your legal fees for the January meeting and grand jury testimony and, if necessary, anything that follows."

"Yes. I know this is serious. I'm asking the firm to advance my legal fees as required by our partnership agreement."

"Given your family mob history in Galveston and Las Vegas, and the Justice Department's hatred of your father, it's no wonder you are being investigated," Allen O'Grady said. "Who are you planning on hiring?"

I had expected O'Grady to refer to my family history. It wasn't the first time he had brought it up, claiming it was one reason I should not become a firm partner. But the dig at my father was something I hadn't heard before. I looked at Bessemer and rolled my eyes, knowing O'Grady wasn't looking and I put my hand on my heart and felt it racing. I almost told him to fuck off, but instead I just sat back in my chair.

Stay calm, take a deep breath. I looked again Harold Bessemer who was shaking his head. Then I said. "Allen, I'm surprised you brought up my family history. I doubt the current FBI knows of my great-grandfather's work in organized crime in Galveston, and I'm not even sure they know that my uncles own casinos in Las Vegas. Like you, the DOJ lawyers may well hate my father- he never has lost a case against you or them. But, I expect they fear him more than they hate him."

"Listen, young lady. The firm is not obligated to advance legal fees to a partner accused of committing a crime."

My mouth dropped open and I blinked at O'Grady. "Allen. I'm sure you know better than that. The government has not accused me of committing a crime. But, even if they did, the firm must advance my legal fees. The partnership agreement does not exclude criminal matters from the advancement of legal fees."

"Ms. Rossi, the partnership agreement provides for the advancement of legal fees only when the legal proceeding stems from the work you were doing for the firm. If you committed a crime, that clearly would not qualify as work you were doing for the firm."

"Allen, you must be forgetting that the firm advanced legal fees for Dennis Anderson back in the 80s when he was caught up in the savings and loan scandal."

Allen O'Grady looked at me, his eyebrows raised, his head shaking and his mouth wide open. I sensed that he and Harold Bessemer were both surprised by what I had said. I smiled.

"Who told you that?" Allen O'Grady asked as he leaned in toward me.

I leaned in myself, only a foot away from his face, grinning. "Dennis Anderson."

"Well, what we've done in the past does not mean we are required to do it again. Times have changed since the savings and loan scandal."

"Allen, you're not saying that the firm would treat me differently than a man. That doesn't make any sense.

"We have no choice. Just this morning when I called the U.S. Attorney's office, they threatened to go after the firm if we pay your legal fees. They could put us out of business like they did the Jergens law firm."

"Whoever made the threat must have forgotten that back in 2008, the 2nd Circuit ruled that the government had violated the Sixth Amendment right to counsel. I'm sure you remember that the

DOJ amended its charging guidelines for prosecuting corporate fraud to instruct prosecutors not to consider a corporation's advancement of attorneys' fees to employees when evaluating cooperativeness. You should tell the U.S. Attorney they are violating those instructions."

"It appears you have done your homework," O'Grady muttered.

He hated that I'd outsmarted him. Still standing, I put my hands on my hips and smiled. "Did you expect anything less from me?"

"Well, if the firm pays for your lawyer, then we get to pick the lawyer and reach an agreement on his or her fees," conceded O'Grady. "We already have someone in mind."

"No, I am picking the lawyer."

"Gina, you can pick whoever you want, but we don't have to pay for him."

"I had planned to choose Jim Hardy, but he told my father he is representing Governor Harrington. I'm waiting to hear from my father who else he would recommend, and I expect the firm to pay that lawyer."

"And if we don't, what are you going to do, sue us?" O'Grady asked in a loud voice while waving his hand at me. "We hired Gabriela Sanchez this morning to represent you."

"The lawyer who defended Duval?"

"Yes."

"Allen, did you hire her because her hourly rate is about half of what a lawyer like Jim Hardy would charge?"

"No. I hired her because she knows her way around the federal court and grand juries."

"I'm sure she does. But, I don't want a woman representing me, I don't want a lawyer as young as Sanchez is, and I don't want a liberal Latina lawyer either."

"You mean a lawyer your own age?"

"Exactly. She can't have enough experience."

"Gabriela Sanchez has tried more cases than almost any 50-year-old litigator in our law firm."

"I'm sure that's true. I prefer that my lawyer be from Dallas."

"Why?"

"She can't be smart enough. The schools in the Valley are likely the worst in the state."

"Did you know Gabriela Sanchez finished third in her Notre Dame law school class? She must be a smart lawyer."

"I don't want a woman lawyer representing me. There's no way she can possibly be mean enough to take on the federal government."

"Well, if you want the firm to pay for your lawyer, you better get comfortable with Gabriela Sanchez representing you."

"I can't believe this. You hired Sanchez without asking me?"

"Yes, she is expecting you to make an appointment to see her after Christmas."

I purposely replied barely above a whisper. "Allen, don't you think you are putting your feelings about me ahead of what is best for our law firm? I would think our law firm would want me to hire the top white-collar defense lawyer in Dallas."

"Jim Hardy is already spoken for. Gabriela Sanchez is likely to become the next top white-collar defense lawyer in Dallas. Ask your father. He'll tell you."

"She's also the lawyer trying to let every Central American and Mexican immigrant into the United States based on phony claims of asylum."

With that, I stood up to leave. I looked at Harold Bessemer, whose expression told me all I needed to know. He did not have the power - or the guts - to challenge Allen O'Grady.

When I reached the door, Allen O'Grady called out, "Gina."

I turned. "What, Allen?"

"Merry Christmas to you, Tony and your son."

I smiled. "Merry Christmas, Allen."

I didn't want Gabriela Sanchez to represent me, but damn if I would pay for a lawyer just to get me out of testifying before the grand jury.

CHAPTER 8

—⚭—

Gina Rossi

I went right from there to my father's office. When I arrived, I walked into the reception area and saw a Christmas tree that almost reached the ceiling. I was surprised to see Connie sitting at the front desk.

"What are you doing here on Christmas Eve?"

"I told your father I would come in this morning. I think he needed some company. I'm leaving at noon.

"Where'd he get the Christmas tree?"

She smiled. "Tom cut it down for him when he cut ours."

"I assume you also provided the ornaments."

"Yes, my mother made many of these, and I wanted a tree for them this year."

"She'd be proud of you. The tree looks fabulous." I snapped a photo and sent it to Tony in a text.

"Are you also responsible for the Christmas music?'

She smiled again and shook her head. I wanted to get your dad into the holiday spirit. He always seems a little down this time of year since your mother died."

"I understand. Anyone with him? I want to talk with him right away," I said as I started walking toward his office.

"I'll let him know you're coming."

"Dad, the firm has already hired a lawyer for me. Allen O'Grady said that if the firm was paying for my lawyer, then they get to decide who represents me."

"Who'd they hire?"

"Gabriela Sanchez."

I paused for his reaction. He perked up in his chair.

"You like their selection?"

He looked up at me, and he must have seen I was not happy. "I do, but to make it work, you have to have an open mind."

"I don't have an open mind. My best legal work is being questioned, my career is on the line, and I don't want a woman younger than me representing me."

"Is it because Gabriela Sanchez is a woman, or because she's six months younger than you?"

"Both. She's not you or Jim Hardy."

"Well, Jim Hardy is taken, and I'm your father."

"But there are bound to be other top criminal lawyers with more experience than Gabriela Sanchez."

"Gina, she has more experience than you think. I know her. I sat in court when she defended Sparks Duval. As talented, determined, and driven as you are, she has the same traits. You'll be a good team."

"Dad, I'm not looking for a teammate. I want a gladiator. I want someone who causes the government lawyers' knees to shake when he walks into the courtroom. I want the lawyer who will persuade them to withdraw the subpoena they issued for me to testify. I don't know

Gabriela Sanchez, but I'm betting their knees aren't shaking when she walks into a courtroom."

"You might be surprised. That may have been true before the Sparks Duval trial-when they underestimated her. After she made a fool out of the DOJ lawyer from the D.C. office, I believe their knees do shake, when she walks into the courtroom.

"I guarantee you she did not vote for Governor Harrington or the President."

"What does that have to do with anything?"

"She and I are not on the same page."

"Gina, I don't care if I'm on the same page politically with my clients. I'm a professional, and so is Gabriela Sanchez. She'll be your lawyer, and you need to be as candid and honest with her as you would have been with Jim Hardy."

"But, Dad. I'm not sure…"

My father interrupted. "Gina, dammit, listen to me. Quit searching for reasons to not hire Gabriela Sanchez. You have two choices. Either you can go along having her as your lawyer, and work with her, or you and Tony can pay for another lawyer out of your own pocket and hope you can get it back from the firm. Before you spend a pot full of money on a lawyer you select, you should at least meet with Sanchez."

I finally had had enough. "Dad, I'm sure you're right. I shouldn't have questioned your judgment." I had other plans to check out. I planned to ask Randall Burke to pay for my lawyer, so I pick one as intimidating as Jim Hardy and my father.

"I need to make a couple of phone calls. Is there a vacant office I can use?"

I first called Anna. She was with her family in San Antonio. When she didn't answer and it went to voicemail, I left a message. "Anna, this is Gina. I hope your phone is turned off because you are spending time with your family. I just wanted to let you know, I care about you and I hope you and your family have a wonderful holiday. Let's talk soon."

I clicked on Randy Burke from my favorites and pushed the call button. Burke and I had already discussed his target letter and my DOJ subpoena when I received it three days ago. He was aware that the DOJ planned to use me to get evidence against him and his pal, the former governor. I told him about my visit with my law firm partners and how my plan to hire Jim Hardy had gone awry.

"Randy, I may need for Burke Construction to pay my lawyer's legal fees."

"You can't testify before the grand jury. You have to keep your work for me private. We need for you to have the best lawyer in town, but Susan tells me Burke Construction can't pay for your lawyer. It's a conflict for us to pay for your lawyer when the Department of Justice wants you to testify against us."

Just what I expected. Susan Delaney would nix paying my lawyer.

"Randy, you're right, I can't testify. That's why I want you to find me the best lawyer in Dallas and pay for him."

"Gina, I told you I can't do that, and I won't."

"What if my lawyer advises me to testify. Don't you want to make sure that doesn't happen?"

"I don't need to remind you that everything said between us is covered by the lawyer-client privilege. If you testify, your law career is finished."

"Did you and Harrington have some deal you hid from me?"

"Gina, if we did, Harrington wouldn't have let you push him further. But, you still can't testify. You know too many secrets, things that could create problems for everyone."

Can't testify? That was an odd way to put it.

"Well, of course I intend to keep what was said between us secret."

When we were ready to hang up, Burke said something that piqued my interest.

"Gina, you and I both know that this case has less to do with the local politicians and current governor being upset about the Cross-Town Tollway project, and more to do with Harrington's political enemies derailing his Supreme Court nomination."

That sounded too much like a cop out and made me wonder whether Burke and Harrington had some kind of deal.

"What?"

"The left-wing Democrats fear that Austin Harrington will be nominated for the Supreme Court by the President, and they are using those in the DOJ who hate the President to derail the potential nomination. If Harrington is under investigation, there's no way the President can nominate him for the next open Supreme Court position."

"Randy you've been watching too many cable news shows. The President's appointees are running the FBI and the Justice Department."

"The President's appointees couldn't stop the Russian probe before it started. The Attorney General recused himself and the Deputy Attorney General appointed a Special Counsel."

"The acting Attorney General has no reason to recuse himself in Governor Harrington's investigation."

"True, but he also can't stop the investigation now that it's public."

"So, the President won't nominate Harrington to the Supreme Court, even if he is never indicted."

"Who knows with this President, but I'd say his chances are between slim and none. He's forever tainted, even if DOJ never indicts him. The left will use the media to make him look like a crook, no matter what happens in the investigation."

I couldn't believe the DOJ wanted me to appear before a grand jury as part of a plan to make Austin Harrington look like a crook.

"If that's their goal, why do they need me?"

"Because you're the poster child who took advantage of Governor Harrington and persuaded him to sign what they believe is the worst deal in Texas history. On social media there have been many claims that you seduced Austin Harrington. They don't need you to keep Harrington off the court. They need you to break our deal."

Next, I called Austin Harrington. When he answered. I said, "Damn Austin, you hired the lawyer I wanted."

"Gina, this isn't funny. They are trying to ruin me to make sure I'm never on the Supreme Court. I've been told they have some sort of plan for each man and woman the President had on his list."

"I'm sorry they are doing this to you, Austin. You'd make a great supreme court justice."

"Gina, Jim Hardy has told me not to talk to you. The government could use that against me."

"Okay."

"I know I can count on you. We can catch up when this nightmare ends."

"Goodbye Austin."

After my calls, I did a Google search of Gabriela Sanchez. I discovered that her father, Roberto, is a lawyer in the Rio Grande Valley. There were many sources on line related to her successful defense of the richest man in Texas, Sparks Duval. I found dozens of video clips of Gabriela Sanchez being interviewed by the local and national news media during and after the case. In every video she wore a different designer suit.

At least she dresses for success. She has expensive tastes.

When I searched images, I found several risqué shots that had run in the *National Tabloid Journal* when they wrote a lurid article about Gabriela Sanchez, just before the Sparks Duval trial started. *Sanchez was no innocent Latina girl from the Rio Grande Valley and she apparently enjoyed the company of both men and women.*

I reluctantly called her office and was surprised when the person who picked up the phone said, "Gabriela Sanchez."

"Ms. Sanchez, this is Gina Rossi, Leo Baretti's daughter. I've been told my law firm has hired you to represent me in the government investigation of former Governor Harrington and my client, Randy Burke."

"Yes, Gina. I received a call from Allen O'Grady last Thursday night."

"Thursday night?" I was taken by surprise.

"Yes, he said you would be served with a grand jury subpoena on Friday and he wanted me to be prepared. I also received a call from your father this morning."

"My father?"

"Yes, he said he had originally recommended Jim Hardy and then discovered that Hardy was representing former Governor Harrington. He asked if I would be interested in representing you, and I told him O'Grady had already hired me on behalf of the law firm."

Why didn't my dad mention this to me?

"Did my father tell you I didn't want you to be my lawyer?"

"No. But he did say your first choice was Jim Hardy."

"That's true, but as a second choice I wanted someone like Jim Hardy or Leo Baretti, not a woman younger than me."

"Why don't you just find someone like your dad or Jim Hardy?'

"Because my firm won't pay $1000 plus an hour for my representation."

"Would it help you if I call Allen O'Grady back and tell him I'm not the right lawyer for you?"

"No. I should have never questioned whether you were the right lawyer for me. I'm sorry. But you may want to rethink representing me. Did O'Grady warn you that I would be a difficult client?"

"Yes. He said you would be one of those clients who thinks she knows more than her lawyer."

"He said that?"

"Yes."

"Well, he knows me. I am a tough boss. I will expect you to do your homework and be as prepared as I would be. Are you sure you want to take me on as a client?"

"I promised I would be your lawyer, and I don't break my promises. I'd like to meet you here at noon on Wednesday. I'll have lunch made here for us. Is a salad with a Salmon fillet ok?"

"Let me get one thing straight with you right now. You have to convince the U. S. Attorney's office to drop the subpoena. I will not violate my client's lawyer-client privilege and Randy Burke won't waive it. I am confident you will take care of that for me."

"Gina, if they would be willing to drop the subpoena, they would have never issued it in the first place. We're beyond getting them to drop it. What is it you could tell them to get your client in trouble?"

"I am a staunchly loyal to Randall Burke and I'm not violating the lawyer-client privilege even with you."

"Then you must know something incriminating. But I agree with you that lawyer-client privilege is sacred, and I will fight for you to save you from being forced to testify. The whole point is to encourage clients to seek legal advice, knowing the conversations will always be private. We can talk about it Wednesday. Are you traveling out of town for Christmas?"

"We plan to visit my husband's family, but I can fly back from Houston in time to meet you at noon."

"I'll see you then. Gina, one more thing?"

"Yes?"

"Do not say anything about this case to anyone, including lawyers in your firm, Randy Burke and anyone else from Burke Construction, Austin Harrington- even your father, and your husband."

"Not even my husband? What?"

"No one – and that includes your husband. I know you are stuck in a bad situation, but you don't want to make it worse and you can count on me to help you."

"Did you know they also issued a subpoena to Anna Lang? She's the associate who helped me draft many of the Hill Country Partnership documents."

"You shouldn't talk to her either."

She's not up to the job. She's making this a bigger deal, just to sound like the expert.

CHAPTER 9

— ✍ —

Gina Rossi

I pulled out of the parking garage onto Field Street. I noticed an overweight man and a blonde woman sitting in a black Escalade parked as if they were waiting for me. When I turned onto Ross Avenue, in my rearview mirror I saw they had made a U-turn and they appeared to be following me.

It takes a lot to scare me, but this gave me a very bad vibe. I had been followed only one other time in my life-by a muscular man with tattoos all over his arms. I thought he might rape me and that scared the crap out of me.

I started figuring out ways to lose the couple in the Escalade. I certainly didn't want them to follow me home. Then it dawned on me they would already know where I lived. They were going to harm me before I was home. So, how could I ditch them without a car chase?

I decided that I might be able to lose them by cutting through the Thanksgiving Tower parking garage. Like I had seen in movies, I sped up and then quickly turned into the Elm Street entrance, tore through the garage, and exited on Pacific Avenue. When I looked behind me, the Escalade was nowhere in sight.

As I sped home, I wondered why those two were following me, and I also realized they must know where I live. About a mile from my house, my cell phone rang. I looked at the screen in my car. No caller ID flashed on the screen. I debated whether to answer and decided to go ahead.

"Ms. Rossi?"

"Yes."

"This is Hannah Locke."

"Who?"

"Hannah Locke. We know you received a grand jury subpoena to testify in the Harrington investigation, and we know the FBI wants to meet with you before you testify."

How did they know that and who were they? I did not reply.

"You should be concerned about your safety and that of your family. There are people who want to destroy Austin Harrington. They want to make sure you testify, and they know where you and your family live. Our people are following you to make sure you stay safe."

"Who are you, and why are you concerned about my safety and my family's safety?"

"I can't tell you who we are or give you specific reasons why we are concerned. I can only tell you there are people who want to put pressure on you, and they will do almost anything necessary to derail Austin Harrington's Supreme Court bid. We think they might harm you, or at least scare you to make sure that you testify to support their claim that Burke bribed Austin Harrington to win the $2 billion Dallas Cross-Town Tollway contract."

Before I could say more, I heard a click.

WTF? I had never been threatened, not even when I was condemned for taking advantage of the state. Now, for the first time, I was stuck in the middle of a political fight and both sides were threatening me. I had not seriously prayed in a long time, but this had gone from just a government investigation to now something scary for my family.

I called my father when I got home and told him what had happened.

"Do you intend to testify?" he asked.

"You know I will not testify."

"You should have called your lawyer and asked for her advice."

"I called you first, because I know I can trust your advice."

"I am your father. Call Sanchez and ask her if you should inform the FBI of threats against you and your family."

"Why should I inform the FBI?"

"Because they can give you, Tony and Mateo around-the-clock protection. You may need it."

Next, I called Randy Burke. After I told him the story, he said, "You need Mario to drive you."

"Why?"

"Because he has a gun, and he knows how to use it."

I envisioned all kinds of bad things that could happen to me if Mario shot someone.

"Randy, I can't believe anyone would shoot me if they want me to testify against you and Austin."

"They likely won't shoot, just threaten to shoot, but better safe than sorry. Call Mario."

"I will, but I still don't understand. Tell me why someone is so interested in my testimony."

"After what happened last time, some liberals want to derail any potential Supreme Court nominee on the President's list, before another Supreme Court seat is open. On the other side, Harrington's supporters want the investigation of their potential Supreme Court Justice to go away and want him declared innocent of any wrongdoing."

"Good luck with helping Harrington. The investigation itself has tainted him. The President will never nominate him to be the next Supreme Court Justice."

"That's true, but there's already a campaign being waged by his supporters. They point to the presumption of innocence and what happened to the last nominee. On the other hand, the more vocal liberals in Congress point out that the Senate confirmed the last nominee. They want to stop Harrington before the President has a chance to appoint him."

"Who do you think is following me, and why do they think they need to protect me?"

"That is a good question. There are only a handful of people who know you have received a subpoena. If her group wants to protect you, whoever they are, they want you to testify. It could be someone connected in some way with the investigation."

I wanted to just make all of this go away so I could celebrate Christmas in peace with my family. The DOJ didn't need me.

"The investigation can certainly go forward with or without me, so I can't understand why anyone would think harming me would change anything. I can't believe I am really in danger."

"You can't be sure," Randy Burke replied. "I simply recommend you pay attention to people around you."

That is hardly comforting.

I sighed. I couldn't believe what was happening to me. I had become a prime target in the middle of a political dispute.

When I arrived at home, Tony and Mateo were ready for the early All Saints Parish Christmas Eve 4:00 p.m. Mass. When we arrived at All Saints, the parking lot was already overflowing. A police officer directed us to a field a block away and we parked there. The 4:00 Mass featured a children's liturgy and the children's choir. I had encouraged Mateo to join the choir, but he was too shy to sing in public, or even just mouth the words in front of an audience. When we arrived, I was in awe of the two large Christmas trees filled with lights and ornaments. Kids did many of the readings and the children's choir sang many of the traditional Christmas carols. At the end of the Mass we all sang all six verses of Silent Night.

After Mass, we drove to Irving. I had gifts for one more family I wanted to deliver. Mateo sang Silent Night in the back seat. I was surprised when he started singing the second verse, and then the third verse.

I had met little Sara Gomez a couple of years earlier when I attended a Big Brothers Big Sisters charity auction. I had taken Sara under my wing. Sara was a nine-year-old girl at the time who had been abused by an uncle. She had given Susan Delaney and me a big hug at the event and won my heart right then and there. I'd asked Sara about her family, but she wouldn't respond. I later learned that Sara needed a great deal of affection and reassurance.

For the last two years I had spent time with Sara at the tennis courts and had helped her get involved in a Dallas Tennis Academy program. Over that time, Sara had slowly come out of her shell.

We finally arrived at the apartment complex where Sara and her family lived. I had visited the apartment many times over the last two years when I picked Sara up or dropped her off.

As we walked to the front door of the apartment, I could hear children's voices. They were singing in Spanish.

I knocked and Sara's mother, Carmen Gomez, answered. Sara stood behind her mom with her two brothers shadowing her.

"Merry Christmas, Sara."

Her eyes were shining, and she spoke rapidly. "*Feliz Navidad*, Ms. Rossi."

I smiled back at her and said, "Mr. Rossi and Mateo and I have gifts for you and Ernesto and Francisco."

That got the boy's attention. Carmen welcomed us in, and Sara and the boys edged closer to us. They came rushing to the door. I handed the three of them wrapped boxes; Ernesto tore open the square box and pulled out the soccer ball.

"Wow, un nuevo balón de fútbol!" he yelled.

Francisco opened his box and jumped up to try on his Brazilian Jui Jitsu Gis.

"No pudeo emperor para mostrarles a los niños nuestro nuevo Gis," he exclaimed.

"En Ingles Francisco," Carmen said.

"I can't wait to show the other boys at our gym our new Gis."

Carmen looked at them waiting. "Tell them thank you," she said.

In unison, Ernesto and Francisco said, "Thank you, thank you."

"I think you have both earned it. The two of you have helped us with our yard work," Tony replied. He pulled a rectangular wrapped box from behind him and handed it to Sara.

"What is it?" she asked.

"Open it and you will see," I replied.

Sara tore the wrapping paper and pulled out the box-a Wilson Burn Junior Tennis Racquet.

There was that smile again.

"Maybe mom will let us play tennis together some time," said Mateo.

"Sara, you have earned this more advanced racquet," I said. "You've worked hard to learn how to play tennis and you keep getting better each time you play. Your mother and I are really proud of you. Just think of how much fun you will have playing at the Tennis Academy in 2019."

As we left, I hugged Carmen and handed her an envelope. Inside the Christmas card, Tony and I had tucked three $100 bills.

"Merry Christmas, Carmen. *Feliz Navidad.* I hope you and your family have a wonderful day tomorrow."

"*Muchas gracias*, Ms. Rossi," Carmen replied, with tears in her eyes. "You have made such a great difference in Sara's life. She is so happy."

I rarely cry, but that night I left Sara's house with tears in my eyes. I love my work, but none of it brought the feelings I experienced watching a young girl who had been hurt get better. I had wanted Carmen to give her children the gifts we had brought, but Carmen told me the children would know she could not afford them.

As we pulled away, there were tears in my eyes. Tony looked at me and said, "You've brought a young girl out of her shell. Her eyes were open wide in amazement and appreciation of your gift."

It had been a good day for me. I hadn't thought about anything other than Christmas.

CHAPTER 10

❧

December 25

Gina Rossi

Every other Christmas Tony and I had shared since we were married had always been a long day, filled with tension, and this one would be no exception. We had spent Thanksgiving with my dad, so we would spend most of Christmas day with Tony's family.

Early Christmas morning 10-year-old Mateo sneaked down the hardwood stairs of our two-story colonial home to get a crack at all of those presents under the big tree in the living room.

Before long, his giggling and the sound of ripping paper woke us up. Tony bolted for the stairs with his digital camera, and I followed with my new iPhone X.

Mateo was tearing into the wrapping paper like a starving raccoon, revealing the Lego Ultimate Building set.

"Cool!" shrieked Mateo.

"There's one more gift for you," Tony added. It's out in the garage."

They headed for the garage to find the Polaris Sportsman Ride ATV. Mateo jumped onto the front seat, smiling like never before.

I had been dead set against this gift, but Tony had assured me that it was safe because of 3 ½ mph maximum speed and the traction on the tires. I had told Tony I didn't feel comfortable with Mateo riding on the ATV in the street.

Tony smiled, thinking how much he would have enjoyed driving an ATV when he was 10.

"Can I ride it on the driveway, Daddy?" Mateo asked.

"Not yet, Mateo, it's still dark."

"But it has lights, Daddy," Mateo argued pointing at the switch to turn them on.

"Mateo, you are up early. Let's wait until everyone in the neighborhood is up."

A couple of hours later, the three of us got into Tony's Ford Fusion and we drove the three miles to my dad's home. I was surprised when my father and his new girlfriend, Marilyn, answered the door. I was even more surprised to see Marilyn's two teenage girls on the couch with their faces buried in their phones. They didn't even look up to acknowledge we were there.

Marilyn was a blonde, just like my mother and me. She was two years older than me and had worked as a legal secretary in an adversary's law firm when my dad first met her. She was always dressed to please my dad. That meant she rarely wore slacks and almost always wore heels.

Marilyn grew up in Tyler, two hours east of Dallas. In photos I had seen of her when she was in high school, she had big hair styled like Farrah Fawcett. Her hair looked a whole lot better since my father started paying for her to have it styled. She was slightly overweight which may have contributed to her oversized breasts. To me she was a gold digger and her two teenage girls were dumber than doornails.

"Marilyn, you look so elegant. Your hair is stunning."

"Thank you," she replied.

"You and your girls got here early this morning," I said.

"We spent the night. We went to Midnight Mass and when we came home, your father insisted that we stay with him."

I sure as hell hope those girls didn't sleep in my old bedroom.

"Apple, Amber, get up and say hello to Gina."

They kept hold of their phones while slowly getting up from the couch. Almost in unison they said, Good Morning Gina. Merry Christmas."

"Good morning girls. Merry Christmas. How was the Midnight Mass?" I asked as they sat down.

Neither girl looked up from their phone. "It was okay, I guess," Apple said.

I'd had enough of this conversation and I walked towards the kitchen where I could smell Mexican food.

Every other Christmas we eat breakfast at my father's home and dinner at Tony's family's home in League City. Each Christmas morning, Consuela brings her famous breakfast tacos, and even more famous pork and chicken tamales, and the family has Christmas breakfast together. This year, my dad was able to make us lattes, using the new Starbucks Verismo machine Tony and I had given him Christmas Eve.

I always looked forward to Christmas at my father's, but every other year I dreaded visiting Tony's family. This year would be even worse, because I'd barely slept since I was served the subpoena to testify. I also had not been hungry, my stomach was in knots. The last thing I wanted to do that Christmas day was to drive to League City, eat Christmas dinner with Tony's family, and then drive back to Dallas alone that night.

After we had been there about 10 minutes, my father's doorbell rang. I went to the door and opened it. Sam and Leah were standing there with Samuel Jr. and Daniele.

I hugged Sam and Leah, then both children.

After they were all in the house, Sam called me over.

"Gina, you look exhausted," he said.

"Sam, I am tired and just have a lot on my mind right now. You know how end of year can be."

"Can you tell me about it? Anything I can do to help?" he asked.

What does Sam know, I wondered? *No way my dad had told Sam anything.* "Sam, it's Christmas," I said. "Let's just focus on that."

Consuela was carrying a box. "Consuela," I said, "you should be home with your family today."

"I always come here to fix Christmas tacos and tamales. Your dad has always made me feel like they are his special Christmas treat. My daughters can start Christmas dinner while I'm here."

"I know, and I appreciate that, and I know my dad does too. He tells everyone that your tamales are the best in the world," I replied.

I approached Tony and took him by the arm into the hallway.

"I think your idea of my flying back first thing tomorrow morning and having Mario pick me up is a good one. I'm not sure how I would have lasted driving back by myself late tonight, or even early tomorrow morning. I'll easily be able to get to Gabriela Sanchez's office before noon tomorrow, and I won't be exhausted."

"I'm glad you are flying. I would have been on pins and needles the whole time you were on the road tonight. Are you sure you're okay with Mateo and me driving back later?"

"Sure, Mario will bring me home in time for dinner."

"What have you told your mom and dad about my going back home?"

Tony had expected the question. "I said you had a big stressful closing on a deal and needed to get back to Dallas to work on it, and that Mateo would enjoy spending the morning with his grandparents."

"You're the best. Thank you for taking care of Mateo, but I'm sure your mother thinks I am awful."

"If she does, she hasn't said so. My mom is just anxious to see her grandson. He's growing up so fast. They want to spend the time with him while he was visiting, even if it is only for the morning after Christmas."

From the living room, Mateo was yelling, "MOMMY, DADDY! Grandpa gave us sweaters for Christmas! ATV drivers don't wear sweaters!"

I saw young Sam and Daniele hugging their grandfather and thanking him for the sweaters. They likely weren't thrilled by sweaters either, but their grandfather would never know.

"I'll take this one," I told Consuela, picking out a pork tamale and exiting the kitchen to look at the sweaters. I felt much better after deciding not to drive back to Dallas that night.

Tony liked the cheese tamales with small pieces of jalapeños in them. He picked one up, unwrapped the corn husk and let it cool for a few seconds. Consuela smiled at him, reminding him that the first time he ate one of her holiday tamales he started to bite into it while it was still wrapped. Thankfully, no one other than Consuela had seen him, and it had been their secret ever since. Consuela had also given Tony her secret recipe including small pieces of chile in the mesa dough, adding a little spice.

I wasn't looking forward to seeing Tony's mother later. She would spend hours wondering aloud why I had to fly home in the morning instead of waiting to drive home with Mateo and Tony in the afternoon.

Silvia Rossi knew her son too well and could figure out when he was not telling the truth, just by staring him down.

As we were leaving, I gave Dad a hug and held him longer than usual.

I whispered. "Dad, she's too young for you."

He looked down at me. "Gina, I can be the judge of that."

I walked over to Sam and whispered. "Sam, don't let Marilyn and her girls take advantage of him."

In a low voice, Sam replied. "She's taking advantage of him, but if she makes him happy, so be it."

When we were outside, Tony said, "Gina, your dad can take care of himself. This too shall pass when he grows tired of her."

"Here's hoping that's sooner rather than later," I replied.

As we drove down Interstate 45, on our way to League City, I had the big dread going. Tony's four sisters and two brothers and all their children would be there. I had once explained that having grown up with only one brother, I struggled to deal with the chaos of so many people under one roof. I claimed Tony's family loved disorder, and he couldn't argue that point.

The holiday meal was never served on time. By the time it was on the table, most of the adults in Tony's family were drunk, and the most of their children were exhausted from playing all day. I was bored and tired and wanted to be at home.

From the driver's seat, Tony put his hand on my knee and looked over to convey that he understood.

"Just find a chair, become invisible, and relax when we get there."

"Easier said than done. There is no chair where I can become invisible."

Mateo was struggling to sit still during our drive. "Daddy, I want to go home and play."

"Tomorrow, son. We'll go home, and you can play the rest of Christmas vacation."

"Can I fly home in the morning with Mommy?"

"No, your grandmother and grandfather want to spend more time with you."

If dealing with the chaos at Tony's parents' house was a challenge for me, it was a far greater challenge for Mateo. In the car, we practiced "stop, relax, think" and taking deep breaths. Before Christmas, I had put several educational games on Mateo's iPad. I hoped he had found one or two that would occupy his time today. He seemed to enjoy the Pitfall game, along with the Kids Chess app. He had always liked playing alone, and those two apps fit the bill.

We finally arrived in League City at about 3 p.m. As we drove through town, I saw restaurant parking lots with no cars, until we passed the King Chinese Buffet. *Who in League City is eating dinner on Christmas Day in a Chinese buffet restaurant?*

Tony smiled. "The thought of eating Christmas dinner at a Chinese buffet should make dining with my family really look good."

I wanted to tell him that I would have preferred the Chinese; at least it would be served on time. Instead, I smirked, and lied. "True, your mom is a far better cook."

Tony's great-grandparents immigrated from Italy to League City and were part of the League City Italian farming community. Tony's great-grandparents grew a variety of truck crops including strawberries, corn, cucumbers, beets, figs, tomatoes, and grapefruit.

Tony's father, Marco, was the Rancho High School principal and his mother, Silvia, was a stay-at-home mom, so he had grown up without much money to spare.

Tony's uncle and aunt owned the local family restaurant Luigi's. None of his brothers and sisters lived in League City. They had also left for bigger cities. Several of his siblings lived in Houston and the suburbs on the other side of Houston. For them, it was a relatively easy drive to their parents' house. For us, it was 4 1/2 hours of one of the most boring highways in Texas.

When we arrived, and after the greetings and hugs, Tony's parents and his sisters and brothers were so absorbed with each other that they paid little attention to me, and that suited me fine. After 20 minutes of catching up with everyone, Tony saw me sitting alone in a comfortable chair with a glass of the Santa Margherita Pinot Grigio Italian wine his uncle and aunt had brought from their restaurant. Between sips of wine, I was plotting my next moves.

"I see you found a chair and became invisible."

"I must have underestimated just how little your family members want to chat with me."

"Don't be a smart aleck."

"I'm not."

We finally sat down to dinner. All of the adults squeezed in at the dining room table, and the children sat in folding chairs at four card tables. In Tony's family the Christmas Eve dinner before Midnight Mass was an important meal. In keeping with the Italian tradition, his family always served fish and vegetables, a lean meal designed to purify the body before the holiday.

Christmas dinner was a different story. Tony's aunt and uncle always created the same traditional meal. The first course was Italian Antipasto, Italian cheeses and crusty bread. The second course was lasagna Bolognese, the house specialty at their restaurant. The main course was braised beef.

Each Christmas by the time we got to the tiramisu dessert, I was so full, I took a pass every time, and this year was no exception.

After dinner, I overheard Tony quietly talking to his mother across the room.

"Gina has to fly back in the morning for a meeting. I thought we would stay until noon and then drive home."

"Why don't you and Mateo spend the whole week with us?"

"Mom, Mateo wants to get back home to play with his Christmas toys, but he's all yours tomorrow morning."

Tony's mom looked across the room at me.

"Gina, I'm glad Tony and Mateo will be spending the morning with us, but I'm sorry for you given the circumstances."

Tony looked at me, and I mouthed the words, "what circumstances?"

"Silvia, I would love to spend more time with you. I just have to get back before noon to prepare for a year-end closing on a real estate deal. Clients don't care about holidays when they need a deal closed by year end."

"Well," she said. "I'm sure you have to put your clients before your son with special needs, that must be really hard for you."

Tony stared at me and shook his head a little.

It pissed me off, but I swallowed hard and slowly replied. "Silvia, yes I have a meeting about the closing, and you're right, it is really hard. Of course, I would far prefer to be home with Mateo. I'm grateful that Tony is able to be with him, and I appreciate him for that." I smiled sweetly and Tony and Silvia gave up.

Five minutes later, we were alone and out of earshot of his mother.

"You didn't tell your mother that I would be preparing to meet with the DOJ and maybe testify before a grand jury, did you?"

"You know I can't lie to her. I told her the truth. But, give me some credit for knowing not to tell her the whole truth. I told her you had a meeting scheduled at noon tomorrow and you wanted Mateo to be able to spend more time with her."

I had to admit that was a good way to say it. "And, I told her my truth. I was being polite. I'm going to bed. I'll get up early and run, shower, get dressed, and grab some coffee and be ready for you to take me to Hobby."

Tony looked puzzled.

"Tony, I haven't slept since Friday, and I want to go to bed early."

"Okay, I understand. I'm sorry that my mother tried to pick a fight with you."

"Tony, she doesn't bother me, but if it bothers you, then you should tell her."

"Easier said than done."

"And that's the problem."

I headed upstairs hoping for peace and quiet and trying to not think about tomorrow or the next several days.

CHAPTER 11

— ⁂ —

Gabriela Sanchez

I woke up early, made coffee and waited for my father to get up. He was driving me to the McAllen Airport to catch my 6:00 a.m. flight to DFW. Finally, at 4:30 I yelled, "Papá, I have to go now."

"**¿Qué deseas?**"

"Papá, did you forget I need you to take me to the airport?"

"No. But tell me again why you have to leave so early."

"I'm meeting a new client at noon today."

"Why do you have to meet him the day after Christmas?"

"It's a she, and she has received a subpoena to testify before a federal grand jury next week and we don't have much time to prepare."

He walked into the kitchen, jingling his keys, and heading for the coffeemaker. I had already brewed a cup of dark roast for him.

He glanced at me quickly. "You're going to let her testify?"

"She's not a target of the investigation, but no, I don't plan to let her testify. I've got to find out what she knows though and why the DOJ wants her to testify. I can't tell you about the case. Just get me to the airport in time to catch my flight."

"Tell me about your client."

"Papá, you know I can't tell you much about her. She's a lawyer. I've heard she is charming, ambitious, and a narcissist. I'm not sure I'll like her."

"You don't need to like her. If liking a client was important, I would have had only a handful of clients over the years."

"I understand, but I'm not looking forward to representing another difficult client."

"Representing difficult clients makes you a better lawyer."

"So you say."

People in the Rio Grande Valley pay little attention to time. I remember when my brother Robert, and his wife, Alexa, missed their flight from Cancún to Dallas and had to pay an additional $800 for a later flight through Mexico City.

When we got to the airport, my father pulled to the curbside drop off, walked quickly to my side and gave me a hug, and said, "Your mother wants you to find Mr. Right, you know."

"Papá, I know, but I don't have time to search."

"Have you tried any of those internet dating sites?"

"No, Papá."

"Okay, come back soon. Your mother might have a couple of young men for you to meet." I rolled my eyes at him. He held my elbow and kissed my cheek.

I was relieved to see the line at security was only about a dozen people, and I easily made my flight, but I couldn't get what my father had said off my mind.

When my plane landed at the DFW airport, I sent a text to my father as we taxied toward the gate.

"I love you, Papá."

Walking quickly through the airport, I saw the front page of the Dallas newspaper. The headline read:

"Grand Jury Investigating Harrington, His Wife and Contractor."

I bought a copy and stood for a moment reading.

"The News has learned that former governor and potential Supreme Court nominee, Austin Harrington, and his wife Laura Ray, are under a grand jury investigation in connection with the award of the $2 billion Cross-Town Tollway contract to Randall Burke, a childhood friend of his. The grand jury is investigating the circumstances of how TxDOT awarded the contract to Burke Construction with no competition.

"The News has also learned that Gina Rossi, Burke's lawyer who negotiated the contract for Burke Construction Company has received a grand jury subpoena for all of her documents related to the Cross-Town contract, and the Hill Country Estates partnership and will testify before the grand jury on January 2."

Since I had time, I stopped by and visited my mentee, Angela Dupree, on my way to my office. Her family lived in a Hispanic neighborhood just south of downtown Dallas, known for its bicycle vendors and mariachi music. I crossed the Margaret Hunt Hill bridge and made two turns and arrived at the Dupree home.

When I went to the door, Angela's older sister greeted me. Angela was right behind her and pushed her older sister to greet me. For the next 15 minutes we talked about what Angela had been doing over the Christmas break from school. Since her parents had to work, Angela was participating in a day camp. She showed me pictures she had painted and books she had been reading. I gave Angela a hug and told her I would see her in school on our mentoring day.

When I arrived at my office, I called Brian Renfro, an assistant U.S. Attorney against whom I had won a case a couple of years before.

"Brian, I'm representing Gina Rossi. Who leaked the grand jury investigation to the press?"

I heard a cough. "I don't know, Gabriela. Do you?"

"No. Was it someone in the Special Counsel's office in Washington?"

"I told you I don't know. I'm just the local attorney. The investigation is all being handled by the Special Counsel's office in D.C."

"Why is this part of the Special Counsel's investigation? It's far beyond his mandate."

"Because Governor Harrington was on the president's short-list for the next Supreme Court appointment, that's why."

"I don't understand what they expect to learn from Gina Rossi that they don't already know."

"They told me we'll know more when we look at her files."

"Well, the Special Counsel's office knows she is the lawyer who drafted the Hill Country Estates partnership documents."

"Yes."

"And they know she drafted the documents when Randall Burke and his wife bought out the governor and his wife."

"Yes."

"And they know she is the lawyer who negotiated the Cross-Town Tollway contract."

"Yes," he said again, his voice beginning to sound impatient.

"Well, what else do they need from her?"

"You left out the most important question. Does Gina Rossi know whether her client gave anything to the governor or made any promises to the Governor in return for his directing TxDOT to award the $2 billion contract?"

"Suppose I tell you she doesn't know."

"The Special Counsel prosecutor will want to hear it from her under oath."

"Is this just a fishing expedition designed to keep Harrington off the Supreme Court?"

"No, it's a serious investigation of a potential $2 billion fraud that Texas taxpayers will be paying for over the next 70 years."

"Well, I'm her lawyer, so make any communications through me."

"Okay, does your client know that her associate, Anna Lang, is cooperating with us?"

"No."

"Tell your client to keep away from Lang."

"I will, but Lang works for her. She has to interact with Lang."

"Gabriela, there is one thing I believe you will like hearing."

"What's that?"

"Jason Daniels was hired by the Special Counsel's office and he is in charge of the investigation. You just might get the chance to go up against him again."

I chuckled. I would like nothing more than to go up against that asshole in court again, but Gina Rossi was just a witness.

"Renfro, unless you tell me differently, my client is just a witness, not a target of the investigation. But, how did Daniels end up in the Special Counsel's office?"

"After you caught him using social media to influence the jury against you and Sparks Duval, and Judge Comstock granted you a new trial, Daniels was demoted by the Attorney General. But, after the Special Counsel was appointed, Daniels used his connections to get an appointment to be part of the Special Counsel's team."

Thinking about Daniels, I replayed what Renfro had just told me. I would only have the chance of going up against him only if the grand jury indicted Gina Rossi.

Does Daniels want to indict Gina Rossi?

At 11:55, Lucinda appeared in my doorway.

"Gina Rossi is in conference room A."

"Did Amanda offer her something to drink?"

"She did. And Raymond made her a French Vanilla Latte. Why are you asking so many questions? She's waiting for you."

"I don't know. I guess because I've never represented a woman and I've never represented a lawyer."

Lucinda looked puzzled. "*Estás nervioso?*"

"No. Not nervous. Just wondering how we're going to get along. I've been told the young women in her firm call her 'the wicked bitch of the west.' I've also been told that she uses her sex appeal to get ahead."

"What's wrong with that? You've been accused of the same thing. You two should hit it off."

She smiled and took off and I picked up my laptop and headed for the conference room.

CHAPTER 12

———— ⟋⟍ ————

Gabriela Sanchez

A minute before noon, I opened the door to conference room A and Gina Rossi stood up to greet me. She was as attractive as everyone had told me, and she dressed to maximize her assets.

"Thank you for agreeing to represent me, she said, "Did Justice Sotomayor make hoop earrings fashionable for Latina lawyers?"

I shook my head. "You must have seen Justice Sotomayor when she was nominated to the Supreme Court. I was wearing hoop earrings long before that."

"You did? That must have taken a lot of guts," Gina said.

"Either guts or I didn't care what anyone thought of it."

"I've heard you work out a lot."

"I do, but you must also work out a lot. I can tell from looking at your shoulders and biceps."

"I do. Guess that's one thing we share in common."

Other than being women lawyers almost the same age.

"You told me you are helping a young Hispanic girl learn to play tennis."

Gina smiled. "Yes, Sara has become like an adopted daughter. She had some bad things happen to her, and I'm trying to help her and her family."

"That's generous of you. *¿Hablas español?*"

"*Sí,*" Gina replied.

"I've heard a lot about you," I said, "and your brother, Sam. Your father talks about the two of you all the time."

"I'd say nice to meet you, but under the circumstances, I'd rather be home with my son, or at my desk at work."

"I understand," I responded. "I know this must be a difficult time for you being subpoenaed to be a witness in an investigation of your client and the former governor."

"Pardon the expression, but it is a fucking horror show. I don't deserve what is happening."

I guess she is not afraid to use the F-word with a stranger.

"Well, I hope you were able to get it off your mind at least for a few hours and enjoy Christmas with your family."

"I did, thanks. And your holiday?" Gina asked in a flat monotone voice.

"My family lives in the Rio Grande Valley. Knowing how important our work together would be, I flew down there on Christmas Eve and then flew back from McAllen this morning so I could talk to the assistant U.S. Attorney before I met here with you."

"Thank you. I appreciate that."

"I'm confident I'll be able to help you. Please, have a seat."

Gina sat down and said, "I'm sure my father told you that I don't suffer fools gladly. The only help I need is for you to get me out of testifying against my client. If you can't accomplish that, then I don't need you."

"I'm working on that. But we have to assume you will be forced to testify. So, we have to spend the rest of the week to prepare for your Grand Jury testimony."

"You aren't listening!" she exclaimed, while crossing her arms. "Your one and only job is to protect me from being forced to testify against my best client. Anything I could offer would be covered by the lawyer-client privilege."

"Gina, no one wants to testify, and maybe what you would have to say is covered by the lawyer-client privilege. But we can't be sure a judge will agree. So, we have to prepare as if you are going to testify. You need to fully understand what you are getting into."

"I do. I've done research on lawyer-client privilege, and I shouldn't be compelled to testify. Would you like a copy of my research?"

"Maybe later. Today, I want to go over the process, and what you might expect, and I want to get to know you better."

"I don't understand. We're not sorority sisters or wine drinking gal pals. Why waste time getting to know me when we need to talk about how I can avoid being forced to testify."

"I understand why you want to get right to the point. I would feel the same way. But, for me to help you, I need to know you."

There was something strange going on during our conversation. Gina's facial expression had changed from calm and composed when we were making small talk earlier. When she started talking about not testifying, her face became stern and her eyes started darting back and forth. I had seen that expression many times when defending politicians in the Valley. I was determined to find out what she was hiding from me.

"Okay," Gina said.

"I've been told that your associate, Anna Lang, is cooperating with the prosecutors. What does she know?"

"Anna doesn't know anything. She just helped me draft documents."

"Did she attend any meetings with you?"

"No meetings that meant anything. Don't worry about Anna."

"Okay. But you can't talk to her about the investigation. If you do, they'll indict you for obstruction of justice."

"I don't need to talk to Anna about the investigation, she knows what to do."

"The U.S. Attorney and the FBI want to meet with you before your grand jury testimony on January 2. You'll find yourself in the middle of the most publicized criminal investigation and political conflict in Texas history."

"I know that about half of the country does not want Governor Harrington to be on the Supreme Court, but why should that generate a grand jury investigation?"

When she said Governor Harrington's name, Gina blinked her eyes two times rapidly. She must know something about Harrington she is not telling me.

"What do you know about Governor Harrington?"

Gina blinked her eyes again. "Nothing more than the public knows. He connects with people and that's why he was elected governor. I don't understand why the Special Counsel is interested in him."

"Maybe the Special Counsel wants to put a feather in his cap. Convicting Harrington would be a big win."

"Okay, I get it."

"After Allen O'Grady called me, I called a reporter who has sources in the Justice Department. He told me the DOJ and FBI officials who were exchanging text messages on ways to stop the President started investigating each lawyer on the President's potential Supreme Court nominees list. But the investigation was put on hold until the day the

Senate confirmed the most recent justice. Supposedly, a whistleblower came forward and claimed that Harrington had granted favors to donors, and that your client helped make the former governor a millionaire as a partner in the Hill Country Estates project."

"That proves it's a fishing expedition," blurted Gina while still blinking her eyes. Austin Harrington has many enemies. The same FBI agents who wanted to have an insurance policy just in case the President was elected now have created an insurance policy to derail Austin Harrington's Supreme Court nomination. My driver showed me the article when he picked me up at Love Field. They're definitely out to smear Harrington."

"But, if your client bribed former Governor Harrington and his wife, their motive doesn't matter. They believe you negotiated the deal of the century for your client because Burke had greased it with Harrington ahead of time."

Gina back straightened as if she were coming over the table after me.

"Burke did not bribe Harrington. I played hardball because I knew the governor wanted to have the Cross-Town Tollway built as his legacy. Tell me about your discussion with the assistant U.S. Attorney."

"Okay. His name is Brian Renfro."

"What could Renfro possibly think I know?"

"They want your files, especially your emails and text messages. The DOJ wants to ask you if your client gave anything to Harrington or promised him anything to get Harrington to direct TxDOT to award the Cross-Town Tollway contract to Burke with no competition."

Gina closed her eyes, another tell-tale sign she was about to lie to me. Then she smiled. It was clearly a fake smile designed to keep me off guard. "There's nothing in the files, and I don't know anything."

"I will have to go through your files. Have someone bring them over to me as soon as possible, and make sure to include copies of all emails and text messages."

"Sure. Don't you don't have a date for New Year's Eve? I'd be happy to set you up with one"

I grinned. "It looks like this year I'll be working to help you. I can't think of a better way to spend the holiday." I gave her one of my own fake smiles.

"They're trying to derail Governor Harrington's Supreme Court nomination and bail on the contract as a benefit."

"That may be true."

"Governor Rogers wants to get Texas out of the deal. He's called Harrington's Cross-Town Tollway contract the worst investment of taxpayer funds in Texas history. He's criminalizing my best legal work-work that resulted in a fair contract for Burke and for Texas taxpayers. Burke did not bribe Governor Harrington. He didn't need to bribe Harrington. He didn't need to-he had me to negotiate the deal."

"I understand you are proud of your work. Let's turn back to what will happen in the next two weeks. I've told the U.S. Attorney's office that I represent you and that any communication with you must be made through me."

"That's good to know."

"One decision we have to make is whether you will take your 5th Amendment right to remain silent and not incriminate yourself when you appear. So far you are not a 'target' of their investigation, you are a subject. Do you know the difference?"

"I did a Google search and talked to my father, but why don't you tell me."

"A target of any federal government investigation is someone who the grand jury indicts almost every time. Randy Burke is a target, and he will likely be indicted. A witness is someone who at least for the moment has information the government needs but who is not in their crosshairs. A subject is somewhere in between. You are not yet a named target, but for our purposes, I have to assume you are one."

"I guess that is the safe way to go."

"Randall Burke received a target letter from the DOJ, right?"

Gina paused and brought her right hand to her chin, tilted her head and raised her eyes.

There she goes again. What is she hiding?

"I call him Randy."

"Okay. And?"

"Randy told me he received a target letter."

"Did you tell him you received the subpoena?"

"Yes."

"Didn't you see in the subpoena that you were not to disclose you had received it?"

"Oops."

"Did you consider the possibility that to save his own skin, Randy Burke might cooperate with the Special Counsel?"

"No way Randy Burke is cooperating. He and Governor Harrington are lifelong friends, they were in business together, and Burke was the governor's largest contributor. He also reminded me of the lawyer-client privilege for our communications."

"When the federal government gets a tip, they like to haul in witnesses who can give them bigger fish. They believe you and your associate, Lang, know something that would contribute to their investigation of Randy Burke and Austin Harrington. While they would like to convict Randy

Burke, their real target is Austin Harrington and maybe his wife, Laura Ray. They'd offer Burke a deal to get Harrington. And they obviously think you know something-you're the one who negotiated the contract and handled the partnership dissolution. Do you know what a proffer is?"

"I've heard my father talk about a proffer term, but no, please explain it to me."

"I strongly recommend against it, but I do need to explain to you what it is."

"Okay."

"The government thinks you are a witness who might have valuable information for its investigation. That's why you are a subject. We could meet with the DOJ in a proffer session. We have to decide whether we think you should cooperate with DOJ. Before they agree, they have to evaluate what you will tell them and how credible it may be. The only assurance you have is that they claim they will not use what you say against you."

"So, if I agree to a proffer, I have to tell them the whole story and there is no assurance that they will give me immunity?"

"Yes, and that is just one reason I recommend against it. Getting immunity all depends on the story and what the DOJ puts into the proffer agreement. They will not guarantee they will grant you immunity."

"There's no way I will make a proffer. I have nothing to tell, and anything I could tell would be protected by the lawyer-client privilege."

Gina blinked her eyes three times and I noted it on my computer. "I thought you would see it that way. But, let's try to determine that for sure over the next week. I plan to meet with Brian Renfro before January 2nd so I can get a better sense of their case and what they might offer you for cooperation."

"I don't have to go to that meeting, right?"

"Right. I'll go alone. The government may believe you know Burke did more than just make campaign contributions and become a business partner with the Harringtons."

"I see."

"If we decide that you will tell your story to the grand jury on the 2nd of January, you must tell the truth, and you must turn over all of the documents the DOJ subpoenaed. If you don't and if they discover you have lied, they will go after you for obstruction of justice."

"Yes, my father told me they would do that, which is another reason I won't testify."

"Good. I want to give you two examples of famous people who were not convicted of the original crime but instead were convicted of lying about it during the investigation. As you might recall, the government did not convict Martha Stewart for insider trading. Instead, they convicted her for lying about it when she was questioned by the SEC and FBI months after the trade. The government also did not charge Scooter Libby with leaking CIA operative Valerie Plame's identity. Libby was the chief of staff for Vice President Dick Cheney and was convicted of lying to investigators, perjury, and obstruction of justice."

"I forgot all about those cases."

"Before we meet with the DOJ on January 2nd, I need for you to tell me everything. Don't leave anything out. We don't know what the prosecutors have discovered. So, I have to ask, does the government have a case against you for anything you did in connection with the Burke Construction State DOT contracts?"

Gina clenched her fists and stared at me. Then she smiled again. "No. Nor do they have a case against Randy Burke."

"Okay, but it seems the DOJ thinks you did something wrong, or that you know about Burke gifts, or favors for contracts in return. They must have some evidence, and we need to find out what it is."

"That makes sense. How will we do that?"

"I will ask them, for starters. I also need for you to think about what potential evidence they might have, and also I want to begin tomorrow by getting to know more about you."

"Look Gabriela, you don't need to know my life story. If you get the subpoena dismissed, I'll buy a bottle of wine and tell you all you want to know about me. Let's just stick to business, okay? Besides, you already know plenty about me and my family."

"That's true. Your father is one of my role models. When I clerked for Judge Comstock, I tried to be in the courtroom every time Leo Barreti was trying a case. Your father told me that you amaze him with all you have accomplished in your life."

She stared at me. "He told you that?"

"Yes."

"Then what else do you need to know about my family and me?"

I smiled but just barely. "I want to know where the bodies are buried-what you are not telling me."

She didn't laugh or even smile. "Your father told me you run and work out at least as much as I do. They are forecasting freezing rain tonight. I belong to the Dallas City Club; let's meet there tomorrow morning, work out, grab a latte and then come back here."

"What time?"

"Let's meet at 6:00. That way we can start here by 8:00."

I showed Gina out, went back to my office and started returning the phone calls. One was from Leo Baretti. He answered on the first ring.

"Leo, Gabriela Sanchez. You called."

"Yes, Gabriela. I just wanted to check on how your meeting with Gina went. Is she being difficult? She can be pretty stubborn and impatient."

"Leo, you know I can't tell you what we discussed."

"Sure, I know that. I just want your impression on how Gina is acting."

I thought about it for a moment. *Should I tell her father what I think?*

"She's keeping something from me."

I heard a sigh, then a deep breath.

"I will talk to her."

"Don't talk to her. Gina and I need to work this out without you directing her. I don't want to press her yet."

CHAPTER 13

Gina Rossi

I normally welcome high-pressure situations, but not this time. I was beginning to think the pressure was getting to me, but that would for always be my secret. I woke up in the middle of the night with an image of DOJ lawyers sitting across the table from me. *What did they know? What did they suspect? What would I tell them? What would I keep from them? No fucking way I'm testifying.*

At 5:00 I woke up to music on my iPhone alarm. Jumping out of bed, I heard the coffee maker whirring as it ground the coffee beans. I ran down, snitched the first cup, and dashed back upstairs. In the bathroom, I looked in the mirror and saw dark bags under my eyes and my hair in a curly mess.

What to wear to Dallas City Club? I picked a UT tee shirt, running shorts, a UT baseball cap, and running shoes.

Back in the kitchen, I grabbed my travel mug, filled it with my second cup of coffee and walked quickly out to Mario's car, waiting at the curb.

"Good morning, Ms. Rossi."

"Good morning, Mario. I'll ride in front with you."

When I settled in the passenger's seat, I noted a gun sticking out between Mario's seat and the console between us.

Someone told him to protect me.

"Damn, Mario, keep the gun hidden. You'll get us both in trouble."

"Yes, Ms. Rossi." He reached down and tucked the pistol into the console.

Fifteen minutes later, Mario pulled into the City Club parking garage. After Mario opened the car door, I reached back for my blouse and skirt and grabbed my gym bag.

I stood at the elevator, anxiously waiting for the doors to open, then I pushed 44 and stood waiting fidgeting. As soon as the doors opened, I made a beeline for the front desk. "Hi, I am Gina Rossi, Gabriela Sanchez's guest." The tanned young hunk behind the desk grinned at me.

"Oh, yes, Ms. Rossi, Ms. Sanchez is expecting you. Have you visited us before?"

"Yes, several times."

"You know where the women's locker room is and how to lock your valuables?"

"I sure do."

"Ms. Sanchez is over running on one of the treadmills."

I looked far across the expansive open area and saw Gabriela running. I headed over and told her good morning.

"Good morning," she replied without missing a breath. "What are your workout plans?"

"I normally run outside, so I'll just join you on one of the treadmills."

"Okay I have only a quarter mile to go, and I'll see you after I do a couple of sets on the weight machines."

As I stepped onto the treadmill, next to hers, I noticed an out-of-shape older man in street clothes, standing over by the wall watching me.

I was pretty sure he was the man in the Escalade who had followed me the day before. My heart sank. *What the fuck? Who is that fat bastard and how did he know I would be working out here this morning?*

I looked at the treadmill settings and chose a seven-minute-per-mile pace. I wanted the endorphins to kick in for an early morning high. If ever I needed it, this morning was the day.

I pulled my earbuds from my shorts pocket and turned to the Pandora country station I had created. "I've Got Friends in Low Places" started and the treadmill gained speed beneath my feet. My steps quickened until I reached the programmed pace. After one mile, I was sweating and chasing the endorphin high. Four miles to go, I felt my chest expand as I sucked in the air. I loved this feeling, but when I glanced toward the wall, the fat bastard was still staring at me.

Thirty-seven minutes later, feeling energized, I started counting down the last 30 seconds of my run. I really wanted to just keep running, but at least now I was ready to start a long day.

As I stepped off the treadmill, I saw Gabriela using the weight machines, I walked in that direction and decided I'd follow Gabriela. At each machine, I set the weights 10 pounds heavier, even if it was more weight than I normally used. After one set, I picked up a mat and started stretching and some core work.

"How long will it take you to shower and dress?" Gabriela asked.

"About 30 minutes, is that okay?"

"Sure, meet you at the front desk and let's stop for a cup of coffee on the way to my office."

CHAPTER 14

———— ⟨ℓ⟩ ————

Gabriela Sanchez

Gina and I got off the elevator, and I pulled out my key fob to open the door. I escorted Gina directly to the conference room and turned on the lights. Gina raised her grandé latte and took a long drink.

"I needed the extra caffeine this morning."

Knowing she was impatient, I decided to get right to business.

"I know that you are anxious to tell me about the Cross-Town Tollway contract, but before we get to that contract, I want to explore how Burke Construction became your client and then work from there to the Cross-Town Tollway contract," I said.

"Before I tell you about how Burke became a client, I want to tell you what I saw that scared me this morning at the Dallas City Club.'

"What?"

"While working out this morning, I saw a fat bastard who was spying on me. He and a woman tried to follow me yesterday. And, while I was driving, I got a call from a woman who told me Tony, Mateo and I were in danger. She claimed they were trying to protect my family and me."

"Protect you and your family from what?"

"I've received death threats from people who don't want me to testify and from people who are most anxious for me to testify. I've been called every name in the book, and some I never heard before. The woman on the phone said some people who would do anything to prevent me from testifying before the grand jury, and the fat guy and woman were following me to protect me. The fat guy must have followed me from my home this morning."

"You've received death threats?"

"Yes."

"We need to notify the FBI."

"I don't want to do that."

"Why not?"

"I don't want their protection. I want them to leave me alone. Mario is protecting me."

"I don't know how the overweight guy was there this morning. They don't let just anyone into the Dallas City Club. You have to show an ID and membership card."

"Someone let him in, and he clearly was not there to work out. He kept staring at me, and obviously didn't care I knew he was watching me."

"What did he look like other than being overweight?"

"I have never been one to stereotype people, but if central casting were looking for someone to play a bodyguard, this guy would be ideal."

"I'll check into it when I arrive at the Dallas City Club in the morning. In the meantime, tell me if you see him again. I'm sorry you've been threatened, but as high profile as this case is, I believe both sides are trying to harass you and scare you."

"I can see that. They're doing a pretty good job of it so far."

"I understand. Can we get back to work now?"

"Sure."

"Tell me how you became the lawyer for the largest construction company in Texas, and one of the top three in the United States."

"The short answer is because I kicked ass and figured out how they could get a case in Denton County dismissed. I did my homework and found the solution to their problem."

"I need more detail than that," I replied. "How did you get the opportunity in the first place?"

Gina told me the story. She had been the token female litigation associate on the Roberson Grant team that made a pitch to Burke Construction, and when everyone else dropped the ball, she was able to save the day.

She said that the Roberson Grant litigation practice group in her firm was a good old boys' club. The old boys assumed the young male associates were capable- until they repeatedly proved they were not. They assumed the women associates were incapable until we repeatedly proved them wrong. As a result, there was only one female partner and Gina was the only female associate in the group.

She thought that when she took maternity leave, she had lost chances to work on big cases because of what she called 'the baby penalty.' For Roberson Grant male lawyers, having children enhanced their careers. For female lawyers like her, it was potentially a career killer.

When no big cases came her way, Gina left the litigation practice group and went to work for David Coleman in the Construction Law practice group. He was an asshole, but she was willing to put up with him.

Shortly after she started working for David, Burke Construction asked the firm to make a pitch to handle a case in Denton County because Susan Delaney, the Burke General Counsel, a leader demanded that women lawyers handle Burke Construction files.

I knew of Susan Delaney. She directed more work to women lawyers than any other company general counsel in the United States.

Allen O'Grady had directed Gina to just show up for the pitch and keep her mouth shut. He didn't include her in any of the preparation meetings. As Gina continued, I sensed what happened at the pitch.

After an hour, I suggested we take a break. I didn't need a break. I wanted to think about how I could prepare Gina to testify. Preparing any witness to testify before a federal grand jury is challenging. It's not a deposition where I get to sit there and hear my client's testimony. I will not be permitted to hear what Gina will tell the grand jury. Gina hasn't told me the whole truth. That's a problem. If Daniels catches her in a lying to the grand jury, he'll indict her for perjury in a heartbeat. The safest thing for Gina to do would be to assert her 5th Amendment privilege against self-incrimination. If Gina took the 5th, Daniels would likely grant her some kind of immunity to force her to testify, and we'd be right back where we started. *Damn.*

Ten minutes later I opened the door to the conference room. Gina was on her phone, but she quickly hung up when she saw me.

"I was talking to Tony," she said, as her eyes blinked three times.

"Okay, where were we? Tell me what happened in the pitch."

CHAPTER 15

— ✵ —

Gina Rossi

I needed the break from talking. Even though it was still cold, I walked around the block. I turned on my telephone and noticed I had received about a dozen text messages. Many threatened me and others were simply vulgar. Some threatened me if I testified. Others threatened me if I didn't testify. I debated on whether to tell Gabriela and decided to make that decision later in the afternoon.

When I returned to the conference room, I saw a man and a woman with aprons on delivering salads with grilled salmon and iced chai lattes. Gabriela's firm was one of the few in Dallas with a full kitchen staff. My firm and most others had lunch catered from local restaurants.

We took some time just eating before we got back to business. I was still trying to size up Gabriela Sanchez. I had decided she knew what she was doing, but I sensed from her facial expressions that she didn't trust me.

"Okay," Gabriela started. "Tell me how you won Burke Construction's business."

"Burke Construction became my client because I did the homework necessary to show them a way to win a case that Allen O'Grady thought was a loser."

"Tell me more," said Gabriela. "I'll let you know if you are giving me too much detail."

"Okay, I told her. "I didn't think I would win Burke Construction as a client, but I was able to do it because I did my homework and came prepared to the meeting with Randall Burke and Susan Delaney".

"The week before the Burke Construction client pitch, I decided to find out what the case was all about. I knew it was a test case designed by Burke Construction to evaluate whether they wanted our firm or one of our competitors to become their chief outside counsel. And I found out that Baxter Development had filed suit against Burke Construction after Baxter had purchased property in Canton County, intending to build a residential subdivision. In preparation, Baxter had subdivided the property, recorded a plat, and obtained a title policy in connection with the purchase.

I explained to Gabriela that when the property was purchased in 2006, there were no signs of a planned road leading from the main highway back to a Burke Construction batch plant. However, unknown to Baxter, the entire property, which had previously been part of a larger tract located in both Canton and Danson Counties, and it was subject to a 1977 roadway easement encumbering several hundred acres of that larger tract. This easement had been recorded only in Denton County in 1977-it was not recorded in Canton County until two years later.

I looked at Gabriela. She was typing notes as I told the story. I told her how Baxter and several lot owners filed suit to prevent Burke from constructing the road. Everything they alleged was true, which made it a tough case to win. I decided to get to the point.

"Allen O'Grady didn't expect me to speak, but he hadn't thought about the possibility that I might be asked a question."

I held back a grin, but Gabriela caught me and nodded. She'd undoubtedly been to meetings like this one where she had been told to keep quiet.

"On the morning of the pitch, I got up and worked out and then put on the sexiest business suit I owned. It was a new champagne blazer, black dress and black heels. I was *ready.*"

"Yeah, I know that feeling." She grinned at me. We both know how this goes.

"When I arrived at the office and went to the small conference room on the 33rd floor, I found Allen O'Grady, Danny Diamond and Rafael Garcia-who I decided was the token Hispanic lawyer. They were practicing the pitch. Danny was talking about our firm. Then Allen talked about the litigation practice group and then finally Rafael talked about the firm's commitment to diversity. Allen reminded me that I was to sit there and say nothing. I came very close to telling him I would just stay in my office."

As I finished, Gabriela heard several buzzes coming from my phone. "Do you need to take a break?" she asked.

I looked at my phone and felt sick to my stomach. I turned the phone towards Gabriela and let her read the recent text messages.

"Have you ever been raped? Testify and u can c if u like it."

"We know how to find u and know where ur boy goes to school. Keep ur mouth shut, or we'll take ur boy."

"Fuck u u whore. U are a piece of government ass if u testify."

"This is just the latest," I said.

"You need to report this to the FBI so they can find these people."

"They'll never find them, and they'll think I want to cooperate."

"Gina, this is serious," Gabriela said. "They're threatening to rape you and hurt your son. Let me call the FBI."

"I said no. I'll deal with it. I have hired a body guard to watch Mateo and Mario, my driver is taking care of me."

Gabriela kept trying to persuade me. I told her to save time I wanted to continue with my story.

"Okay. You were telling me about the awful PowerPoint slides."

I laughed and explained to Gabriela Sanchez how bad the PowerPoint slides looked. I had anticipated death by PowerPoint because there were so many words and bullet points on them.

"When it was time for us to leave for the Burke Construction offices, I discovered there wasn't room for me to ride in the car that Allen O'Grady had ordered. So, I drove myself to the Burke offices. I thought I would look foolish arriving after everyone else. I made a grand entrance. When I walked in, Susan Delaney and Randy Burke got up from their side of the table."

I decided that Gabriela didn't need to know that Randy Burke had looked me over head to toe and when he reached out to grab my hand, he whispered that Judge Harrington had spoken highly of me.

"What happened?"

I was lost in thought when I heard Gabriela say, "Gina, tell me what happened."

I thought about it and remembered the details and started telling what I remembered.

"Susan asked Allen whether we were ready to tell her and Randall why they should hire Roberson Grant to handle the Baxter Development case. O'Grady thanked her and introduced Dave Diamond who spent the next 15 minutes using his bullet point slides boring everyone in the room while telling Burke and Delaney things they already knew from the Roberson Grant website. When I looked over at Susan and Randall Burke, they were shaking their heads and grimacing. Dave Diamond was so glued to his slides that he didn't see it."

It had been excruciating. I had to keep from laughing out loud and Gabriela smiled too long which signaled to me she wanted me to get to the bottom line.

"When Diamond finished, Allen O'Grady stood up and started his PowerPoint presentation. His first slide showed the number of Roberson Grant litigators in Dallas. He must have included lawyers from industry practice groups who litigate, because I knew there were fewer on the 33rd and 34th floors than shown in his slides."

I told Gabriela that his presentation was intended to illustrate the significant cases the firm had won, but that curiously, none of the cases involved either construction or real estate.

"His next several slides were the website photos of the top litigators in the group. I was surprised he had failed to include Stephanie Osborne, the only woman equity litigation partner.

"That was a big mistake," I told Gabriela. "Susan Delaney knew Stephanie Osborne and when Allen wrapped up, Susan asked him to share what he knew about the current state of the construction industry."

I almost snorted remembering his response.

"What was funny?" asked Gabriela.

"The sonofabitch looked confused by the question," I laughed. "Allen folded his arms across his chest like he was pondering an answer. After a long pause, he told her that since our city and state were attracting companies from New York and California, the contractors were building many homes and office buildings." Gabriela laughed out loud, obviously picturing Allen O'Grady standing there totally caught off guard without the slightest clue.

"Susan just closed her eyes and shook her head," I went on with the story. "Allen started fidgeting. He unfolded his arms, put his right hand in his pocket and started jingling his change. He does that whenever he's rattled."

Gabriela seemed more interested, and I continued telling the story. I told her that Rafael's presentation on diversity had been a disaster. I didn't blame Rafael. After all, he couldn't say much about our firm's diversity when the firm did everything possible to minimize diversity. At the end Allen forced Rafael to read our firm's commitment to diversity. Since I had it almost memorized, I recited it to Gabriela.

"*Roberson Grant embraces diversity as a hallmark of the firm and is committed to recruiting, hiring, developing and promoting attorneys without regard to gender, race, disabilities, age, religion, national origin, sexual orientation, social or ethnic group. We recognize that our ability to provide clients with the highest quality of service in the local, national and international marketplace is strengthened by a diverse workforce, among whom differences are accepted and valued.*" I looked at Gabriela. "You know where this is going, right?"

"I know Susan Delaney, so yes, I can picture what happened next."

"With that slide on the screen, Susan asked how many litigation equity partners we had in our Dallas office. Rafael looked at Allen for the answer. Allen stood up and said we had 37 litigation equity partners. Susan asked him how many of the equity partners were women, and Allen folded his arms back over his chest again and replied, 'one.'"

Gabriela and I both grinned, then she said, "Get to the part where you saved the day."

Okay. "Susan asked Allen to tell her what he thought about their case against Baxter. I could have really helped him answer had he given me a chance."

Gabriela interjected. "But, he didn't. So how did he respond?"

"As I'd expected, Allen told her it was a tough case and that jurors from Canton County would be biased because they didn't like Burke Construction's local asphalt and concrete plants. Both the judge and the jury would likely think Burke should have recorded its easement in both counties. And, he concluded that since Burke had recorded it *after* Baxter Development purchased the property that showed Burke understood it should have been recorded in both counties."

Gabriela smiled. "I thought most trial lawyers oversold their own clients' cases. Did you jump in?"

"No, I sat quietly just waiting for Susan to ask what I thought. Finally, she did. Allen interrupted before I could start, telling Susan he had not asked me to evaluate their case. I plowed ahead. I explained I had done some research and I believed we could get the court to dismiss the case. I couldn't look at Allen, but I could hear his breathing. I decided to throw Allen a bone and I said that he was right in saying that if the case got to a jury, they would likely be prejudiced against Burke Construction and filing the easement after Baxter purchased the property would give the local jury a hook to decide against Burke. Then, I paused for just a moment and told them there was an old 1893 case where the state supreme court had held when a single tract of land spans multiple counties, recording in any of the counties is sufficient to provide constructive notice of the easement spanning two counties. Then I looked right at Susan and Burke and said we would be able to get the case against Burke dismissed."

Gabriela, eyebrows up, smiled ever so slightly. "That's quite a story. If Daniels asks you to tell the story to the grand jury, I recommend you get right to the point."

"I'm sorry. You asked for the whole story."

"Yes, and it was important that you tell me the whole story."

I had left out very little. She didn't need to know what Randall Burke said to me or that he was giving me the once over.

"I bet when you got back to the office, you were in big trouble with Allen O'Grady."

"That's an understatement. When I got to his office, his face was still red, he was perspiring, and his right eyebrow was twitching. He told me to sit down and just to show him I said I preferred to stand up, so I was looking down at him."

"What did he say?"

I remembered distinctly and I told her.

"He told me I had fucked up big time and had undermined him and made him look like a fool in front of our client. He reminded me that he had instructed me to keep my mouth shut and just sit there, and I had defied him. At the end he told me he should have never allowed me to be on the team."

"You were asked a question," Gabriela interjected.

"Well, I told him I would have sat there quietly, but Susan had asked me a direct question, and she expected me to answer her question."

"He couldn't argue with that."

"But he did. He said I should have responded that he was covering that question-or I could have told him about the 1893 case before we had left our office. I reminded Allen that I would have told him about the case had he invited me to participate with the pitch team preparation. He purposely had excluded me, so I never had a chance to tell him."

Gabriela leaned in and said, "I get it. He was mad at you for a problem he had created."

"Mimicking what he had said to me, I told him. I should have just let him make a fool of himself and our firm. I won't bore you with more details. Let's just say, Allen was madder than hell at me, and by that point, I didn't care. I got up to leave, and as I was walking away, he stopped me saying he had one more thing before I left."

"I bet I know what he wanted," Gabriela said.

"Yeah, he asked for the cite to the 1893 case. All I could do at that point was smile and hope he didn't see it."

I told Gabriela that after I got the case dismissed, our firm's management committee voted to promote me to partner. David Coleman gave me the details on the vote and needless to say I was not surprised when I learned that Allen O'Grady had voted against me and argued at length that I should not be promoted. He even claimed he should get credit for bringing Burke Construction in as a client."

But he was outvoted-in fact he was the only one who'd voted against my promotion, but it just seemed to make him even more vindictive against me. As one of the few young women promoted to partner, I had a target on my back, and I had to prove myself each day. It had been worth it-for the first time my father treated me like I was a hotshot lawyer like him. I had brought in the largest, best-known contractor in all of Texas."

I thought that O'Grady might have been the whistle blower. But, if he was, why would he have hired Gabriela Sanchez to represent me? That was troubling.

We both looked at our watches at the same time. It had been a long, tiring day.

"Let's call it a day," she said. "Can we get started tomorrow at 8:00?"

"Sure, I will be here at 8:00."

"Want to meet again at 6:00 at the Dallas City Club?"

"Sure."

"Good. Be prepared to tell me more about the Cross-Town Tollway contract tomorrow."

CHAPTER 16

Gabriela Sanchez

I arrived at the Dallas City Center at 5:45 so I could get a head start on Gina and sit in the jacuzzi while she was finishing up. She arrived at 6:00.

When I finished my five-mile run, I started with the weight machines. I loaded weights on each end of the leg press, lay back flat and then pushed up and back 30 times. I went from there to the leg curls machine and then to the leg extension machine. After that, I picked up a mat and spent 10 minutes on planks and other cores exercises. After 15 minutes stretching, I headed for the locker room and the jacuzzi.

When I walked back to my locker wrapped in a towel, I froze in my tracks. Gina stood in front of her locker birthday-suit-bare. Several women were eyeballing her ample and eye-catching rear end.

Gina looked up and her eyes met mine. I turned away, looking down at my gym bag. A young, attractive woman continued to stare at Gina, even when their eyes met. I admired Gina's boldness, but it was weird to see my client naked. She had to know that made me uncomfortable.

Whew. I wasn't expecting to see my client naked as a jailbird.

Gina, touched my arm and said, "I thought the purpose of separate locker rooms was for us to feel comfortable being naked."

At first, I was at a loss for words. I replied, "You're right. You should feel comfortable being naked in the locker room. But, recognize that others feel more comfortable if you cover yourself with a towel."

When Gina and I walked out of the City Club, we crossed the street and over to the Starbucks on the corner. We ordered lattes and muffins, stuck the green plastic stoppers in the lids and walked to my office, chatting about the weather, Dallas traffic and our New Year's plans.

"We have lots to cover today," I said. "And I want to focus on it, so we won't have to spend New Year's Day together."

"I am game for that," she said with a smile.

"I also have some news. Yesterday after you left, I received a call from Ken Sanders."

"Sanders?"

"Yes, he represents Randall Burke and Burke Construction in the grand jury investigation. He told me that first thing this morning they plan to file a motion to quash your subpoena, asserting the attorney-client privilege and work product protection. Those are the standard arguments, so nothing out of the ordinary. Having your client argue the point will make the judge think twice before forcing you to testify."

"So, I won't have to testify?"

"We'll see. The government will contest the motion, as if it were an insult to file it."

"When will the judge rule?"

"Before January 2, especially since the government wants to complete its investigation of the governor. We still have to assume you might be forced to testify, so I want to get back to learning all about your work on the Burke highway contracts and the loans and gifts, plus the Hill Country Estates partnership."

Gina explained to me that when she'd first become a lawyer, her father had told her that a lawyer who is well prepared will defeat a more talented lawyer who is not. "I'm insatiable about research," she said. "I worked with Burke on big highway and bridge projects throughout the United States. Each time I learned what the state wanted."

"And what did they want?"

"The states wanted the huge projects built as fast as possible but paid for over many years after the currently elected officials are long gone. I helped Burke win projects from Boston to San Diego and Seattle to Miami, and in between. I was on the road three out of four weeks each month, and I was making more money than I ever dreamed possible."

"How did your husband respond to all your travel?"

"He would have preferred that I make less money and never traveled. But Burke was one of the largest contractors in the country, and was trying to win the biggest and most complex projects around the country."

I asked her to go back to Texas and tell me how the Cross-Town Tollway project had come up, and how she had gotten involved.

"I learned about the project," she said, "and the state had wanted for years to build it-the road needed to be widened to six lanes each way. Burke and two other contractors had submitted proposals before my time, but the problem lay in how to finance the project. I did some research and I talked to my brother Sam. He told me Merit Finance, an Australian financial institution, was interested in providing financing and partnering with contractors on U.S. toll projects. After I arranged a meeting, Randall Burke and Merit formed a partnership to go after the

Cross-Town Tollway project and Burke gave me the credit for putting it all together."

"You must have been excited."

"For the first time Randall Burke told me I was a great lawyer and he appreciated my work. Prior to that he'd spent more time studying my legs than my legal work."

"The only problem is that Governor Harrington championed a $2 billion contract and there was no competition. How did that happen?"

"I wanted Harrington involved. I knew him and I knew I could persuade him. I reviewed every design-build and public-private partnership contract the TxDOT had awarded to contractors. All the State DOT officials talked about was how fast the construction could be completed. They were far more interested in time for completion than they were in the cost. Because Burke Construction had far more equipment than any other contractor, it could offer to complete the projects in significantly less time than any other contractor. That would be the key to Burke's winning the $2 billion contract."

"But, what about the financing?"

"I knew that Burke needed to both build and finance construction of the $2 billion Cross-Town project. Sam had found Merit, the Australian financing partner before any other contractors did. Having their financing in place maximized Burke's chances of winning. But, Burke's ability to complete the project in far less time than any competitor also made it next to impossible for the other contractors to compete. Burke didn't need to bribe Harrington to win the contract. Randall Burke and I both knew there would be no competition."

"How could the two of you be sure of that?"

"The construction industry in Texas is a tight-knit group. There are only a few secrets. When I had secured Merit to finance the project, the other contractors were caught off-guard and not prepared to compete. They needed more time-and I did everything possible to make sure they didn't have it."

"What exactly did you do?"

"I put Governor Harrington's interests ahead of my own and by doing so I achieved what I wanted. I met with Harrington several times, and I convinced him that completing the Cross-Town Tollway project was a key to bringing large companies to Texas to create more jobs. At the time, he was considering a Presidential run. He needed a big success story to promote him."

"You said you met with him several times. How many times exactly?"

"At least five or six times."

"Where did you meet?"

"In Austin and here in Dallas. I persuaded him to create the 'Texas Roads to Destiny' program."

"You were the one to come up with that slogan?"

Gina sat up in her chair and smiled while cocking her head like a cat. Yes, I created the slogan, I first pitched it to Laura Ray Harrington. After she spoke to her husband, I pitched the idea to him. 'Texas Roads to Destiny' made it easier for me to negotiate the Cross-Town Tollway contract."

I saw her steely-eyed determination. Harrington must have seen it when she negotiated with him. She had convinced me that when she set her mind to something, she would stop at nothing to make it happen.

"Or, as the press puts it, allowed you to take advantage of the state," I said.

"They said I did a better job negotiating than the state representatives, and I did." countered Gina. "The press gave me credit for negotiating a great deal for Burke Construction and Merit Project Finance. I'm proud of that press."

"Gina, when you testify, you have to look at the grand jurors. Otherwise, they'll think you are lying."

"Gabriela, you're right, thank you. But I don't need any eye contact advice. I'm not testifying."

"Then, look at me in the eye when you're telling me your story. Otherwise, I will question whether you are telling me the truth."

She glared at me.

I sensed I could get closer to the truth now, so I pushed her. "But other than Governor Harrington wanting the 'Texas Roads to Destiny' to catapult him into the White House, what was the value of the project to the state?"

"Texas Roads to Destiny and no income taxes caused a couple of big California and New York companies to move here. All you have to do is drive on any of the roads from north Dallas to Frisco and you know they need to be widened or new roads completed as soon as possible. Burke and its joint venture partners completed the $2 billion contract one year ahead of its proposed schedule."

Is she taking credit for the corporate moves that created the $5 billion mile?

"You negotiated the deal by yourself?"

Gina straightened her back. "I did indeed. Burke would have accepted far less than I was able to get, and the Australians couldn't believe what I had accomplished."

I frowned. Gina noticed. Her face darkened a little. "What's wrong with what I said?" she asked.

"Nothing. I was thinking about how the grand jury might feel about what you said."

"I told you the truth. You don't want me to lie to the grand jury, do you? I was the one who convinced the state to agree to a better deal than what Burke was ready to accept."

"I thought you said you were not going to testify."

I'm not, unless Randy Burke waives the lawyer-client privilege. And if he does, you don't want me to lie, do you?"

"No, lying would be a big problem. But some of the grand jurors will despise your mastery and great work-it resulted in them paying higher tolls to get to work every day."

"True, That's one more reason you have to get me out of testifying."

"Your client is working on that."

"If any of the grand jurors read the news or watch TV, they already know I am the one who is responsible for the tolls they are paying every day."

"Did you take advantage of your state?"

"I represented my client to the best of my ability, and I persuaded the governor that my offer was in his best interests."

"So, the end justified the means."

"I don't like your insinuation. It was a deal. Harrington could have said no, or the state could have negotiated a better deal. That is what they are trying to do now, but it is too late."

I smiled and shook my head at her. She didn't have the slightest clue how the grand jurors would look at her great success. "Yes, the local politicians, and the new governor and the media have all taken to publicly shaming you for negotiating too good a deal. They claim it is the worst deal the Texas DOT has ever negotiated."

"I wear their shame with honor. Some local politicians threatened to black-ball him in all 50 states. It's all just bullshit designed to get Burke to offer better terms."

"All right then. Is there anything else I need to know about how Burke was able to negotiate such a sweetheart deal with the State DOT?"

Gina glanced sideways to her right – a tell-tale sign she was getting ready to tell me another lie or half-truth.

Gina turned back and looked right at me and began. "No. The bottom line is our state had needed the Cross-Town project for many years. When the State DOT started looking into it, the project would not have been completed for at least 12 years using the normal federal and state financing. I came up with the idea to make it a toll road and, with Sam's help, I found a Merit to finance the project for Burke Construction. Because we were the only group submitting a proposal, I negotiated the best deal I could for my client. The State DOT and local government officials love the project, but they hate the deal. Burke didn't need to bribe the governor. End of story."

It wasn't quite what I had expected, but if she could stick to that and do it sincerely, or at least appear to say it sincerely, it might work.

"Let's break for lunch and get back together at 1:00. Will that work for you?"

"Sure, I'll see you at 1:00."

As soon as she left, I called Leo Baretti.

"How's it going?" he asked.

"We have a problem, and I'm not sure I can solve it by myself. I may need your help."

"How can I help?"

"You know I can't tell you what Gina has told me, but she's been too smooth with her story. She is hiding something from me, and maybe lying, I don't know whether it's important or not."

"I understand. Gina's upset that anyone would think there was a bribe involved in what she believes is her best work."

"She needs not be so prideful about her deal."

"I'll talk to her. I'll let her know the grand jury doesn't want to hear about what a great deal she made for her client."

"Thank you. But please do it in a way that Gina doesn't think you are telling her what to do because she is still trying to prove to you that she is a superstar lawyer and can handle this on her own."

"I'll do my best, but I've told her what to do her entire life."

"Thanks for making my point."

CHAPTER 17

Gabriela Sanchez

When we returned to the conference room, Gina sat down looking like she was in deep thought. Before I could start, she pointed at me. "I want to share a feeling with you. May I do that?"

"Sure, go ahead."

"I know you are a truly outstanding lawyer. I can tell that simply by spending time with you. But, I'm still not sure I want you to represent me."

I shook my head, smiled at her and leaned forward. I wanted to reply that I wasn't sure I wanted to represent her, but instead I said, "Okay. Let's talk about that."

"All I need for you to do is keep the government from forcing me to testify, and here we are spending all of this time going over what happened. You called my father during lunch and talked about my testifying before the grand jury. If you are thinking that I will testify, then I don't want you."

"Gina, you may be forced to testify. It could happen. Or your client could waive the lawyer-client privilege. Your client is the one to argue lawyer-client privilege, not you - it isn't your privilege to argue. We have limited time here, and we have to prepare."

"And you told my father to talk to me about my testimony."

I reluctantly admitted that I had.

"I talked to your father at lunch because he asked me to let him know how he could help us. Look, if you are unhappy with me, find another lawyer. But you don't have much time."

Gina sighed. "Damn, damn, damn. You 're right. I'm sorry. I should have never questioned you representing me. But look, if you plan to talk to my father at any time in the future, I want to know in advance, and not after the fact."

Her hand covering part of her face gave away that she wasn't really sorry, and she didn't think I was right.

"I promise I will tell you first."

"Then fine, let's continue."

"Gina, let's go through this step by step. You told me you found Merit, the Australian finance partner and convinced Randall Burke to submit a proposal. What did you do next?"

"He called Governor Harrington and suggested he meet with me."

"Well, that's unusual, isn't it?"

"How so?"

"It would make more sense if Burke met with Harrington himself rather than sending his lawyer. Did he send you so he would not be personally involved?"

"He sent me because I could push the governor further. They've been friends since grade school, you know."

"Where did you meet?"

"I met him in Austin."

"Was this the first time you had ever met with him?"

"No, I may have met him when he was a judge and I was in law school. I believe he judged a moot court competition. I met with Harrington and his wife, Laura Ray, when we put together the Hill Country Estates partnership. And, I met the two of them many times after that."

"What can you tell me about Austin Harrington?"

"As you know, he's a great communicator. He could have made millions of dollars practicing law, but he chose to run for the Texas Supreme Court, and after spending a few more years in private practice, he decided to run for governor. He has a big ego. I know his long-term plan was to run for President in 2020. The 2016 Presidential election changed his path, though. Overall, he's a good guy and I admire him."

"What can you tell me about Laura Ray Harrington?"

Gina cringed.

"Laura Ray is an attractive woman in her early 50s. She was once a Dallas Cowboys cheerleader. That's when Austin Harrington met her."

I pulled my laptop towards me and started searching for photos of Laura Ray as a cheerleader. Gina continued.

"Laura Ray is needy, greedy and she covets what Jenna Burke has - money, designer clothes from Neiman Marcus, jewelry, and a fancy Mercedes."

"So, you don't like her."

"I didn't say that. Laura Ray is easy on the eyes and the woman knows no strangers. She's the life of any party. But she is a thorn in Austin's side, and for that matter, Randall Burke's side too. Laura Ray was dead set against Harrington running for Governor to the extent that his staff thought she was sabotaging his campaign."

"Interesting. Why?"

"She wanted him to keep earning the big money practicing law. The pay as governor pales in comparison."

"I'm sure she was not happy when he was elected."

"No. She and Austin Harrington were not then, and are not now, happily married. I doubt they sleep in the same bedroom."

"He's making upwards of $3 million in private practice now. Hasn't that made her happier?"

"Well yes. But the last thing Laura Ray wants is for him to be appointed to the Supreme Court."

"Are their marital problems known?"

"The governor's staff members certainly were aware of the problems. His chief of staff once told me Laura Ray refused to play the political games."

"What political games?"

"Austin Harrington frequently showed up in homeless shelters to serve meals. He was always trying to portray himself as 'Mr. Good Guy.' Laura Ray Harrington never joined him because she thought it was just a show. She was right."

"It's the Hill Country Estates partnership that drags Laura Ray into the investigation. Are you aware of anything else she ever received from Randall Burke?"

"Laura Ray frequently sent me emails asking for money from the partnership. That created all kinds of conflict because Burke wanted to put the money back into the development. She also asked Burke for gifts and loans - many times."

"Well now, did Burke give her anything?"

Gina looked away. "I've been told that Burke paid for Laura Ray's inaugural dress, and I'm sure he bought her much more over the years, but I don't know all of the details."

"Did you see Austin Harrington any other times before the Cross-Town project meeting?"

"Several times. We were friends for some time before the Cross-Town Tollway Contract. Whenever he visited Dallas, Fort Worth, or anywhere in between, he'd invite Tony and me to meet him for dinner, and whenever I traveled to Austin, I let him know and he'd invite me to dinner. I've sat in the Burke Construction box with him at Cowboys games and UT football games."

"So, you and Tony met him for dinner how many times up here in the DFW metroplex?"

Gina raised her hand to her face and paused before she spoke-another tell-tale sign what she was about to tell me was either a lie or a half-truth.

"I'm not sure how many times I ate dinner or met with Governor Harrington here in Dallas."

Huh, she said I, not we... Was it more than social?"

"You said, I not we. Did you eat dinner alone with Austin Harrington?"

She paused again.

"If it was on a week night and Tony and I couldn't get a babysitter, I ate alone with Austin. If it was a weekend or we were able to secure a babysitter, then Tony and I ate with Governor Harrington."

"Did Harrington ever make a pass at you?"

"What?"

"Did he ever make a pass at you?"

"What does that have to do with anything?"

"Some people have theorized that you took advantage of Harrington because he made a pass at you."

"I didn't take advantage. I followed his lead."

I didn't understand. "What does that mean?" I asked her.

"It was pretty simple. One time when he took me to dinner in Dallas, he looked down at my feet and said, 'nice shoes.' I had four-inch heels on that night. From that night on, I always wore heels when I knew I would see him. I even wore heels with jeans to the Cowboys games."

"You were flirting with him."

"I used one of the tools that were available to me."

"You were flirting."

"No. I was building a personal relationship with a man who admired my looks and my shoes."

"When did you realize that Burke would submit the only proposal to build the Cross-Town Tollway project?"

"I knew right away as neither of the other two contractors that had submitted earlier proposals currently had the financing.

"So, the state had no option but to accept Burke's proposal -or not build the Cross-Town Tollway."

"That's not exactly true. The state could have delayed the contract and let other contractors find financing."

"But you had convinced the Governor that building the Cross-Town Tollway project right away would give him a better chance to run for President."

"Yes, but that was when the entire country was expecting the President to lose the election. That all changed when he shook up the world and actually won. Austin Harrington was on his first list of potential Supreme Court Justices."

"Did you make notes, or is there any written record of your meetings with Governor Harrington?"

"No."

"Why was that the case?"

"Our discussions were informal. I'm telling you it was friendly and social. There was no reason to make any notes or write anything about what we discussed."

"Did you exchange emails with Harrington?"

"No."

"Text messages?"

"Only about where to meet him."

"When you negotiated the contract, you didn't negotiate with Governor Harrington?"

"Not at the beginning, no. I negotiated with John Randolph, the lawyer that Governor Harrington appointed to represent TxDOT."

"On any other Burke project, did you ever personally negotiate with a state governor?"

"No."

"Why?"

"Because no other state governor tied his future to transportation."

She yawned, put both fingertips on her eyes and took a deep breath.

"Let's call it a day," I told her. "Tomorrow is Saturday, are you okay getting together here in the morning? Then you can spend the afternoon with your family."

"Can we cover the rest of what you need in the morning?"

"Yes, I think so. I want to discuss in detail your negotiations with Randolph and Harrington. Bring any notes or documents you have and overnight please try to recall the specifics of your negotiations."

"Okay." She looked at her watch. "Want to go downstairs and get a drink or a glass of wine?" she asked.

"I thought you told me you didn't want to be wine drinking buddies with me."

"I need to get the edge off before I go home, and I don't want to go for a drink alone."

I really didn't want to have a drink, but I thought it might be a way to get her to relax, and I might learn something that will help me represent Gina.

When we arrived at the doors to the Maximus, I looked in and saw several of my partners at tables and standing at the bar. There was no really quiet place for the two of us to talk.

"Let's go to the Starlight Room at the Grand Hotel," I suggested. "We can find a quiet spot to talk there."

We walked underground over to the Grand Hotel and went up the carpeted stairs. When we walked into the Starlight Room, only a few patrons were sitting at the bar, and just one table was occupied.

A tall, blond young man with sparkling blue eyes near the bar looked at us and smiled at Gina.

"Hi, Sophia."

She froze for a moment like she had seen a ghost. Then she smiled and said "Hi, Liam," and she turned away.

We sat in a small booth in the corner, and within a minute, one of my favorite waitresses, Gladys, appeared at our table.

"Hello Ms. Sanchez and Ms. Rossi, what can I get for you?"

"Could I have a Pellegrino with a lime?" I asked.

"Ms. Rossi, a Grey Goose Cosmo?"

"Yes, Gladys, thank you."

"I see you've been here before. Why did that young guy call you Sophia?"

"Sophia is my middle name. Some people like it better and Liam is one of them."

"How do you know Liam?"

Gina squirmed in her seat and slid down ever so slightly.

"I'm his mentor. We've met here several times."

Ten minutes later, I had only finished about half of my Pellegrino and Gina had started her second Cosmopolitan. "May I ask you a personal question?"

"Yes."

"Why aren't you married? You're a beautiful woman and have a great career."

"Why are you interested in that?"

"You put your career first and that's the reason you are single."

I laughed. "Have you been talking to my mother?"

"What?"

"My mother has encouraged me more than a few times to get married and have her grandchildren."

"So, why haven't you?"

"Look, we're all different. We have different talents, goals, aspirations, and problems. I don't want to settle for just anyone. I want the right one. He hasn't come around yet."

Gina crossed her arms and gazed over toward the bar.

Finally, she looked back at me. "You spent most of the summer helping the illegal children and their mothers in McAllen, and El Paso. I'm surprised your firm let you do it. Was it because you were constantly a guest on CNN and MSNBC?"

She thinks I only do things to further my career. "No," I told her. "and I was surprised when TV reporters caught up with me in McAllen and asked me for an interview."

"It wasn't only one interview. Your photos were on the front page of the newspaper, and you were on TV every time the liberal media covered the caravans coming to the United States."

"Well, the reporter had a photographer with him. I went to Tornillo near El Paso in November because there were 3,800 children being held there in tents. You don't think I went there to get a photograph on the front page of the newspaper?"

"So, how did you help them?"

"I helped children deal with the immigration system once they were taken into custody by immigration officials. I helped some families in McAllen seeking asylum so they could stay in the United States. In June I was trying to reunify families separated by our government."

"So, you favor open borders, and just letting anyone in our country?"

"No, of course not. That's a silly accusation the conservatives make against anyone trying to help the children. You're not buying that are you?"

She didn't respond.

"Look, thousands are fleeing crime in Central America. Children are being killed, and girls are being raped in record numbers."

"So, why can't they settle in Mexico? Why do they have to come to the United States?"

"Many of the refugees *are* seeking asylum in Mexico."

"I heard you convinced a judge to issue an injunction requiring the government to reunite the families."

"Children were separated from their parents. The media covered it extensively. At least 2,300 children were separated from their parents."

"But, a lot of the adults were posing as parents. They weren't really parents."

"I wouldn't say a lot, but I'm sure some were posing as parents."

"Did you represent some of the men in the caravans?"

"No, I was busy with other things when they started arriving in November."

Gina gestured to Gladys with her empty glass, and I decided it was time to leave.

"Gina, I have a dinner engagement," I said. "I'll see you in the morning."

"You have a date? Is it with Christopher Duval?"

I shook my head and dropped twenty on the table and started walking toward the door. "See you in the morning."

"Wait, is it true what they said about you in that National Tabloid Journal article. Are you really bisexual?"

"Gina, there are some things that are just not your business."

"Here's one thing that is my business."

"What's that?"

"I know why you do the volunteer work."

"Why do you think that is?"

"It's no pressure. You're in your comfort zone in the Rio Grande Valley, and the people you are helping worship you. You don't have to prove yourself. In Dallas, helping me, you're back in the high-pressure zone. You're not absolutely sure you are up to it."

"Don't worry," I told her. "I thrive on proving myself in high pressure situations."

When I reached the door, I looked back, and the blond young Liam had walked over and put his arm around Gina.

When I got home, I did a quick search on the Roberson Grant website. There was no lawyer named Liam in the list of attorneys. I then searched the name Liam and Dallas attorney, no one with that first name came up in the search. Liam is not really a lawyer.

Why would she lie about Liam? What else is she lying about?

CHAPTER 18

Gina Rossi

I woke up early on Saturday morning with somewhat of a hangover. I looked forward to working out at the Dallas City Club. Mario arrived at 5:30 to pick me up.

"How do you feel this morning?" he asked.

"I'm feeling fine, Mario."

"You were out pretty late last night."

"I know, Mario. I ran into some friends at the Grand Hotel. I wanted to spend some time with them."

"Mr. Burke was worried about you."

"You told Mr. Burke what time you brought me home?"

"I'm sorry I had to because while I was waiting for you, he asked me to make a pick-up at the airport."

"What else have you been telling Mr. Burke?"

"Nothing other than you are safe. Mr. Burke is worried sick that someone wants to hurt you, especially after you told him about the text messages you've been receiving."

"He told me you'd protect me."

"And I will, but I'm not with you 24/7."

Fifteen minutes later, Mario pulled up in front of the City Club.

"What time do you want me to pick you up?"

"I don't know. I'll call you."

When I walked out of the locker room, Gabriela was already on the treadmill. She was one of only a few working out early that Saturday. *Must be Saturday after Christmas.*

It was cold again, so I decided to run on the treadmill. I wanted to push myself, so I set the pace at 6 minutes and 45 seconds per mile rate. After I made 5 miles, I was energized and ready for weights and core exercises.

In the locker room, I noticed Gabriela had a towel around her when she came back to her locker from the shower. I gathered she was trying to send me a message, but I didn't care. I remembered the look on her face when she saw me without a towel.

After we got dressed, we stopped for a latte on the way to Gabriela's office.

On the way to her office, Gabriela asked: "May I ask you a question?"

"Isn't that what you've been doing since we met?"

"Yes, but I mean a personal question."

"Go ahead."

"I did a search for Liam and discovered he's not an associate in your law firm. How are you his mentor?"

"What? Are you accusing me of lying to you? How can you represent me if you think I am lying to you?"

Gabriela's face turned red. "I didn't understand how you were mentoring him."

"Gabriela, you must trust me," I told her. "If you have to know. I am mentoring Liam as part of the Dallas Bar Association mentoring program. I'm a volunteer. What did you think I was doing with him?"

"He wasn't looking at you like you were his mentor."

"How was he looking at me?"

"He never took those blue eyes off of you. He was like a schoolboy infatuated with his teacher."

"Maybe he is, but that doesn't mean I'm returning the favor. You don't trust me."

"Actually, you're right," she said as if I had given her the opening she wanted. "I'm pretty sure you're hiding something from me, and I fear it might be something that could get you into trouble."

"I'm sorry I am leaving you with that impression. I'm telling you all you need to know to represent me," I replied. "I hope that is good enough, but if it isn't, do you think you can really represent me?"

"We're beyond that point, Gina. I'm here to help you. It's up to you to enable me to do the best I can representing you."

No. It's up to you to get me out of testifying against my client.

"I'm glad to hear that. I'm doing my best. Let's get to business so I can get home this afternoon."

"Okay. After I left you yesterday," she began. "I got a call from Brian Renfro, the Assistant U.S. Attorney. He told me that Jim Hardy is putting pressure on the DOJ in Washington to drop the investigation against Governor Harrington."

"I assume that's what any lawyer would do."

"Yes. Hardy has a good argument."

"What's the argument?"

"Do you remember when the former Virginia governor and his wife were convicted of taking a bribe?"

"No."

"The former Virginia governor and his wife received over $175,000 in gifts from a political donor who wanted meetings with state officials.

A jury convicted them. Then, after the appeals court affirmed the conviction, the Supreme Court unanimously overturned the conviction."

"That's good, right?"

"It might be good for Governor Harrington, but it's not good for you. Renfro believes you are the only one who knows whether the state awarded Burke the $2 billion contract in return for making Harrington and his wife millionaires from the Hill Country Estates investment. You had many personal discussions with both Burke and Harrington.

"But, my discussions with Burke are protected by lawyer-client privilege."

"Gina, Renfro knows that, but he is prepared to show they are not privileged because you were helping Burke commit a fraud when you advised him on the purchase of the Harringtons' interest in the Hill Country Estates partnership. He told they met with your associate Anna Lang and they believe she will help their case."

"That's a bunch of crap. Anna doesn't know anything that would help their case."

"It may be, but I need to review those files right away. Renfro has asked Judge Parsons to conduct an in-camera review of your files and to question you to determine whether you were helping Burke commit fraud."

"How does that work?"

"Judge Parsons will review the files. The government will have a chance to submit questions to him that he may ask. He has scheduled the in-camera questioning for Monday. That's why I need the files today."

"Will Renfro ask questions Monday?"

"Neither the government nor anyone from Burke Construction will be permitted in the courtroom, and they won't be given a transcript of your testimony."

"That is good, right?"

"Yes, if the government lawyers were allowed to witness your testimony, or get the transcript, they would use what you say against Burke or Harrington and maybe even you. If Judge Parsons thinks you offered advice to help Burke get the Cross-Town Tollway contract in return for getting a windfall on the Hill Country Estates buyout, or any other benefit Burke gave Harrington, he will direct you to testify in front of the grand jury. On the other hand, if he believes you were just acting as Burke's attorney and giving the company and Randall Burke advice on what the law is, then he will grant the motion to quash your subpoena. You will need to persuade him."

"I can do that. Jason Daniels wants me to lie so they can taint Harrington before he is nominated to the Supreme Court. You have to persuade Judge Parsons and let me know what I should and shouldn't say, and I'll take care of the rest."

"That's what we have been working on all week."

"What if I refuse to answer Judge Parsons' questions?"

"Judge Parsons will hold you in contempt and send you to jail until you agree to answer the questions."

"I understand."

"Okay, yesterday we were talking about your negotiations with John Randolph. I want to learn more about that. "Could John Randolph be the whistleblower?"

"No way. He was appointed by the governor. I negotiated the contract terms with him and with the TxDOT Transportation Secretary."

"But he has received lots of heat for 'giving away the farm.' If he is under investigation, he may be willing to deal to save himself."

"Given his history with Governor Harrington, that seems a little far-fetched," I replied.

Gabriela Sanchez looked at me.

She thinks I am holding something else back. I can tell.

"One of my running friends," I told her, "practiced law in the same firm as Randolph. She told me he was a brilliant lawyer. But then she also said he had some issues. When I asked what issues, she told me I would have to learn about that from other sources."

"I've heard Randolph is a real ladies' man who wears $5000 suits and drives a Tesla luxury car. That's a little rich for a lawyer working for the TxDOT."

I laughed.

"He's a wealthy man," I told her. "When Randolph was in private practice, he made a ton of money doing the legal work on major construction projects throughout the United States. He demanded top dollar and he got it. He took the State DOT job to further the Governor Harrington's transportation agenda. I'm sure Randolph expected to be named Secretary of Transportation if Harrington had been elected President."

"How did you deal with him?"

"Do you want an honest answer?"

"Absolutely."

"I dealt with him the same way I dealt with Governor Harrington. I got to know him and made him my friend. I smiled a lot, and always looked my best."

Gabriela rubbed her forehead and shook her head.

"I see what you are thinking. No, I didn't have sex with Randolph," I told her. "I talked about Tony and Mateo. I didn't want him to make unwilling advances or disrespect me in any way, and I made that clear from the beginning. I played to his ego and figured out what he was passionate about. I knew he worked out, so I told him he looked great and asked what he did to stay so fit. I knew he was a Cowboys fan, so I read everything being written about the Cowboys, going all the way back to when they played at the Cotton Bowl. Instead of flirting, I would say I made him feel comfortable with me."

"Comfortable with you?"

"I've always gotten along far better with men than with women. Every deal I have ever negotiated for Burke Construction involved persuading a man to reach an agreement. You think I was flirting, or even sleeping around. I'm telling you I'm simply a good persuader and I use what works well with men. What does any of this have to do with my potential grand jury testimony?"

"You may well be asked how exactly you persuaded Governor Harrington and John Randolph to enter into a contract that some say is the worst deal in Texas history."

"Well, I wouldn't tell them anything I just told you about how I persuaded them. I'll stick to the more basic facts - we desperately needed the Cross-Town Tollway contract to deal with the increased traffic in Dallas, and Governor Harrington wanted it to be the centerpiece of his Texas Roads to Destiny program."

For the next four hours, Gabriela Sanchez grilled me about every aspect of the Hill Country Estates deal and the Cross-Town Tollway contract. Sanchez specifically wanted to know what Burke Construction and Randy Burke likely had about the deal in their files and on their computers. I was getting tired, but I was prepared. *No way Judge Parsons' questions could be this tough.*

Finally, at noon, the courier brought the files from my office. Gabriela looked at me.

"Let me share some advice. Like me, you speak at breakneck speed, and sometimes you start to answer before the full question is out. Make sure you hear the end of the question. Take a deep breath, pause, and then answer slowly."

"Thank you. That's a good reminder. When I get going, I speak quickly because I think quickly."

"When asked about the nature and purpose of your advice to Burke, make it broad and general because the prosecution must tie the advice to the crime. If Judge Parsons believes that the only thing Burke wanted to know was whether his buyout of the Harringtons' interest in the Hill Country partnership *at a premium* could somehow be considered a bribe, and you said it could, the judge will likely conclude that Burke used your advice to commit a crime. The more detailed Burke's questions and the more detailed your advice to him, the more likely the judge will find that your advice furthered a crime."

"Look, Burke sought my advice to help him make sure the payment to Harrington when he was running for governor complied with the law."

"I understand that."

"If I answer the questions Judge Parsons asks, what happens if he then orders me to testify?"

"You'll be in a Catch-22. If you appear and testify to the grand jury, you and your client won't be able to challenge Judge Parsons' ruling. But if you refuse to testify, he can hold you in contempt and throw you in jail or send you to the Federal Prison Camp.

CHAPTER 19

———— ❧ ————

Gabriela Sanchez

After Gina left, I thought about what had happened. I had made an assumption that Gina had lied to me about Liam, and while I was embarrassed when Gina called me out for making the assumption and came up with a reasonable explanation, I knew she had lied, but calling her on it again would only create more problems. She may be under a lot of pressure, but she always acts composed, like it is no big deal.

Thirty minutes after Gina had gone, I called in two associates who I trusted to start reviewing Gina's and her law firm's files on the Hill Country Estates partnership and the Cross-Town Tollway contract, along with some other contract files that were included in her package. I told them to create a privilege log of documents they believed would qualify as lawyer-client privileged documents and to bring to my attention anything unusual they found. I also told them to look specifically for anything that might indicate that Randall Burke had given Austin Harrington anything at all with the expectation of something in return.

I started reviewing the files and emails. The first thing that struck me was that when the Hill Country Estates partnership was formed, Gina had advised Randall Burke that if he and his wife contributed the

Harringtons' share, that would be considered a gift - and Burke and his wife would have to report it and pay a gift tax.

Gina also had posed a question in an email to Burke. *Where will the Harringtons get the money to contribute their share to the partnership?* Burke had replied that Harrington had made lots of money during the short time he had been in private practice, and Burke knew Harrington and his wife would contribute their share.

When Harrington then announced he was running for governor, Gina had advised Burke to dissolve the Hill Country Estates partnership.

Burke had asked for her advice on whether he and his wife could buy out the Harringtons. Gina had replied: *If you and Jenna want to purchase the Harringtons' interest, we need to hire an appraisal expert to evaluate the fair value of the Harrington's share of the partnership.* Burke had sent a reply saying he knew the fair market value of Hill Country Estates land and there was no need to spend money getting an appraisal.

Gina was clearly well-prepared in every matter she had handled for Burke. Her preparation undoubtedly gave her confidence to be bold in her negotiations.

I started to piece together what had happened. Randall Burke had retained Gina Rossi and her firm to represent the company because Gina anticipated things others missed and she was a master negotiator with no fear of failure. But, when it came to her legal advice in connection with his business dealings with Austin Harrington, it seemed that Burke pretty much ignored what she advised him to do.

Had Gina only flirted with John Randolph or if it had actually gone further. She seemed willing to do whatever it took to make the best deal for her client. I couldn't figure out how she had been able to get both Governor Harrington and Randolph to cave-in on the tolling of the old road while the new one was being built. I didn't understand why Burke had been upset with her when she pushed Randolph and Governor Harrington to include tolling on the old road while the new one was being built. Merit Financial praised what she had done.

There were a few emails between Gina and Governor Harrington. As she had claimed, she was the one who came up with the "Texas Roads to Destiny" program. Before Burke submitted the proposal on the Cross-Town Tollway, Gina had suggested the idea to Harrington. So, Gina first persuaded Harrington that "Texas Roads to Destiny" was his ticket to the White House. Then she found a finance partner for her client Burke, helped the team submit the only proposal, and twisted Harrington's and John Randolph's arms to get even a better deal for her client.

I was specifically looking for a smoking gun, and I didn't find one in her files or her law firm's files, but I did understand why the government needed her to testify. Ever since the Supreme Court decision in the former Virginia Governor's case and the mistrial and dismissal of the New Jersey Senator's case, it had become increasingly difficult to convict a government official. Gifts from friends no longer were enough to convict a public official. The government now was forced to show that the gift was directly related to an official action taken by the government official.

In this case, Harrington had gotten involved in the solicitation and the award of a $2 billion contract to his lifelong friend, but the Hill Country partnership and buyout were all done before he became governor. Harrington and Burke would both deny any connection between the two events, and the government believed that Gina Rossi was the one person who would know whether Harrington had interceded on behalf of Burke in return for the Hill Country Estates payout.

Questions kept nagging at me. *Did the former Governor and Burke meet or talk about the contract behind the scenes? Why did Gina negotiate the contract? If Randy Burke had bribed the Governor, why was he so upset when Gina pushed for a better deal?*

I came up with a theory answering some of my questions. Either Randall Burke or Gina Rossi had something on Governor Harrington that gave Gina leverage to get a better deal on the Cross-Town Tollway contract. That was the only theory that could explain how she was able to convince Governor Harrington to agree to tolling the freeway during construction. The Texas Department of Transportation had been against the idea. John Randolph was against the idea. Randall Burke was willing to enter into the contract without the added tolling. *What does Gina Rossi have on the former governor?*

CHAPTER 20

December 30

Gina Rossi

At 8:45 a.m. Mario pulled up to the curb outside Gabriela's office building. We were both ready. I was trying hard to not be nervous, or at least not show any of my nervousness. Gabriela and I settled into the back of his Lincoln. I was dressed in my power suit, a jacket, blouse and pencil skirt.

There was a lot of traffic heading north out of Dallas to Plano. At 9:30 Mario turned into the Federal District Court parking lot off of Preston Road in Plano, Texas. Gabriela told me she had not set foot in the modern small courthouse since she had clerked for Judge Comstock 10 years earlier. It was much smaller than the Dallas Federal Courthouse, and the lighting always seemed much brighter.

As we got out of Mario's car, a dozen or so reporters and cameras, and a group of protesters descended upon us.

"What do you plan to tell the judge this morning, Ms. Rossi?" one of the reporters asked. The protestors were chanting "Shame" and carrying signs and placards with the words "No Toll No Way." One carried a sign with Gina's photo and Harrington's and the words "Guilty as Charged."

Mario hustled around to the front of his car and started pushing a path through the crowd. One of the protestors hit him on the side of the head with a sign. I looked at Mario reach inside his jacket and was worried he would pull out his revolver. Instead, he pulled out a handkerchief and wiped his forehead.

"Did your client pay Governor Harrington to let him submit the only proposal on a $2 billion contract?"

"Why are you refusing to testify and help the Special Counsel find out the truth?"

"What are you hiding?"

"One of the protestors yelled "Bitch" at me. Then the group chanted "Bitch" in unison.

I grabbed the back of Mario's suit jacket and inched myself closer to him as he kept shoving us through the crowd.

Cameras flashed in my face and at the protestors. I knew I would be one of the lead stories on the evening news that night and on the front page of the Dallas newspaper in the morning.

When we got through security, I asked Gabriela, "How did the press and protestors know I would be here this morning?"

"Someone apparently leaked your appearance to the media."

I had to stop and gather myself before we walked into the courtroom. I wanted to go to the bathroom, but I figured female news reporters would be waiting for me there.

Judge William Parsons was appointed in 2009, shortly after President Obama took office. He had grown up in a Dallas suburb where he had been a star tailback. But Judge Parsons apparently was not good enough to receive a scholarship from the University of Texas or A&M, so he had gone to school and played football at Trinity University in San Antonio.

In his sophomore year, Parsons suffered a career-ending knee injury and spent his remaining time at Trinity focused on his studies. After college, he received his law degree from the University of Texas. Before being nominated for the Federal District Court, Parsons had practiced law in a large Dallas law firm, where he had gained a reputation for being a ruthless, take-no-prisoners litigator.

In his nine years on the bench, Judge Parsons had proven he was no friend of the FBI and the Department of Justice. But he had also developed a reputation for punishing white-collar criminals. He routinely sentenced white-collar defendants to the maximum punishment allowed, as if to send a message to their friends.

Gabriela had appeared before Judge Parsons before and she was convinced that after he questioned me, in-camera, he would order me to testify before the Grand Jury on January 2. My father echoed Gabriela's prediction.

At 10:00 a.m. sharp, Judge William Parsons entered the courtroom. Gabriela Sanchez, and the court reporter and I stood up.

"You may be seated."

"Ms. Rossi and Ms. Sanchez, I think the two of you know why we're here today."

"Yes, Your Honor."

"Well, let me get this background information on the record before we proceed. We are here today in connection with an ongoing grand jury investigation in the Northern District of Texas. Ms. Rossi received a subpoena to testify and produce her Burke Construction Company and Randall Burke client files. Both Ms. Rossi through her lawyer, Ms. Sanchez, and Burke Construction, through its lawyer, Ken Sanders, filed a Motion to Quash the subpoena, essentially arguing that if Ms. Rossi is required to testify and produce client files, that will violate the lawyer-client privilege.

He continued explaining for the record that the government had replied stating that Ms. Rossi could be required to testify before the grand jury because her client Burke Construction intended to commit a crime or fraud, by bribing former Governor Austin Harrington, to obtain TxDOT highway construction contracts, and that the otherwise-privileged communication between Burke and Ms. Rossi was made in furtherance of that illicit purpose. The government also presented evidence which it claims shows that is what happened. I found that the government's *ex parte* submission met the threshold required for me to question Ms. Rossi *in camera*, meaning outside the presence of both the government and Burke Construction and their lawyers.

"And so that brings us to why we are here today," he concluded.

"Your Honor?"

"Yes, Ms. Sanchez."

"May I look at what the government's *ex parte* submission that you said met the threshold to cause you to examine Ms. Rossi *in camera*?"

"No, Ms. Sanchez, that would violate the Grand Jury's secrecy."

"Your Honor, not having the submission violates Ms. Rossi's right to due process."

"Ms. Sanchez, for now, Ms. Rossi is a witness, not a defendant, or even named a target of the investigation. You are not entitled to the submission."

"Yes, Your Honor. Our understanding is that even though the court reporter will be taking down and transcribing Ms. Rossi's testimony today, the transcript will be placed under seal and not disclosed to the government."

"That's right. And it won't be disclosed to Burke Construction or its lawyers either."

"Thank you, Your Honor."

"Ms. Rossi, please come up here and sit in the witness chair and let Ms. Garcia swear you in."

I got up from the counsel's table and slowly walked to the witness chair. I walked up two steps, sat down on the cushion in the wooden chair and looked out at Gabriela Sanchez, who raised her thumb ever so slightly.

"Ms. Rossi, please rise and raise your right hand. Do you swear or affirm to tell the truth, the whole truth, and nothing but the truth?"

"I do."

"You may be seated, Ms. Rossi. At the beginning here, I want to ask you some background questions. You'll easily get the gist of them."

"Yes, Thank you, Your Honor."

For the next 20 minutes, Gabriela learned more about my background than I had ever told her during our interviews. Judge Parsons established that my father was Leo Baretti, my brother was Samuel Baretti, and my mother had died in a car accident when I was 10. He learned that after my mother died, I had been raised primarily by my father, my grandmother, and my father's housekeeper. Yes, my father was the famous Dallas lawyer, Leo Baretti. Yes, Samuel Baretti was the well-known Dallas investment banker, and yes, my husband, Tony Rossi, was a Dallas lawyer with Legal Aid.

Judge Parsons then turned to my legal career.

"Ms. Rossi, when were you admitted to practice law in Texas?"

"In 2001, Your Honor, after I graduated from the University of Texas law school."

"And that year you started work with the Roberson Grant law firm here in Dallas."

"Yes, Sir, I started in September of that year."

"You are now one of the firm's partners, is that right?"

"Yes, Sir."

"And what year did you become a partner?"

"That would be 2008, Your Honor."

"And you've been a partner ever since?"

"Yes, Sir."

"Burke Construction is one of your clients?"

"Your Honor, in our firm we would say Burke Construction is a firm client. I am the lawyer responsible for the company and Mr. Burke."

"When did Burke Construction become a firm client?"

"In 2007, Your Honor."

"And how did Burke Construction become a client?"

"They were being sued by a developer in Denton County. Susan Delaney, the company general counsel, sought proposals and presentations from outside law firms. We were one of the firms, and we were the firm selected."

"And did you take responsibility for that case?"

"I did, Your Honor, and we got the case dismissed and won on appeal."

"I see. Is that how Burke Construction became a firm client and your client?"

"Yes, Sir."

"And shortly after that, you were promoted to partner in Roberson Grant, is that correct?"

"Yes, Sir."

"And since that time, Burke Construction has been the only client for whom you are responsible, is that correct?"

Gabriela stood up. "Judge Parsons, I understand you are going after a little background information here. But I believe whether or not Burke Construction is Ms. Rossi's only client is not relevant."

"Ms. Sanchez, this question was submitted by the government lawyers. They think it is relevant and I agree. I'm going to have Ms. Rossi answer."

"Yes, Your Honor," I replied. "Burke Construction is the only firm client for whom I'm the responsible attorney."

"I want to take a 15-minute break here," he said checking his watch. "I have a short conference call on another case."

When we walked out of the courtroom I turned to Gabriela. "So far the questions have been pretty easy to answer."

"That's because all he has focused on so far is background information. Don't expect the questions to be as easy when we go back."

CHAPTER 21

Gina Rossi

Twenty minutes later I was back in the witness chair.

"Ms. Rossi, are you ready to continue answering questions?"

"Yes, Your Honor."

"Okay. I have asked background questions about how Burke Construction became your client. Now I want to focus on more specific questions. You helped Burke Construction on major highway and bridge projects throughout the United States, is that correct?"

"Yes, Your Honor."

"Ms. Rossi, how much in fees has Burke Construction paid the firm, this year?"

"I don't know exactly, Your Honor, we're at year end so lots of money comes in these last few days in December."

"Last time you checked, how much had Burke Construction paid the firm this year?"

"Slightly over $4 million in fees."

"They are a big firm client and you are the responsible lawyer?"

"Yes, Sir."

"And what would happen to you if Burke Construction left the firm and went to another firm?"

"I don't understand, Your Honor."

"If Burke Construction left your firm and went to another firm, would you be paid less?"

"I don't know, Judge."

"If you were promoted to partner because you became the attorney responsible for Burke Construction, is there a chance you would be fired or demoted if they went to another firm?"

"I don't think so. Our firm doesn't treat our partners that way."

"Would you be worried if Burke Construction fired the firm and went to another law firm?"

"I'm not sure worried is the right word. I would be concerned about why Burke would fire us."

"Ms. Rossi, after you successfully handled the Denton County work, describe some of the other work you have done for Burke."

"As you mentioned, there have been a lot of work on public-private partnership deals in Texas and throughout the United States. These deals are called P3 projects. I negotiated the contracts for all of these deals. I spent months investigating potential P3 projects throughout the United States, Canada, and Mexico."

"Did Burke Construction enter into contracts to build highways in Canada and Mexico?"

"No, I convinced Randall Burke that he would be crazy to cross either border when there were many big P3 projects right here in the U.S."

"During the time that Austin Harrington was governor, how many contracts was Burke Construction awarded without bidding?"

I tried to count the number in my head. Finally, I answered, "several, Your Honor, but I am not sure of the number."

"Was Burke Construction awarded a contract every single time it submitted a proposal?"

"I'm not sure, Your Honor. You would need to ask TxDOT."

"Ms. Rossi, is it true that Burke Construction was awarded contracts even in cases where it did not submit the lowest cost proposal?"

"I'm not sure, Your Honor."

"Do you know of any cases where Burke Construction was awarded a contract when it did not submit the lowest priced proposal?"

"Yes, Sir."

"More than one time?"

"Yes, Your Honor, but Governor Harrington had nothing to do with the award of the contract."

"How many trips did you make to Austin in connection with TxDOT public-private partnership projects?"

"A whole bunch. I can't tell you an exact number. I was traveling to Austin at least once a month, and sometimes more often, for several years."

"And who were you visiting on those trips?"

"In some cases, I was visiting Governor Harrington, because he was spearheading the Cross-Town Tollway project. I also visited William Jenkins, the Chairman of the Texas Transportation Commission, and I met with John Randolph, who was the lawyer responsible for the projects."

"Did you get to know Mr. Randolph?"

"Of course, every large Texas contractor and every contractor lawyer knows Mr. Randolph."

"Did you give Mr. Burke business advice suggesting which P3 projects to pursue?"

"I wouldn't call it business advice. It was part of the legal advice I gave Mr. Burke. Before Burke submitted any proposals, I would spend many months studying the viability of the projects, because they were so risky and many of them had not been financially viable."

"Did you advise Burke on its unsolicited proposal on the Cross-Town Tollway Contract?"

"Yes, I did."

"Why did Burke submit an unsolicited proposal?"

"In part, because Governor Harrington - and Governor Carson before him - made the Cross-Town project the highest priority in their administrations, and in part because I searched and found the finance partner that Burke needed to fund the project."

"You found the finance partner?"

"Yes, Sir. My brother first made me aware of Merit Project Finance, an Australian firm. I did a lot of research and talked to a Merit V.P who told me that Merit was looking to finance projects over $1 billion in the United States."

"Why didn't any other Texas construction company submit a proposal?"

"I don't know, Your Honor. You'd have to ask them."

"Did you talk to any of those construction companies?"

"When, Your Honor?"

"When your client submitted an unsolicited proposal on the Cross-Town Tollway project."

"I'm not sure, Your Honor. I may have, but I don't remember the timeframe."

"Ms. Rossi, the government believes you asked Ronan Construction to submit a proposal so that your client's $2 billion proposal would not be the only one."

"Your Honor, Ronan Construction had submitted a proposal years ago when the idea for the Cross-Town Tollway project was first discussed. I may have asked their general counsel if they planned to submit a proposal this time."

"Did the Ronan general counsel tell you they did not plan on submitting a proposal because your client had it locked up with the governor?"

"I don't recall his ever saying that. I do recall his asking how Burke was able to find financing during the recession though, and I told him I had found the financing."

"Beyond any technical issues, what were the most significant challenges on that project?"

"Figuring out a way to make it financially viable was the biggest challenge."

"How was funding a challenge?"

"After I found Merit, I had to find a way to make it financially viable. As the project stood at the time, the numbers didn't work, and the Australians were ready to back out. Without funding during construction, the tolls would be too expensive when the project was completed. Also, if the existing highways did not have tolls, that would drastically reduce the number of cars paying tolls on the new highway."

"What were other challenges?"

"During the construction, a new governor was elected. So, there was the risk of dealing with the new administration. There was loud public outcry against the project by groups that were against toll roads. Some local government officials were against toll roads and they found a friendly media to state their case."

"Tell me more about the financing."

"There were bonds, state funds, federal funds, Burke and Merit's equity and toll revenue collected during construction."

"How did the state happen to agree to allow your client to collect tolls on an existing highway, during the construction period?"

"As I noted earlier, there was no way the project would be financially viable without those funds coming in during construction. Without those toll funds, Burke and Merit would have put up $200 million before any money from tolls even started coming back to them. We anticipated that about 18 percent of the funding would come from tolling the existing road during the five years of construction."

"And the public was outraged by that arrangement?"

"I never used the term 'outraged.' Many were unhappy. But many more were unhappy with what they were told the greater tolls would be without those funds. The tolls during peak periods were reduced from $2.85 to $1.85. When the public was still upset by paying a toll at all on the existing road, Governor Harrington agreed to increase the state's share of the funding."

"And that delayed the tolls on the existing highway until after he left office?"

"I'm not sure of the timing, but that sounds about right."

"If Governor Harrington had not personally been involved, the Cross-Town Tollway deal would have never closed. Is that a fair assessment?"

"I think that's a safe assumption."

"And your client's risk was reduced when Governor Harrington convinced the legislature to appropriate more funds and delay the tolling of the existing road, isn't that true?"

"Sure, if Burke correctly analyzed the cost to build the Cross-Town project, it was less risky when the state appropriated more money. Burke's exposure to shortfalls from the tolling was reduced."

"And Burke did not change its price or change the agreement to reflect it was in a better, less risky position?"

"No, Burke was willing to take the original risk. The state increased its funding to alleviate a political problem its agreement with Burke had created."

"Did Governor Harrington ask Burke to negotiate a reduction in compensation to account for that better, more certain deal?"

"No."

"Did Burke ask for your legal advice when the state delayed tolling of the existing road?"

"I wouldn't call it legal advice. Randall Burke knew he had no legal obligation to change the contract. He asked for my business advice on whether it made business sense."

"What did you tell him?"

"That those who were upset about the tolls wouldn't be any less upset by his making a concession."

"So, Governor Harrington directed TxDOT to award a contract to Burke Construction with no competition and then he reduced Burke's risk without even asking Burke for anything in return. Is that about the size of it?"

"No, not at all," I told him. I shifted a bit in my seat, remembered what Gabriela had told me about not jumping to an answer and carefully went on. "TxDOT asked for other proposals, and no other contractor was willing to take the risk."

"In spite of you asking them to submit proposals?"

"I believe TxDOT and the governor asked. I didn't ask."

"Governor Harrington asked contractors to submit proposals."

"Yes, at the Texas Contractors annual meeting, the governor spoke on his 'Texas Roads to Destiny' plan and encouraged all contractors to participate."

"Were you the primary person who met with Governor Harrington and John Randolph during the negotiation of the Cross-Town Tollway project?"

"Yes."

"Burke Construction has an in-house general counsel. Why didn't she negotiate the contract?"

"Because I had come up with the 'Texas Roads to Destiny' program. When I suggested to Mr. Burke that the company submit a proposal for the Cross-Town Tollway, he said they couldn't because they could not find the financing. I found the financing. I worked months with the Merit Project Finance crunching the numbers to figure out what would be financially viable. I spearheaded the team that put together the proposal. Since I was the one who made it possible to build the project, I was the logical one to negotiate the contract."

Judge Parsons smiled. "So you were the one responsible for what has been described as the worst deal in Texas history."

I looked him right in the eye. "It's not the worst deal in Texas history, but yes, I am responsible."

"Did Randall Burke ever say to 'do whatever it takes' to convince governor to approve of the Cross-Town proposal?"

I looked at Gabriela Sanchez for help.

She stood up. "Your Honor, I object. That's an unreasonably broad question."

"Ms. Sanchez, it gets to the heart of whether Ms. Rossi's client bribed the governor. I'm going to direct Ms. Rossi to answer the question."

I paused again and spoke carefully.

"Your Honor, Mr. Burke never used those words with me. I told him I was convinced I could persuade the governor to approve of the contract, and I was committed to doing whatever it took to make a deal."

"Whatever it took?"

"Your Honor, I meant whatever it took legally and ethically to make a deal."

"Did you, on behalf of Mr. Burke and the Burke Construction joint venture, give Governor Harrington any money or anything of value?"

"No, Your Honor."

"Did Mr. Burke give Governor Harrington any money or anything of value?"

"No, not that I am aware of, Your Honor."

"You are not aware, or Mr. Burke never gave Governor Harrington any money or anything of value?"

"I can't be absolutely positive; I wasn't with the two of them at all times they were together."

"Do you know of gifts that Burke made to Governor Harrington over many years?"

"Your Honor, I know they are friends. I know they have been on hunting trips together. I know they go to University of Texas football games together. I know they go to Dallas Cowboys games together, and I know Randy Burke contributed to the Governor's campaign. But I'm not aware of any specific gifts."

"Who pays for the hunting trips, University of Texas football game tickets and Dallas Cowboys game tickets?"

"I'm not sure."

"But you know it was the Burke Construction box at UT and Cowboys games and it was the Burke Ranch where they went hunting, right?"

"Yes, Your Honor. I'm pretty sure that's correct."

"Did you work on the Hill Country Estates partnership agreement?"

"Yes. I drafted it."

"Did Anna Lang help draft it?"

"Yes, Your Honor. Anna had a minor role in the drafting."

"Did Randall Burke and his wife own the Hill Country land before they formed the partnership?"

"Yes."

"Why did the Burkes make Governor Harrington and his wife partners?"

"I'm not sure."

"Didn't you ask Mr. Burke when you created the partnership agreement?"

"I believe I did."

"And what did Mr. Burke tell you?"

"He said Ms. Harrington had complained they were broke, and that Austin Harrington was not making enough money as a judge in Texas."

"Did Governor Harrington and his wife contribute their share to start the partnership?"

"As far as I know. The Harringtons wrote a check for their share."

"Do you know if Mr. Burke gave the governor and his wife the money to write a check?"

"He didn't."

"How can you be sure?"

"Because I asked Randall Burke and he told me the Governor Harrington and his wife took money from his 401k to fund their share."

"Were you the lawyer involved in the Harringtons' sale of their interest to Mr. Burke?"

"Yes."

"How much did Mr. Burke pay the Harringtons for their share?"

"$7.5 million."

"How was that amount determined?"

"I believe Randall Burke and Governor Harrington negotiated the amount."

"Were any evaluations made of the value of the Harringtons' share?"

"Not that I am aware of."

"Why?"

"Because the two of them had known each other for a long time and trusted each other. Also, keep in mind that the Harringtons' sale to Randall Burke and his wife took place before Austin Harrington announced that he was running for governor."

Judge Parsons spent the next two hours grilling me on each and every detail of the Cross-Town Tollway contract. Finally, he looked like he was wanting to wrap it up.

"Ms. Rossi, didn't you find it odd that Burke Construction submitted the only proposal for the Cross-Town Tollway contract, even after Governor Harrington asked for more proposals?"

"No, Your Honor."

"And didn't you find it odd that Randall Burke and his wife, let Governor Harrington and his wife become partners in a multi-million-dollar development project in the Hill Country?"

"No, Your Honor."

"And, didn't you find it odd when the Burkes purchased the Harringtons' partnership share that in spite of your legal advice, Randall Burke chose not to hire a real estate appraiser to determine the value of the Harringtons' share?"

"No, Your Honor."

"One final question, Ms. Rossi. Has anyone threatened you or your family about your testifying before the grand jury?"

I felt my heart racing and put my right hand over it hoping it would slow down. I looked at Gabriela Sanchez for help. She sat still, her face expressionless. I didn't know what to say.

"Your Honor," I said as calmly as I could. "I've been told that we are in danger, and I've received threats from people who want me to testify and threats from people who don't want me to testify. I've been told people are protecting me and my family."

"Who are those people?"

"I have no idea."

"Did they say who they were protecting you from?"

"No, they said some people did not want me to testify. I assume it's the same people who have threatened me."

"Okay. Ms. Rossi, you may return to your seat. And if anyone threatens you – at all - I want to know about it right away."

After I had sat back down next to Gabriela, Judge Parsons looked down at us, and said, "Since time is tight, I will have my ruling to you this afternoon or no later than tomorrow."

And with that, we stood as the judge exited the bench.

"He's going to direct me to testify, isn't he?" I asked.

"I believe you can count on it. We need to prepare." Gabriela replied.

"Prepare for what? I don't give a damn if he orders me to testify, I'm not testifying. So there is nothing for us to prepare."

CHAPTER 22

———— ❦ ————

Gabriela Sanchez

Mario was waiting for us outside the courthouse. On the way to his car, protestors yelled at us. One man pushed Gina and she fell to the ground. I helped her up, while Mario reached out and grabbed the man. I thought Mario was going to punch him, but the man slipped away. As another man reached out for Gina, a policeman stepped in front of us and escorted us to Mario's car. I was shaking, but Gina looked like nothing had happened. She turned her head to say something and I stopped her.

I regained my composure by the time we got back to my office. Over the next two hours, Gina and I sat in the conference room waiting to hear from Judge Parsons.

"You know," said Gina. "We share a lot in common."

"We do?"

"We are both in our thirties, the daughters of trial lawyers. We both beat the odds and became partners in big law firms known for not promoting women. We both work hard, and we don't suffer fools gladly."

I processed what she had said. *I hope I don't crave attention as much as you do.*

I thought we shared some things in common on the outside, but I didn't want to be anything like Gina on the inside. She was cold and calculating.

During the Sparks Duval trial, my father had told me that my ambition had made me a different person than I had been growing up in the Rio Grande Valley. If I had not understood what he was telling me before, I understood now.

"When did you decide you wanted to become a lawyer?" Gina asked.

"When I was about 10-years-old," I replied.

"That young?"

"When I was little, my father gave me a set of golf clubs and told me he wanted me to become the next Lorena Ochoa. I worked really hard because that's what he wanted me to become. He wanted my brothers to follow him in law."

"What happened?"

"They didn't want to live his life."

"Why?"

"He was never home. He worked hard but didn't make a lot of money because many of his clients couldn't pay him. My brothers liked computers, and I wanted to be like my father."

"Did he encourage you?"

"No, if anything he did the opposite. He believed practicing law in the Rio Grande Valley was no career for a young woman. I would say Latinas face a challenge practicing law anywhere in the United States. That's why there are so few Latina partners in law firms."

"And is that why you were determined to become a lawyer?"

"It motivated me, and I received scholarships for college and law school. Otherwise, I wouldn't have been able to afford either one."

"So, what brought you to Dallas?"

"It was the money, and it was because after clerking for Judge Comstock, he told me I needed a bigger stage to work on to prove myself. Why are you asking me all of these questions?"

"Because I want to make sure my lawyer wants, no, *needs* to win my case as much as I do."

"Have I passed your test?"

"We'll see."

"May I ask you a question?"

"Sure, ask away."

"Do you find it hard to compliment to the women in your law firm?"

Gina's eyebrows raised a notch, and her mouth gaped open, one of her icy looks I had seen before. She started to speak and stopped.

I returned one of her fake smiles and suggested that she go home.

Gina Rossi

I had thought I could turn on the charm and get Judge Parsons to see things my way, but I was pretty sure my charm offensive had not worked.

I arrived at my home at 5:00 p.m. and my cell phone was ringing. It was a local TV reporter.

"We want to interview you."

"I don't think I can let you interview me."

"Why?"

"I can't disclose client confidences."

"I won't ask you anything about your representation of your client."

Thirty minutes later I was on Skype doing an interview.

"Ms. Rossi, can you tell our viewers why you are refusing to testify?"

"Sure. I will read this to you. The principle of confidentiality, as set out in the legal ethics rules states that: "A fundamental principle in the client-lawyer relationship is that, in the absence of the client's informed consent, the lawyer must not reveal information relating to the representation. ... This contributes to the trust that is the hallmark of the client-lawyer relationship." A violation of the ethics rule may lead to disciplinary sanction. It would be unethical for me to testify and violate that privilege."

"What do you have to say to the protestors who have harassed you over the last week. They are demanding that you testify about corruption during Austin Harrington's tenure as governor."

"They don't care about corruption. All they care about is smearing Governor Harrington so he will never be appointed to the Supreme Court. They have threatened violence and that has forced me to have a body guard 24/7."

"What have they threatened to do?"

"If I refuse to testify, they say they will kidnap my son, rape me and kill my husband."

"Have you reported the threats to the FBI?"

"No, because they already know about them."

At 10 p.m., the interview was aired as the breaking news story. The story included, video of the protestors standing in front of my house.

As soon as the interview aired, my cell phone rang. Randall Burke's name flashed on my screen.

"What in the world were you doing on TV?"

"I wanted to explain why I was not willing to testify."

"That's fine for you, but the reporter made it sound like you are refusing to disclose something I did that was illegal."

"No way."

"Watch the recording again. You'll see what I mean. No more interviews."

"Ok."

"So, what happened in court today?"

"What happened is Judge Parsons grilled me for over four hours like I was some kind of criminal and then he told us he would rule either this afternoon or first thing in the morning. Since I haven't heard anything yet, I assume I will hear in the morning."

"You know that you can't testify, right?"

"I know what you have told me, but I may be forced to testify."

"You can't be forced to testify, and I want you to remember that I gave you a one hundred-thousand-dollar bonus."

"That was for helping you win the Cross-Town Tollway contract. It has nothing to do with whether or not I testify."

"I gave it to you because you are my lawyer and I trust you to keep our business together confidential."

"You didn't bribe Austin Harrington, so what is there for me to keep confidential?"

"My lawyer says the government plans to look at the totality of what I have done for Austin Harrington over many years, and they plan to force you to disclose all of the details of what I have done over the last 10 years."

I thought for a moment. *If he hasn't done anything wrong, why would he worry about me testifying?*

Before I could respond, he said, "Gina, your career as a lawyer here in Dallas depends on you not testifying against your one and only client. Austin Harrington and I expect you to keep your mouth shut."

"That's fine, but if you listened to the protestors outside my house, you'd say the safety of me, and my family depends on me testifying. Which would you choose?"

CHAPTER 23

Gina Rossi

The next morning, after running outside, I was sitting at my table drinking coffee when my cell phone vibrated. I knew right away who was calling and what she would say.

"Gina, I have some bad news."

"Judge Parsons is ordering me to testify."

"Yes. Let me read what he said: "Based upon the court's review of the Government's Ex Parte Affidavit and the Attorney's in camera testimony, the court finds a reasonable basis to suspect that the Client intended to commit a crime when Client consulted the Attorney and could have used the information gleaned from the consultation in furtherance of the crime."

"That's bullshit. Can we appeal?"

"We can appeal, but it's complicated. We can't do it right now. Judge Parsons' order for you to testify isn't immediately appealable. If you wish to object, you must refuse compliance, be held in contempt, and then appeal the contempt order."

"Be held in contempt? That makes no sense. I shouldn't have to do that."

"I agree, but that's what you have to do if you want to appeal. On the other hand, if you agree to testify, Burke Construction has the right to appeal before you testify."

"I'm not testifying unless Randall Burke waives the lawyer-client privilege and he isn't about to do that. He and Austin Harrington do not want me to testify."

"What about the threats you are receiving?"

"I think they are just that-threats. All talk-no action. Do I have any other options?"

"Yes, you could exercise your Fifth Amendment rights not to incriminate yourself."

"But I haven't done anything wrong. Plus, won't taking the Fifth put me at risk of losing my license to practice law?"

"You and I know you've done nothing wrong, but you asked if you had any other options and that would be the only option other than testifying or refusing to testify and being held in contempt."

"What do you recommend?"

"Are you willing to testify?"

"No."

"Then I recommend letting the judge hold you in contempt and appealing his ruling. If you are held in contempt, I will ask the judge to stay his order until your appeal can be heard. If he is willing, you won't be sent to prison. Our other alternative is having me tell the DOJ lawyer that you plan to exercise your Fifth Amendment rights."

"If I take the Fifth, will I have to do that in front of the grand jury?"

"No, I can tell Brian Renfro and he will tell the DOJ headquarters prosecutors."

"Give me a few minutes to talk to my father and think about it."

"Gina, one more thing."

I know what's coming.

"No more TV or newspaper interviews. You are on the front page of the Dallas newspaper this morning."

"That was my plan. I wanted to explain why a lawyer should not be required to testify against her client and make a point that protestors outside my house are harassing me."

"I know that, but you can easily slip up and disclose something that is privileged."

"Okay. Okay. I get it. This keeps sucking worse, but I can handle it."

We hung up, and I dialed my father's cell number.

"Dad, it's Gina."

"Has the judge ruled?"

"He ordered me to testify."

"I thought he would. I'm sure Gabriela will ask him to stay his order so you can appeal."

"She doesn't think Judge Parsons will stay his order. I need your advice."

"Okay."

"Randall Burke has told me in so many words that if I testify my career in law will be over."

"He threatened you?"

"Not directly, but he got the point across. It doesn't matter. I don't intend to testify. I believe the judge was wrong. Burke never sought my advice to help him bribe Governor Harrington and not get caught. Plus, I've been told that my family and I are in danger if I testify, and I've been threatened by protestors if I don't testify."

"*What?* Who is threatening you? I'll take care of it right away."

"Dad, there's nothing you can do. I haven't even figured out who has warned me that we are in danger and the protestors who demand I testify have been on TV, but none of them have threatened me in front of a camera."

"I'm still going to dig into this. Let's hope it's not a real threat to your safety and it's all designed to scare you."

"I'm not scared, but I'm afraid of what they might do to Mateo. I want to appeal Judge Parsons' ruling. The only way I can do that is to refuse to testify and be held in contempt."

"And be sent to jail?"

"If Judge Parsons is unwilling to stay his order until the Fifth Circuit decides, they can take me to jail in Dallas or the federal women's prison in Fort Worth when I refuse."

"Have you thought about taking your Fifth Amendment rights not to incriminate yourself?"

"Yes, but I've done nothing wrong. Suppose the DOJ offers me use immunity. They can't use my testimony against me, but I'm right back where I started."

"True, but if they don't offer you immunity, you wouldn't have to testify, and you wouldn't have to be hauled off to jail."

"Dad, it's wrong to force a lawyer to testify against a client. This has become the DOJ's favorite weapon. If I testify, I'll never be able to practice law in Dallas again."

"Sounds like you've already made up your mind."

"I have."

"Then, there's nothing left for us to discuss."

After hanging up, I called Gabriela Sanchez back.

"Gabriela, I'm not going to testify and I'm not pleading the Fifth."

"Okay, I'll call Brian Renfro. I suspect Jason Daniels will want to have a hearing in front of Judge Parsons, likely as early as tomorrow morning."

"So be it. I'll be there."

"You realize you may be spending New Year's Eve and Day in jail or prison."

"It's New Year's Eve today. Judge Parsons may have already left for the day. Can't you put off telling Renfro until January 2?"

"I'll do that but be prepared for the worst on January 2, especially since the DC Special Counsel prosecutor will have spent New Year's Day on an airplane."

I made another call to Randall Burke.

"Hi, it's Gina again."

"What's new?"

"What's new is people who don't want me to testify have threatened me and people who demand I testify have threatened me. That group camps out in front of my house and follows me wherever I go. My photo is on the front page of the Dallas newspaper this morning and I'm going to be found in contempt and sent to Dallas County Jail or to a federal prison in Fort Worth. What's new with you? Did you and your family have a nice Christmas?"

"I appreciate what you are doing for me."

"I'm not doing it for you. I hate that you will benefit from what I'm doing."

"Then why are you doing it?"

"Because I expect you to compensate your most loyal friend and advisor and to let the world know what I am doing for you. I want you to get me on the national news each day I'm sitting in a prison for you."

"I appreciate what you are doing, and I'll forget what you said about not wanting to do it for me. But, also keep in mind that it's just plain wrong in America to force a lawyer to testify against her client."

"I assure you I will be giving that lots of thought while I'm sitting in a jail cell. How much do you believe you should pay me for each day I'm in jail?"

I heard a sigh. "I've always taken good care of you, and I will again."

After I hung up, I made one more phone call. This one was to Charlotte Bain, the Dallas newspaper reporter who had been writing about the grand jury investigation. Contrary to the promise I had made to Gabriela, I wanted to talk to the reporter.

"I'm not sure if Judge Parsons will allow the press to cover his interrogation of me when I refuse to testify before the grand jury. But if he does, I think that might be a far more interesting story than the phony one about Randall Burke bribing Austin Harrington to be awarded the $2 billion Cross-Town Tollway contract."

"Thank you. Maybe I'll see you in court on Wednesday."

"I have a favor. Please let your friends in the national media know about this story."

CHAPTER 24

Gina Rossi

I woke up at my usual time on New Year's Day. I was doing some research on preparing to go to jail or prison tomorrow. What would I need to pack?

I put on warm running clothes and went to the kitchen. I was glad to see the timer on the Keurig Coffee Pot had turned on. I dropped a Sumatra K cup in the slot, pulled the lever down and punched the button for a large cup.

That morning I really needed coffee. Even though Tony and I had not gone to the New Year's Eve party at the North Metroplex Country Club, we had managed to down two bottles of our best Amarone red wine. More accurately, I figured I had drunk about a bottle and a half of the two bottles, and to my surprise I found Tony ready for one last wild and crazy frolic before I would be leaving the house for an undetermined length of time.

I didn't exactly remember what all we had done before going to sleep, but I did recall thinking that it shouldn't take the threat of my going to prison to bring out the beast in him.

After finishing my coffee, I walked out the front door. There were no protestors in sight. Maybe the 30 degrees temperature kept them at home. I took off jogging down the street. After a minute I was running faster, and after five minutes I was running at even a faster pace. I was determined to run ten miles that morning in under eight minutes per mile, but I discovered I had run the first two miles in thirteen minutes and forty-five seconds.

Then I spotted a man running behind me. He was running fast enough to catch me. I was sweating and felt my heart racing like I had never experienced before. *Is this from being afraid of being caught or stressing over what will happen to me?*

As the man got closer, I felt light-headed and noticed my fingers tingling. I looked at the heart rate app on my Apple Watch and discovered my heart rate was much higher than normal. I knew it was time to stop and rest, but I was too afraid to stop. I wanted to call Tony, but the man would catch me. Finally, I thought if I didn't stop, I would pass out.

I stopped, bent over and tried to catch my breath. I looked up and saw a young man likely in his early twenties right in front of me.

"Ma'am are you okay? Can I help you?"

I sighed in relief. "Thank you. I think I'm okay now. I'll call my husband and have him come pick me up."

"Do you want me to wait until he gets here?"

"No, please go ahead. I'll be okay now."

I dialed Tony's cell phone.

"What were you doing?" he asked.

"Running, but I thought a man was chasing me. I was afraid and my heart started beating too fast, and I almost fainted."

"That's no good. Was he chasing you?"

"No. He even offered to help me until you got here."

Ten minutes later, Tony found me.

"You need to come home, drink another cup of coffee and rest."

I looked at Tony. "I don't have time to rest. Whatever you do, do not tell my father that you had to rescue me because I was hyperventilating."

"I hadn't even thought of telling him. But, you still need to take it easy."

"Mommy, are you okay?" asked Mateo.

I turned. He was biting his lip. I reached out my hand and touched his.

"Mateo, I'm fine. I just wanted you and your dad to come pick me up, okay?"

He didn't look convinced so when we got home, I gave him a big hug and whispered in his ear.

"Mommy is okay and happy to be able to spend the day with you."

This was not how I had planned on spending my New Year's Day. Instead of making cookies with Mateo and watching college football playoffs with Tony, I was preparing for my likely incarceration. I had downloaded the instructions from the federal Bureau of Prisons website, and I was reading them intently.

As I was packing my duffel bag, my cell phone rang. I looked on the caller ID said it was Allen O'Grady.

Whatever could he want on New Year's Day?

"Gina, the DOJ has advised us that you're not cooperating."

"Allen, if they mean I'm not testifying against my client, they are right."

"That's not a wise move for you or for our firm."

"You want the firm to be accused of selling its top client down the river to the feds?"

"No, but more important, I do not want the feds coming after our firm. You need to convince Randall Burke to work out a deal. If he doesn't, he'll be indicted, the jury will convict him, and you could lose your license to practice law."

"Allen, I know you are right, and I'll tell him you said that. But, I can't picture him paying a big fine and admitting to something he didn't do, and something that would ruin his best friend's career."

"If he doesn't, you and our firm may be indicted."

"Is that what the DOJ lawyers told you? That's the last thing I would want to happen."

"Not in so many words. They let us know they didn't look favorably at our firm since you aren't cooperating, and they said we should not be paying your legal bills unless you cooperated."

"Allen, if DOJ is threatening our firm, that is a violation of Burke's constitutional rights and my constitutional rights. We should fight them."

"Gina, tell that to the Supreme Court after you, Burke and Harrington are convicted, and our firm is put out of business."

Before I could tell O'Grady to go screw himself, I heard the click of him hanging up on me.

I called Randall Burke again.

He seemed upset and asked why I had called him on New Year's Day.

I told him Allen O'Grady had told me the DOJ had threatened our firm if I didn't cooperate."

"That's not my problem," he said. "You know your career is over if you testify. No one will hire you."

I told Burke I understood. He had made that crystal clear.

"And the firm doesn't have on its server the private communications between us, right?" he asked.

"Right."

"Then don't bother me on New Year's Day. You know what you need to do tomorrow. Just do it, and you will be amply rewarded."

Oh boy, Burke is going to give me a bonus for going to jail for him. Bastard!

"Allen, I'm truly sorry to have reached out to you on a holiday. I hope you have a great day."

I wasn't the least bit sorry, but I saw no reason to tell him what I honestly thought.

I spent the next hour playing Uno with Mateo. When we were putting the cards away, my cell phone rang again. It was Gabriela Sanchez.

"Hi, Gabriela."

"Hi, Gina. I've been thinking about what has gone on the last two weeks and I want to share a theory with you."

"Okay."

"I believe Randall Burke is having Mario protect you from the protestors so he can spy on you."

"What makes you think that?"

"The other day at the courthouse when you went in, I hung back for a moment, and I heard Mario call Burke."

"How do you know he called Randall Burke?"

"Because I heard him say Mr. Burke when someone answered the phone."

"This whole idea of you not reporting threats against you to the FBI and instead having Mario protect you was so he could spy on you for Burke."

"I don't believe that Mario would ever spy on me."

"Didn't Burke recommend you have him drive you years ago?"

"Yes."

"And, didn't Burke suggest that Mario drive you when you were followed a few days ago?"

"Yes."

"And who pays Mario? You, your law firm, or Randall Burke?"

"Burke."

"So, who do you suppose Mario is loyal to? You, or Burke?"

"Mario may be loyal to both of us. I know he genuinely cares about me and protected me these last several days. But, you've made a really good point."

"Does Mario also know Austin Harrington?"

"Sure, Mario has driven Harrington several times when Harrington was visiting Dallas."

"Both Burke and Harrington have good reason to have Mario spy on you and report back to them, under the guise of protecting you."

"That's true."

"Gina, I believe Mario is protecting you from the protestors, so you won't testify."

"The trouble is, the protestors have camped out near our house, followed me, followed Mateo and whenever they see me, they have chanted vulgar slogans. Mario can't be with me all the time."

"I think the threats from both sides are meant to scare you. Randall Burke doesn't want you to testify because he believes you might give the prosecutors ammunition to indict him and Harrington, or you know something that might implicate him in another way. You have not told me what worries him."

"You are right. That's because there's nothing I can say that would incriminate Burke or Harrington. Burke has given Austin Harrington many gifts and has supported his political ambitions. It's no secret."

"You must think overnight about whether you are making the right decision."

"I will, but I've made up my mind."

Before bed, I decided to talk to my father. So, I drove to his house. We talked for the next hour about what lay in store for me. As I was leaving, he took my arm, looked into my eyes and said, "I know tomorrow will be a difficult day. I am very proud of you for standing up to the government on the sanctity of the lawyer-client privilege. You've shown you have lots of guts."

I wanted to cry, but I held back the tears. "Thank you, Dad. That means a lot to me."

CHAPTER 25

⚮

January 2

Gina Rossi

At 10:00 a.m., Gabriela Sanchez and I walked into Brian Renfro's office at the federal courthouse. When we arrived, Jason Daniels was sitting there with Renfro.

I knew the history. Jason Daniels had prosecuted Sparks Duval when Gabriela defended him. After the jury found Duval guilty, Gabriela had convinced Judge Comstock to order a new trial on the basis that Daniels had inappropriately used social media to influence the jury. Daniels was criticized in the press and was demoted from his post in Washington, but he was not fired. Gabriela told me that when Daniels learned she was representing me he had convinced his boss in Washington to assign this investigation to him.

"Ms. Rossi, Ms. Sanchez has advised us that if I take you in to the grand jury, you will refuse to testify in the Harrington and Burke investigation. Is that correct?"

"Yes, it's the only way I can appeal Judge Parsons' ruling."

"Did Ms. Sanchez advise you that if you exercised your rights under the Fifth Amendment, we would give you use immunity - and nothing that you tell the grand jury would be used against you."

"She did, and I did nothing wrong. So, I have no need to exercise my rights under the Fifth Amendment."

"Well, Judge Parsons is expecting us, we might as well go upstairs to his courtroom now."

Fifteen minutes later Judge Parsons came out of his chambers and sat on the bench.

"You may be seated. Ms. Rossi. Mr. Daniels and Mr. Renfro report that you have refused to testify before the grand jury and produce the documents that were subpoenaed. Is that true?"

"Yes, Your Honor."

"Ms. Sanchez, have you advised your client of the consequences for her refusal to testify?"

"Your Honor, Ms. Rossi was aware of the consequences and I reminded her of them."

"Mr. Daniels, given what you have heard, are you still demanding that Ms. Rossi testify and produce the documents in the subpoena?"

"We are, Your Honor. Her refusal is impeding the grand jury investigation."

"Ms. Rossi, before I hold you in contempt of my order to testify, I would like to see you alone in my chambers. Is that okay with you, Ms. Sanchez?"

"Yes, Your Honor."

"Ms. Rossi, would you be willing to talk with me in chambers?"

"Yes, Sir."

"Then come let's go."

Once in his chambers, Judge Parsons took off his robe and placed it on a hanger on the backside of his office door.

"Ms. Rossi, you can sit right over here. Would you like some coffee?"

"No thank you, Sir."

"Ms. Rossi, I know Ms. Sanchez has told you in detail the consequences of your refusal to testify before the grand jury. I want to understand why you are refusing."

"Your Honor, the lawyer-client privilege is sacred. If I testify and it is later found on appeal that you were wrong, the genie is out of the bottle."

I waited for him to respond. When he didn't, I continued.

"With all due respect, Sir, this is a bullshit investigation and your order directing me to testify is wrong. It's unfair to Governor Harrington and to my client. But worse yet it is unfair to me. You are impugning my character. You are saying I helped my client commit a fraud. I believe you owe me an apology."

"Ms. Rossi, keep your cool and don't swear and don't raise your voice at me. I am following the law."

"Judge Parsons, I may not be a criminal lawyer, but I can read, and I've read that when the court orders a lawyer to testify, the judge must find that the allegation of attorney participation in the crime or fraud has some foundation in fact. By making this ruling you are saying I participated in the crime. If someone you respect accused you of helping a client commit a fraud, you wouldn't be keeping your cool."

"By ordering you to testify, I didn't conclude you helped your client commit a fraud. All I concluded was there was a reasonable basis for me to conclude your client may have used your services to commit a crime. He sought your advice, and when you gave it to him, he didn't take it."

Bullshit.

"Judge, I read the cases. No one will make the distinction you made. I will forever be tarnished by your ruling. You are forcing me to be held in contempt. That's just plain wrong. Have you ever ordered a male lawyer to testify before a grand jury on a matter he handled for a client?"

"Ms. Rossi, how dare you insinuate I am ordering you to testify because you are a woman."

"I think you answered my question."

"You'd better stop arguing with me."

"Or you will hold me in contempt and send me to jail?"

"Yes, I'll add to your time in jail, after the grand jury completes its work."

"Judge, my client conversed with me believing what he told me and the advice he sought would forever be confidential."

"I understand the lawyer-client privilege, Ms. Rossi."

"I would never help a client commit a fraud. Randall Burke didn't do anything wrong. He never intended to bribe Harrington and he didn't come to me to figure out how to get away with it. With all due respect Sir, you made a bad decision when you concluded the government and my *in-camera* testimony met the crime-fraud exception to the lawyer-client privilege."

"Isn't that for the grand jury to decide?"

"Your Honor, you and I both know the grand jury decides whatever Mr. Daniels tells them to decide."

"I don't necessarily agree. But, still, why refuse to testify?"

"Because I have to refuse and be held in contempt before we can appeal your decision to the Fifth Circuit. If I testify and later the Fifth Circuit finds you were wrong, my reputation as a lawyer is forever lost. I will never have another client."

"Ms. Rossi, I think you know the Fifth Circuit is not going to overturn the judgment I made. I don't think it has ever happened in a grand jury proceeding."

"I don't believe that is true, Your Honor. My father told me that you have the right to stay your decision until the Fifth Circuit rules. That way I wouldn't have to leave my son and rot in a prison."

"I also have the right to send you to Dallas County Jail or the federal women's prison. Mr. Daniels or his bosses in Washington could decide to indict you for obstruction of justice and criminal contempt."

"And if I testify before the grand jury and don't say what Daniels wants to hear, he will indict me for perjury. You and I both know this investigation is nothing more than an attempt to keep Austin Harrington off the Supreme Court and to overturn the Cross-Town Tollway contract in the process."

"I would give the DOJ more credit than to do that."

"Your Honor, it wouldn't be the first time, and you know it."

"Is Mr. Burke worth going to jail over?"

"Your Honor, it has nothing to do with who the client is. It's the principle we have always had in this country that when a client seeks help from a lawyer, their communications are privileged. It's the client's privilege, not mine, and this client has chosen not to allow me to waive it."

"It sounds to me like you want to be a martyr."

I bit my lip.

"Judge, I have great respect for you. I want you to right a wrong by letting me stay home until the Fifth Circuit Court rules. That would be the fair thing to do."

"No. It would reward you for not obeying my order. Have you talked to your father about this?"

"Judge, you know I talked to him. He didn't like that I would likely go to jail or to federal prison, but he understood and respected what I was doing. I wish you'd understand and respect it also."

"Do you realize you could stay in jail or prison for the duration of this grand jury's term?"

"Judge, you know my father is an outstanding lawyer. I know all the consequences, and you don't need to remind me."

"Ms. Rossi, I want to give you one last chance. I want you to call Mr. Burke right now and ask whether he is willing to waive the lawyer-client privilege to save you from going to jail."

"That's a waste of time. Randall Burke knows you've ordered me to testify, and he specifically told me not to."

"Go into my conference room and call him."

"Okay, but I already know his answer."

"When I sat down in Judge Parsons' conference room, I dialed Randy Burke's private number."

"Randy Burke."

"Randy, this is Gina."

"Hi, Gina."

"I'm sitting in Judge Parsons' chambers."

"Mario told me."

"Mario told you?"

"Yes."

"Has Mario been spying on me and reporting to you while he's been driving me these last two weeks?"

I heard Randall Burke cough.

"No, he told me he took you to the federal courthouse this morning."

"Are you having Mario protect me from the protestors who demand I testify so you can spy on me?"

"No, Gina. I would never do anything like that. You are my lawyer. Why are you calling me from Judge Parsons' chambers?"

"He told me I had to call you one last time before he puts me in jail."

"For what purpose?"

"He wants me to testify and not go to jail for you. You say you did nothing to help Austin Harrington with an expectation of his interceding with TxDOT to award the Cross-Town Tollway contract to you. I know of nothing you did either."

"But you know that for the last eight or nine years we've been focused on building the Cross-Town project, and you know my wife and I allowed Austin and Laura Ray to become partners in the Hill Country Estates Development, so they could make lots of money. You are the only one who can connect the dots, and with your testimony, the grand jury will too."

"I don't believe they will do that based on anything I might say. But, if I understand you, you want me to tell Judge Parsons that you are not willing to waive the lawyer-client privilege."

"You sound angry."

"I am angry. I'm going to jail, or prison and Mateo will forever wonder why his mother was behind bars."

"I'm sorry about that."

Bullshit.

"I know you are sorry, but you are sitting comfortably in your office. I guess the next time you hear from me, I'll be in jail or prison. Make sure and come visit me."

"I assume you aren't being serious."

"No, I would love for you to see me in my prison garb. Goodbye."

"Goodbye, Gina."

I knocked on Judge Parsons' door.

"Come in." As I entered, Judge Parsons asked, "What did he say?"

"That he's not waiving the privilege."

"And you still choose to have me find you in contempt?"

"Yes, Sir," I replied, "Would you have asked me that if I were a man?"

"Of course."

" I ask that you reconsider."

"I'm sorry I couldn't change your mind. Are you willing to report to the women's federal prison in Fort Worth this afternoon?"

"Can we quit talking about this. I shouldn't have questioned your judgment – it was out of place."

"You're right. Will you show up voluntarily?"

"Yeah."

"Let's go back in the courtroom and go on the record."

I walked into the courtroom where I found Gabriela Sanchez still seated at the counsel's table.

"I have to report to the women's federal prison in Fort Worth this afternoon. I want my father to take me. Please call him."

Judge Parsons entered the courtroom. "All rise."

I looked around and the courtroom was packed with reporters. I saw a man in the front row drawing on a sketch pad, since cameras are not allowed in federal courtrooms.

"Please be seated. I want to get on the record what has happened. While we were in chambers, I asked Ms. Rossi to call her client and ask once more if he was willing to waive the lawyer-client privilege. She did, and he refused."

"Then I asked Ms. Rossi one last time if she would comply with my order and testify before the grand jury. She advised me she would not testify. Is that correct, Ms. Rossi?"

"Yes, Your Honor. My client did nothing wrong, and I didn't help him commit a fraud or bribe the former governor."

"Ms. Rossi, I direct you to answer my questions yes or no. Do you understand?"

Gabriela grabbed my arm and squeezed. Parsons looked at Daniels.

"Mr. Daniels, is the government willing to excuse Ms. Rossi from testifying?"

"No, Your Honor," he said. "She is a key to our investigation."

"Ms. Rossi, I'm afraid you have given me no choice but to order that you be placed in confinement at the Federal Women's Prison in Fort Worth until such time that you agree to testify, or the grand jury is excused. Do you understand, Ms. Rossi?"

"Yes, Your Honor."

Gabriela stood up. "Your Honor?"

"Yes, Ms. Sanchez?"

"Could you possibly stay your decision until the Fifth Circuit rules, or put Ms. Rossi on house arrest and require that she not leave her home?"

"Ms. Sanchez. Ms. Rossi already asked that. One of the reasons we hold recalcitrant witnesses in contempt and put them behind bars is to encourage them to change their minds and testify. Another reason we do it is to deter other potential witnesses from refusing to testify. If I stayed my decision or allowed Ms. Rossi to stay in her own home, she certainly would not change her mind about testifying, and it certainly would not deter other witnesses from refusing to testify. So, no. She's going to prison."

"Yes, Sir."

"Ms. Rossi has advised me she is willing to voluntarily report to the minimum-security prison for women in Fort Worth this afternoon and I have alerted the staff to expect her no later than 3:00 p.m. Ms. Sanchez, can you assure me she will report as ordered?"

"Yes, Your Honor, I have called her father and he will be taking her."

"Well, Ms. Rossi, I'm sorry about this, but it is your decision. Court is adjourned."

"Judge, I was never asked for legal advice on how to win a contract by bribing the governor. This is not right."

I looked back at the reporters to make sure they heard what I said. Gabriela grabbed my arm more, forcefully this time and led me out of the courtroom. She whispered. "Don't say another word."

I pulled away. "What will Judge Parsons do, throw me in jail?"

When we opened the courtroom doors, Gabriela and I were greeted by at least a dozen news reporters with cameras and lights, and a group of protestors behind them

"Ms. Rossi, why did the Judge direct you to go to jail for violating his order?"

I turned to respond.

"Keep walking," Gabriela Sanchez hissed in my ear, again grabbing my arm.

"Why are you refusing to testify?"

"What are you hiding?"

"Did Randall Burke threaten you?"

"Ms. Rossi, did you know someone has already created a Twitter hashtag #FreeGina?"

"Does your father know you refused to testify?"

"What does Roberson Grant think?"

Gabriela Sanchez stopped for a moment and the news cameras focused on her.

"Ms. Rossi has nothing to add to what you already know. She believes in the lawyer-client privilege and is willing to fight for her client's right to that privilege. She has an appointment this afternoon and needs to get going. Could we please have some room here? Thank you. I'm sure after this is over, Ms. Rossi will be happy to speak with you."

We finally reached the elevator, and when it opened, Gabriela and I stepped in. Down at the first floor, we encountered more reporters who had not been in the courtroom.

"Please let us exit the building. Make room."

"Is Ms. Rossi willing to be interviewed while she is in prison for contempt?"

I started to answer, but Gabriela interrupted me.

"Ms. Rossi has nothing to say at this time," Gabriela Sanchez told those near me.

After we finally made it through the press, we faced a group of protestors. They were holding signs reading "Shame Rossi Shame. They clapped in unison and chanted "Go to jail, Go to jail." One protestor shouted, "Harrington's a crook, Harrington's a crook.

Gabriela Sanchez opened the passenger front door of my father's Mercedes. I got in and closed the door.

"How did they know what is happening?" Leo Baretti asked.

"If I had to bet, I'd say the Jason Daniels or someone on his staff leaked it," I lied.

"You'll most certainly be in the news for a while," he said.

CHAPTER 26

Gina Rossi

While we were driving, I waited, knowing my father would at some point offer his advice. I predicted he would start before we got to Arlington.

"Are you willing to listen to my advice?"

"Dad, you know I want your advice."

"Are you afraid?"

"Yes, I am afraid of how I will be treated, but I can take care of myself."

"You have to act humble. You are no better than anyone incarcerated in the prison, or certainly any of the guards. The guards will know you are a lawyer. They will know you are my daughter. They won't like you and they will try to bait you."

"Why will they try to bait me?'

"Because if they have any discipline problems with you, that will give them the justification to come down on you like a sledgehammer. Don't act angry. Don't act upset."

"That's good advice. I will do my best to keep my cool."

"You are going to be given some menial task that you won't like, and you can't complain about it. Do the work and keep smiling."

"I can do that."

"To get along with inmates, ask questions, listen to them, be interested in their stories."

I hadn't thought of that one.

"Good idea. I'll try."

At 3:00 p.m. sharp, my father and I arrived at the prison.

After signing in, I said goodbye to my dad. I gave him the longest hug I had ever given anyone. His lips were pressed together, and his head bowed as if he had just lost a big case.

"Dad, cheer up. I'll be okay. I've always landed on my feet." I wasn't really sure that was true, but I wanted him to believe I could handle what was to come.

"I'm proud of you standing up for the lawyer-client privilege. I'm not sure I would have been willing to go to prison."

That was all I needed to hear. I reached out and hugged him again.

"Stay in touch with me and be prepared for the media to come here wanting to interview you."

"Okay." I turned and an officer in charge of Receiving and Discharge, whose badge read Fleming, greeted me.

"Ms. Rossi, before you go to your quarters, you will be searched, urinate in a cup, photographed, fingerprinted, issued clothing, medically screened, issued an operations handbook, and then you will be assigned to a bed. Do you understand?"

"Yes, Ma'am."

"Then come in here and take off all of your clothes. We will be keeping your clothes and issuing you prison clothes. We will search you and watch you urinate into this cup."

After I was naked, Officer Fleming looked me over.

"Squat and cough."

"What?"

"Squat and cough."

"Why?"

"Ms. Rossi, let me offer you a piece of unsolicited advice. Outside you are a lawyer. Maybe even a famous one. In here you're an inmate with a number like everyone else. If you want to get along in here, when you are told to do something, just do it. Don't ask why."

"You're right. I appreciate your advice." I grimaced, squatted, and started coughing. I had been naked in front of women many times, but this was humiliating.

"Okay Ms. Rossi, it doesn't appear that you have any drugs stuck up your private parts. Come over here for fingerprinting and a photograph."

After the fingerprinting and photographs, I was issued khaki slacks and shirts, socks, 2 pairs of underpants, 2 bras and a pair of work shoes. Then I was handed bedding: sheets, a blanket, and a pillow. After that, an inmate named Connie Peterson showed me to my cubicle sleeping quarters, where I saw three bunk beds. I was assigned one of the top bunks. That was no surprise, I had read that the newbies always get the top bunks.

"This is where you'll sleep tonight. Tomorrow you'll be permanently assigned to a cubicle."

I expected Connie to leave, but she sat in a chair and continued talking as I placed sheets on my upper bunk.

"I hear you're a lawyer," she said.

"Yes."

"In here it's considered rude to ask an inmate what's she's in for, but since you are a lawyer and should know better, I have to ask. How did a lawyer get sent here?"

"It's a long story."

"Well, we have all kinds of time. What's your crime?"

"I didn't commit a crime."

"That's what all newbies say. I didn't do it."

"I wasn't sent here for committing a crime. I was sent here for refusing a judge's order to testify to a grand jury."

"Wow, you refused to be a snitch. I didn't know someone could be sent here for that. Since you're a lawyer, when the word gets around, the women in here will be in line to get your help."

"Does the word have to get around?"

"Yes. The women in here want a lawyer to help them get out."

"But, I'm not a criminal lawyer."

"No matter. You are a lawyer."

"What have the women in here done to be sentenced to prison?"

"Most are in here for petty drug offenses. Did you know that Marion Jones served time here?"

I had heard of Marion Jones, but I could not remember why I recognized her name.

"Yes, Marion Jones. She won three gold and two bronze medals in the 2000 Summer Olympic games, and then spent six months here for lying to investigators about using performance-enhancing drugs. Along with her role in a check-fraud scam."

"Yes, I remember Marion Jones now."

"Did you know we have a law library here? And you'll always find people in there working on their cases. I'm sure they will want your help. Don't act like you are better, or smarter than anyone here."

"I won't. I don't think I'm better than anyone here."

"Do you have children?"

"I have a son, Mateo. What difference does that make?"

"So are many of the mothers in here. Those without husbands looking after their children are the ones who will most want your help."

"I'll do what I can to help them."

"You will wake up every morning at 6:00. Your first week will be orientation. Then you will be assigned some kind of job. Don't expect the job to be anything like what you did as a lawyer."

"Okay."

"Have you watched Orange is the New Black?"

"Yes, why?"

"Then you know that several times during the day and night the count will be taken. That's one of the few accurate things in that show. You may also know we eat dinner early around here. After dinner is free time. You could watch TV, but the TV room is so crowded, you won't likely be able to get in there. When you get up in the morning, if you want to get a shower, you better get there right away. It gets crowded quickly when 150 women here want to get a shower."

"What else should I know?"

"There are the written rules and the unwritten rules, and neither is applied uniformly. Since you're good looking, you'll be approached to have sex."

"Should I be worried?"

"You should be worried about getting caught, because if you are caught, they'll throw the book at you."

"What if I say I'm not interested?"

"You won't get hurt. This isn't like TV. Women are looking for companionship, friendship and emotional support. That can be worse than those looking only for sex. My advice is to say you're happily married with a son. That's better than being a good-looking single girl."

"Are the women in here from North Texas?"

"Many are. I think the feds try to place mothers with children from North Texas here so the children can visit. There are only so many spots, and you're taking one of them."

"I'd be more than happy to give mine up."

"Not if they sent you to Dallas County Jail."

'I guess you're right about that. Is there a running track here?"

"Yes, you will be able to exercise and run if that's what you want to do. But you made a mistake turning yourself in on a Friday, you won't be able to get things from the commissary until Monday."

"I don't need running shoes."

Connie got up to leave. "Thanks for your advice. I appreciate your kindness." I told her.

"I'll keep an eye on you the first couple of weeks. Let me know if anyone bothers you."

That night I lay in my bed wide awake. So, it really didn't bother me when the counts were taken at 11, 2 and 5 o'clock. *What will orientation be like?*

CHAPTER 27

Gina Rossi

I was awakened the next morning after just an hour or so of dozing. After a shower, I got dressed in my khakis and walked down the hall to the dining room, which I learned was called the "chow hall." It reminded me of a big cafeteria on a college campus. I stood in line at the serving bar and discovered I didn't get to choose what I ate. When it was my turn, an inmate assigned to the food service department placed a bowl of oatmeal, two slices of white bread and a glass of skimmed milk on my tray. I was nervous about where I was supposed to sit. I saw Connie and she invited me to sit at her table with her friends. She introduced me as the lawyer, which seemed to get their attention.

After breakfast, I reported as instructed to Admissions and Orientation. Right away I figured out what it would it was going to be like to not be free.

I was not accustomed to following rules. I thought of what my father had told me. I had to be able to follow the prison's written rules - it was those unwritten prisoner rules that worried me. I decided it would be vital to figure out what they were by observing and asking questions.

After visiting the Admissions and Orientation office, I was directed to the counselor's office. My assigned counselor was a fifty something year-old African American lady named Nia Summers. She explained that she was there to provide mental health counseling, education and help to adjust when the inmates left prison.

"Ms. Rossi, since you aren't in here for any specific time, and we have limited resources, we can't see the value of more orientation for you. Are you ready to be assigned a job?"

"Yes, Ma'am."

"I think we'll start you cleaning the kitchen and dining hall after meals."

"Yes, Ma'am."

"At any given time, there are 800 to 1100 inmates here. Only about 200 of them have a high school diploma or GED. Of that 200 about half have any education beyond high school."

"Yes, Ma'am."

"I recommend that you keep your being a lawyer to yourself. Otherwise, you will be inundated with requests by inmates."

"Ma'am, I think it's too late for that. Most inmates knew I was a lawyer before I even arrived here. I guess they must have seen it on TV. I've already been approached by several inmates."

"Do they claim they are innocent?"

"I've discovered that most of the women are in her for petty drug offenses. No, what they claim is their court-appointed lawyer either didn't care or didn't have time to defend them. From what I've seen, they may be right."

"I guess that's because they were involved in what you call petty drug offenses."

"I want to help them."

"Go right ahead - in your free time."

"Thank you, Ma'am."

"Ms. Rossi, let me take a moment to tell you about the inmates you may encounter. We have all types, all races, and sexual orientation. As a white, married woman, you are in the minority here, but about 85 percent of the inmates are mothers, and they want to see their children. Many will seek your help, but some may want to mess with you because you're a lawyer. They may think you believe you're better than them."

"Do I act that way?"

"No, but it doesn't matter. As you might imagine, we have lesbians here. You will see and hear them. Because you are attractive, they will seek you out. Stay away from them, and they'll figure out you're not interested."

I was curious about sex with a woman, but I decided to keep that thought to myself.

How could anyone have lesbian sex in here? No place is private enough.

"I'll talk a lot about my husband and son. Maybe that will give them the idea I'm not interested in women."

"Maybe. Do you have any questions for me?"

"No, Ma'am."

"You may be excused, inmate. Now that you are finished with orientation, we are assigning you to the B dorm which is mostly with Hispanic women, Asians, and Middle Eastern women."

"Why aren't you assigning me to the dorm with white women?"

"That's the A dorm. We think you will be safer with Hispanic women. When you answered your questionnaire, you stated you speak Spanish. You'll be able to communicate with most of the women in B. We are putting you in a cubicle with one other inmate. Her name is

Gloria Ramirez and she's 50-years-old. I don't want to see you back here until the day the judge lets you out of here, do you understand?"

"Yes, Ma'am. Thank you."

I was led back to a cubicle in the B dorm. When I walked in, Gloria Ramirez looked up from her bunk.

"Oh, they decided to give me the lawyer," she said with a heavy Spanish accent.

"I'm Gina Rossi, Ms. Ramirez."

"I know who you are. You've been on TV the last couple of days with some people saying you have no business being here. I've been here close to two years, and no one has said that about me."

"I'm sorry about that, Ms. Ramirez."

Gloria pointed. "There's your locker and over here are the hooks you can use."

"Thank you, Ms. Ramirez."

"Don't call me that. Call me Gloria."

"Yes, Gloria."

Over the next few days, I began to get to know Gloria. It was clear, she did not want to share anything personal about herself, her family or the reason she was locked up. But, she had many questions for me. One afternoon she asked questions about my father, my mother, my brother, Tony and Mateo, I finally asked her: "Gloria, why do you want to know so much about my family?"

"Well Señorita, I've only known you a few days, but I think as successful as you are, you are missing something essential in your life, and I want to figure out what that is."

I was dumbfounded by the statement.

"*Puedo ver*. I can see it in your face and eyes. You are unhappy."

"You expect me to look happy while I'm rotting away in here?"

"No, Señorita, I can tell you've not been happy for a long time. *No has encontrado sentido en tu vida.*"

"That's not true. I find meaning in my life every day."

"You are a Christian?"

"Yes."

"You are Catholic?"

"Yes."

"I have spent more time reading the Bible since I have been here than in all the years before. *Entonces sabes que Dios es amor.* God is love. But, God needs someone capable of loving him back. You haven't taken time from your busy, successful life to love God and love your neighbor. As hard as you have worked, as successful as you are, as much money as you have made, you have not found meaning in your life."

I couldn't sleep that night. Gloria had me pegged, but how could she tell? What had she seen in my eyes?

On Saturday, Tony came to visit at 10:00 a.m. It had been easy to get my family members on the approved visitor list. Gabriela Sanchez was also on the approved visitor list.

Gloria had told me about the rules for the visit. An embrace and kiss within the bounds of good taste were permitted at the beginning and end of our time together, and I could hold Tony's hand. Anything beyond that was prohibited.

Tony had received permission to bring me another pair of running shoes. He kept leaning away from me, which made me think he was uncomfortable being there. We talked about Mateo. Then I asked, "How do I look?"

"You look fine. Why? How are you doing?"

"This is a humbling experience for me. I've learned a lot about myself, and I've learned a lot about life from people less fortunate than I am."

"What have you learned about yourself?"

"I have always craved being the center of attention and being applauded for my great work. Here, the last thing I want to do is be the center of attention. Because I've had so much time to reflect on life, I've learned I can be confident without seeking the praise of the people around me."

"That makes sense."

"I hate following orders, and that's what I have to do here 24/7. Then there's the boredom. I have never been more bored in my entire life. I often reach for my cell phone and realize I don't have it, or my iPad, or my computer. I can't wait for each day to be over and after dinner, I count the minutes until I go to bed, except I'm unable to fall asleep for several hours."

Tony had heard that line before.

"If you are bored, how do you plan to spend your time here?"

"I plan to run on the track, exercise, and do yoga as much as I can. Since I'm living with the Hispanic women, I'm sure they will help me become a better Spanish speaker. I had hoped to read, but I don't feel like it so far."

"At least you have a plan."

"I don't deserve to be here. I've done nothing wrong. I'm just a pawn in an investigation. Many of the women here didn't really do anything other than be caught in the middle of some drug deal. Their sentences are ridiculous, and they should be home with their kids. I plan to help them."

Tony covered his face with his hands and frowned.

"Being away from you and Mateo, and not being able to work is the worst part of being locked up in here. I may have to prove myself again."

"Gina, why don't you just agree to testify?"

"Damn Tony. I've told you a dozen times now. Because the prosecutors have already decided that Burke bribed Harrington to win the Cross-Town Tollway contract, and they won't believe anything I say to the contrary. They'll prosecute me for perjury if I don't tell them what they want to hear."

"Well, Mateo asks about you. He wants to see you. I want to bring him here to see you."

"Don't ever let him see me in this hell-hole dressed like a convicted criminal. He would never understand that I didn't do anything wrong."

"I won't, but Mateo does not understand why you are not at home."

"Tell him that my work keeps me away from home and that I promise to spend more time with him soon. I miss him and I can't wait to be home with the two of you."

"I still say you should agree to testify and get out of here."

I just shook my head.

"Okay. So, what is this like? How are you treated?"

"The food sucks. I noticed a lot of it is well beyond its expiration date, and I plan to never eat a hot dog the entire time I'm here."

"Is there anything healthy served?"

"Not much. I'm already losing weight."

"How are you treated?"

"There aren't enough guards. There are nurses and administrators here pushed into duty as guards with no training. I can see fear in their eyes. There is frequently major conflict and drama among the women."

"Why?"

"There are three TV screens in the whole prison, and I've seen inmates fight over what show is playing."

"Do you watch TV?"

"Never. I don't want to get in the middle of the fights."

Time passed quickly, and soon it was time for Tony to leave. I held him, gave him a kiss and went back to my dreary existence.

"Tony, you look exhausted."

"I am exhausted. I want to give you moral and emotional support, but it's challenging taking care of Mateo when he is afraid you are gone forever."

"I know that can be exhausting. Thank you for helping him feel secure. I'll call and talk to him the first chance I get."

CHAPTER 28

Gina Rossi

When I returned to my cell, Gloria Ramirez was sitting at a desk reading a Spanish novel.

"Gloria, may I ask you a question?"

"Yes, Señorita."

"Why haven't you asked for my help to get you out of here?"

She smiled a little, closed her book, and shifted the chair around to face me.

"In our culture, the family is everything, and we do what we can to help each other. We would never ask a stranger for help when we know there is no way to repay the stranger for the help."

"I will help you. I promise."

"How?"

"I have the connections that can help you."

"Why do you want to help me?"

"Is the reason important?"

"Yes. I don't want your pity or sympathy."

I shook my head and looked into Gloria Ramirez's eyes.

"Gloria, I want to help to right a wrong, and I will be able to do it. You shouldn't have been taken away from your family for these many years. Have you ever heard of Alice Johnson? She was serving a life sentence until the President commuted her sentence at the request of Kim Kardashian. After the favorable publicity, the President asked for a list of others who should be granted clemency. He's looking for cases of injustice, and I plan to submit your name."

There were tears in her eyes.

"God bless you."

"Tell me your story. Why were you arrested?"

"It's a long story."

"We have lots of time. I'm listening."

"My husband, Andrés, became a drug addict shortly after our second child was born. I worked as a housekeeper in a hotel, and he could not hold a job. At some point, I found crack cocaine and confronted him. I told him to stop, and I know he tried, but he didn't. When the police came looking for Andrés, they arrested me as well. I was supposedly the person in the middle between the big-time drug dealer and my husband."

"Were you?"

"I was the person who connected the two. I never sold drugs myself. I made a bad decision. They tried to get me to tell them who the kingpin was. I refused. Andrés told them and cut a deal. He was sentenced to four years and I was convicted of conspiracy and sentenced to 24 years in prison."

"That's unbelievable. It wasn't fair. You shouldn't be in here."

"*Nunca me dijeron que podría ser sentenciado a cadena perpetua.*"

"You were never told you could be sentenced to life in prison?"

"No." Gloria Ramirez held up one finger and pointed it toward herself. *Fue mi primer crimen.*"

"It was your first criminal offense?"

Gloria Ramirez nodded.

She continued telling me in Spanish that she was convicted of conspiring to traffic 20 kilos of crack cocaine and the judge gave her the maximum sentence of 24 years' imprisonment.

"Did you even know what crack cocaine was?"

"No, no no."

Later that day, I called Randall Burke.

I told him who it was, and he said he almost didn't answer since he didn't recognize the caller ID.

"I'm glad you answered," I said. "I only have so much time during the day to be able to make phone calls."

"I know being stuck in there must be difficult for you."

"It's difficult because I miss my son and he doesn't understand why I am gone or where I am."

"I'm sure you didn't call me to catch up, what prompted you to call me from prison?"

"I want you to contact the President and ask for leniency or a pardon for Gloria Ramirez."

"Why should I do that?"

"Because you owe it to me for going to prison instead of testifying before the grand jury and getting you in trouble. I'm sitting here in the Fort Worth prison because you demanded that I not testify before the grand jury. For a second thing, the President is looking for cases like this to get the favorable publicity. For a third thing, Gloria Ramirez is no criminal, and she should be home with her family."

"This call is being recorded, right?"

"I'd bet it is."

"Then I'll keep my thoughts to myself. I will contact the President."

CHAPTER 29

Gina Rossi

Two weeks later, a guard stopped at my bed and touched my arm and woke me from a sound sleep. I was confused and groggy and could barely get my eyes open. He grabbed my hand.

Startled, I raised my head and slowly opened my eyes.

"Rossi, you're leaving here this morning."

"What? Why?"

"Rossi, no one told me why. They told me to get you ready to leave and that was it."

"Okay."

I looked down at Gloria Ramirez, still tucked in her bunk.

"Gloria, I'm going to get you out of here. You can count on me."

Gloria lifted her head, and her eyes met mine. She was not smiling. I climbed down and gave her a hug.

"Gloria, you've made a difference in my life. I promise you I will do whatever it takes to get you out of here and back with your family."

Finally, she smiled ever so slightly.

An hour later I stood at a counter in the clothes I had worn when I arrived collecting my other personal items.

"Do you know if someone told my husband I would be leaving here today?"

"I don't know, Rossi. There's a young, dark-haired woman waiting for you. That's all I know."

Gabriela Sanchez is taking me home? Why?

When I pushed open the door into the visiting area, Gabriela walked toward me.

"Gabriela, it's nice of you to pick me up, but why didn't Tony come for me?"

"He took Mateo to school and had a court appearance."

"Why have I been released?"

"I thought you might have agreed to testify."

"No way."

"Then the grand jury must have been discharged. You can no longer be held in prison since the order to testify applied to a grand jury that is no longer in existence."

"Did they indict Austin Harrington or Randall Burke?"

"No, that would have been a huge news story."

"Well, that's certainly good news."

"You would think, but I am concerned Jason Daniels and the FBI aren't giving up that easily."

"What could they do?"

"They could convene another grand jury and issue a subpoena for you to testify again."

I shook my head. "Then, we'd be right back where we started."

"I'm afraid that's true. But, for now, you're going home."

"And, I am most hopeful this saga is over, and I won't need your help any further."

On our way home, I was excited to be seeing Mateo and Tony. More than anything, I wanted to convey to Mateo that I had not abandoned him. But, I was still confused about how I'd been released and why Gabriela didn't seem to know much.

When we got home, as she parked alongside the curb, she told me, "Gina, make sure your outside video cameras are working and on."

"Why?"

"You want to make sure you capture video of anyone coming to your door."

"Okay." I wasn't sure exactly what she was thinking. I thought it might be to capture the protestors who were already gathering along my street.

I walked quickly to the front door. It flew open and Tony greeted me, and Mateo ran up and jumped into my arms.

"You're home." I said. I thought you would still be in court.

"I picked up Mateo as soon as my hearing ended so we'd be here when you got home."

"Mommy, where have you been?" he asked excitedly.

"I've been away for work."

He started crying. "Mommy, please never leave us for so long."

"I won't leave again, darling. I promise."

Mateo was still sniffling.

"Would you like for me to fix spaghetti for our dinner tonight?"

Mateo smiled for the first time.

"Yes mommy, please, please, please!"

I spent the entire afternoon with Mateo. We worked on a model building kit of construction equipment I had purchased before Christmas.

I had read that building the models would enhance Mateo's hand-eye coordination, fine motor skills, problem-solving skills, and spatial awareness. There were 480 pieces to put together, and that number and the complexity seemed to overwhelm Mateo. We took frequent breaks and spent some time playing outside since it was a beautiful, sunny day.

About an hour before I wanted to start the spaghetti, Tony joined us and with his help, we finally completed the backhoe and the wheel loader.

At 6:00 the three of us sat down for dinner. To celebrate my return, Tony opened a fine Italian Brunello. I hadn't had a drink of alcohol for several weeks. I promised to drink only one glass of the wine. It was a great day with Mateo, and I was anticipating a romantic night with Tony.

I got up early the next morning and ran five miles outside. When I returned, I started fixing breakfast for Tony and Mateo, and they sat at the table waiting, bacon sizzling.

Just as I set plates on the table, I heard loud knocking at our front door. As I approached to open the door, a man yelled, "Gina Rossi, FBI, open the door!"

I opened the door. A dozen FBI agents with vests and drawn automatic assault weapons greeted me with a line of video cameras and spotlights not far behind them. Before I could say anything, the FBI agents were pushing past me into my home with video guys recording their entrance.

The leader pulled my arms behind my back and put handcuffs on me. I looked at him and he said, "Gina Rossi, you are under arrest for obstruction of justice and criminal contempt."

Mateo was crying, protesting to Tony who stood with his mouth open.

I stayed calm. "Tony, take Mateo to the bedroom and call my father and call Gabriela Sanchez. They will know where they will take me and what to do."

Tony pulled Mateo aside.

"Gina Rossi, we also have a search warrant to take your computer hard drives, your tablets, cell phones, and any other electronic devices you may have here."

I was pushed out my front door to the waiting news video cameras and spotlights in my face.

I rode in the back of the car to the federal courthouse. When we walked through the front door, Gabriela was there waiting for me.

"I want to speak to my client," she told the FBI agent.

"You can have about 30 minutes before we bring her in front of the judge."

An FBI agent took the handcuffs off and led us to a room and closed the door. I tried not to cry thinking about how they had terrified Mateo.

"Gina, I have a pretty good idea what happened, but tell me anyway."

"We were sitting down to breakfast when a dozen FBI agents arrived with guns drawn and warrants to arrest me and take my computers, and other electronic devices in my house."

"The FBI didn't need to make a spectacle of it," she said.

"Why didn't you insist that they call you and I would turn myself in?"

"I told Brian Renfro. He promised that if they were going to arrest you, he would call me. Daniels must have arranged for the FBI bust, and purposely didn't let Renfro know."

"The bastard. After months of dealing with protestors, now every neighbor knows I was arrested. I will be the lead story on the evening news, with video of them taking me out of my house in handcuffs."

"I understand. Did you have all your video cameras on like I suggested?"

"Yes."

"Then, we should be able to show what they did to you and your family. I want to see the video. Then I will figure out a way to leak it to the press."

"They terrorized my son. He was already upset because I was gone for a month. Now, he is scared to death."

"That's why I will leak the video to the press. Everyone in Dallas will know they terrorized Mateo."

"That's fine, but how could Daniels possibly issue a warrant for my arrest after the grand jury concluded?"

"Because they want to put pressure on you to bring them something on Harrington and your client, Randall Burke. They made the big show to scare the crap out of you, and they will go through everything on your computer and other electronic devices to find something you wrote or received that will show anything that looks like Burke gave something to Harrington expecting Harrington to give him something in return."

"They won't find anything like that."

"Then they will want to find something they can use to squeeze you. They may even be looking at Tony's computer to see if he has done anything wrong so they can use something he has done to threaten you."

"Tony has nothing to do with any of this."

"I know, but that won't stop them from using him as a bargaining chip if they find anything. They may even threaten your brother since he brought Merit Financial to you."

"This is unfucking believable. I can't believe I am living in America. What can they find on my computer?"

"Anything you have on it, including your logins and passwords to websites, and lots of things you think you have deleted. They can get it. Is there anything I need to know about?"

"There are no communications with Randy Burke or Austin Harrington on my computer that you haven't already seen."

I started picturing what they would find.

"Gina, what else is on your computer you don't want anyone to see?"

"We don't have time to go over it now. I'll tell you when we are finished here."

There was a knock at the door. Gabriela got up and opened it. My dad walked in, and I jumped up and hugged him.

"Gabriela, can I have some time alone with my dad?"

"Sure."

She left, and I looked expectantly at my dad.

"I assume you know the whole story, likely more than I know."

"I know that the Special Counsel believes you can tie their case against Harrington together and they're trying to put the squeeze on you by indicting you. They would work a deal for your testimony."

"You know I can't and won't testify. You even said you were proud of me."

"That was back when you were only going to prison until the grand jury finished. Now, you could be found guilty and spend several years in prison - as a convicted felon. If that happens, you will never practice law again."

"Dad, this isn't right. Sam was right in the middle of the biggest banking scandal ever, and all they did was interview him. I'm trying to uphold the lawyer-client privilege, and Judge Parsons refused to stay his order for me to testify. Then, after the grand jury is dismissed, Daniels indicts me."

"Sam didn't do anything illegal when he was in New York."

"Dad, you really believe that? They all committed fraud and only one went to jail. During the 80s over a thousand went to jail in the savings and loan scandal here in Texas."

"Gina, I'm not going to argue with you about Sam or the past. We have to focus on you and your future. You may need to testify to save yourself."

"Even if I testify, the Special Counsel wants me to lie, and he won't be satisfied unless I testify the way they want."

"That may be true, but you aren't testifying, so what difference does it make?"

"None, I guess."

"Well, here is something for you to think about if you haven't already."

"What's that?"

"If you don't give in before your trial, I believe you will have to testify to defend yourself in your obstruction of justice and criminal contempt trial."

"I don't want to testify."

"I know that, but you'll have to if you want the jury to find you not guilty."

"I want you to defend me."

"I understand, but that's a mistake. The press would have a field day writing about how daddy has jumped on his horse to save his daughter. Plus, I have complete faith in Gabriela Sanchez. She beat Jason Daniels in the Sparks Duval case. She knows how to get under his skin, and that will be important to defend you successfully."

"Are you sure she will take care of me as well as you would?"

Leo Baretti shook his head. "You have my word. I've already talked to Gabriela. She's on top of things, and she told me she needs to learn more about you. For your own sake, open up to her and help her defend you. She needs to know everything that might be brought up at the trial."

"I'm sure you are right. But, I can't tell her everything."

"You damn well better, or plan on being away from your husband and son for a few years."

CHAPTER 30

Gabriela Sanchez

Gina's court appearance took less than 30 minutes. The judge ordered a $100,000 promissory bond for bail, which she would have to pay only if she failed to comply with the terms of her release.

As we walked out the front doors of the federal courthouse on a sunny and seasonally warm January day, we were met by dozens of reporters and video cameramen and women.

"What do you have to say about your indictment, Ms. Rossi?"

I stepped in front of Gina and spoke. "This is a travesty and a prime example of a Special Counsel gone amok. What started as an investigation has become a circus, and Gina Rossi is stuck right in the middle of it. She defended her client's right to hold his conversations and interactions with her as privileged, and the court could have stayed the order until we could appeal. Instead, the Special Counsel insisted that Gina be sent to federal prison. When she continued to insist on upholding the lawyer-client privilege, the Special Counsel's office convened a grand jury and indicted this brave woman. This morning, a dozen FBI agents in protective vests and drawn automatic weapons terrorized Gina, her husband, her little son, while you in the media were shooting video that will undoubtedly be played on the news tonight."

"Sooner or later," I said, looking straight into one of the cameras, "we will have a countdown to justice for Gina Rossi and her family. She will be vindicated. You can count on it."

"Ms. Sanchez, the Special Counsel's office has said Ms. Rossi is an essential witness in a vital criminal investigation. She refused to testify. They say it's an open and shut case of contempt and obstruction of justice."

I looked at the reporter and replied, "This is not a valid criminal investigation. It is a politically motivated fishing expedition. They don't have evidence and they think Gina Rossi can supply it. Thankfully, the Special Counsel's Washington office will not have the final say. Citizens right here in Dallas, Gina Rossi's hometown, will."

As we continued walking, Gina's cell phone rang. She showed me the "Fox News" caller ID." I remembered my media appearances in the Duval trial. I shook my head at her and motioned her to decline to take the call.

When we finally got to my office, and settled down, I asked Gina, "What did you start to tell me that the FBI and Daniels might find on your computer?"

"I have a profile on Ashley Madison."

"Ashley Madison?"

"Yes. Ashley Madison. I'm sure you know what it is."

"The website for married men and women cheating?"

"I wouldn't describe it that way. I'm more happily married because of it. My participation has nothing to do with our case."

"What makes you think your identity is private?"

"Since the hacking in 2015, Ashley Madison has carefully protected the privacy of their members. I have a username for my profile, not my real name."

"And what is your username?'

"HotTexasGal."

"Is your photo in your profile?"

"Yes, but my face is so blurred that no one would know it is me."

"They have your computer, with your Ashley Madison profile and activity. The government will soon know everything about your Ashley Madison dalliance and will likely find some way to make it public. Take down that profile immediately."

"Damn. Could I use your computer?"

I didn't think our IT staff would allow a login to Ashley Madison. I tried logging in and was blocked and showed the blocking to Gina.

"You can use my iPhone. I will turn off the office connection."

For the next several minutes Gina was on my phone typing. Finally, she said, "I've deleted my profile."

I wasn't sure how to discuss this development. I began, "Look, it's none of my business, but since your Ashley Madison profile and encounters could become public, I need to know why you joined Ashley Madison."

"Okay, if you have to know. We've been married for some time, and over time our tastes have differed. I want our sex life to have more variety. Tony doesn't. I want sex more often. Tony is happy with sex no more than once a week. I am ambitious and demanding at work, but in bed, I want to be controlled by a man. Tony doesn't get that. After I signed up for Ashley Madison, we stopped arguing about sex. You might say it saved our marriage."

I'm not a marriage counselor. I don't want to get in the middle of Gina's marriage.

"Not if Jason Daniels, the FBI, or an online lover decides to out you."

"I've never shared my real name. I haven't had affairs. I only have sex. Sometimes it takes less than an hour. The married men I have sex with still love their wives and I still love Tony."

"I understand all of that. But what if Tony finds out?"

"He'd divorce me, especially if his mother found out."

"Then you better start preparing your confession to him."

I could see she was coming up with a plan.

"Okay. I think that's all I need to know about Ashley Madison."

"This is bullshit. It all started when I was served with a Grand Jury Subpoena, and now the FBI and Justice Department have all of my electronic devices and know everything about my private life, and to put pressure on me, they might threaten to disclose I was an Ashley Madison client."

"I'm sorry. I wish I could help. That's a lot."

"It's a fucking disaster. I will be the lead story on every Dallas TV station tonight, and I'll be the headline in the newspaper tomorrow. I need a drink in the worst way."

"Don't drink." Go, find a computer and make sure your Ashley Madison profile has been deleted."

After Gina left, I started back to work. Fifteen minutes later my phone rang.

"Gabriela, this is Aubrey Gall from the *National Tabloid Journal.* I'm sure you remember me."

"How could I forget. You're the reporter who printed vicious lies about me and embarrassed my mother so much that she is still suffers from depression."

"I gave you the chance to refute what we had been told, and you can't deny that the photos we published of you nearly naked were you."

"I can't deny that, but you violated my right to privacy and whoever gave you the photos should be in jail. I know you didn't call me to talk about old times. Do you plan to print something about my father?"

"No, I want to talk to you about Gina Rossi. She's become a national celebrity, and we want to do a story on her. Our source is a man in Dallas who says he met her on the Ashley Madison website"

Damn! That was fast. I bet Liam was the source.

CHAPTER 31

Gina Rossi

As soon as I was perp walked and indicted, Gabriela pushed for a speedy trial, and we began preparing. Because of the controversy around my arrest and the media interest in my case, almost every night a talking head was on each of the news channels discussing me and the case. Each night, the photos of me in my running clothes with handcuffs leaving my house were on each channel.

We provided my home video which showed the whole scene from a far different perspective. My video made it look more terrifying and unnecessary.

There were arguments back and forth on whether the raid was appropriate or whether I should have had the right to self-surrender. Some former prosecutor claimed that I was not allowed to self-surrender because I was a flight risk. Who in their right mind would believe that?

Another legal commentator claimed the raid was appropriate because I might have destroyed evidence. That guy didn't take into account the point that I would have destroyed evidence long before the day I was released from prison.

When asked to justify the overkill of raiding and arresting a mother with her husband and young son at home, some former FBI agent claimed that some of his most dangerous arrests had been of white-collar criminals like me.

Night after night, the more liberal news media defended the raid and attacked me for not testifying. They presented it in such a way that it was assumed that Burke had indeed bribed Austin Harrington to win the Cross-Town Tollway contract. They called the case against me an open and shut case and claimed I had valuable information that would contribute to the investigation and I had refused to testify even after a judge had ordered me to do so.

Gabriela had experienced it before, and she feared the strategy was to taint the jury. I experienced more than just fear. I was livid.

I wanted to go on TV and defend myself, but I couldn't. Jason Daniels had convinced the judge to issue a gag order. Neither Gabriela nor I could discuss the case with the press. The government had lined up lawyers for each liberal news outlet. My father found several Texas lawyer friends to speak to the media as often as they could. At least they were all Texas lawyers and the talking heads on the other channels were New York or California lawyers.

Finally, it was time for the trial. Gabriela knew about my Ashley Madison secret, but I had still not told her my deep, dark secret that kept me from testifying. I started to tell her my story.

"It all started when I was in college and traveling to Las Vegas. I was trained and became a flight attendant on my uncles' casino private jet."

"I didn't know casinos had private jets. I guess I never thought of the possibility."

"When I turned 21, during the summer between my junior and senior year in college, I worked as a flight attendant on my uncles' private jet that transported high rollers to their casinos in Las Vegas and to other exotic locations. Behind their back, we called them whales.

I explained to Gabriela that it had been the perfect summer job. I worked only a few hours, and I could lie by the pool in Las Vegas or any exotic location we landed. I continued working for them during the summer between my first year and second year in law school, and when they asked, I worked on the weekends until I got married."

Gabriela seemed curious to learn more about the high rollers. I told her I had been amazed at how differently whales viewed money. Several times they had invited back to the "private" gambling rooms, reserved only for them and I had watched many times bets of $10,000 or more on one spin of the roulette wheel, or one roll of the dice, or one hand of blackjack. Some of the high rollers are well-known and worth over a billion dollars, so losing $10,000 on one spin of the wheel meant nothing to them.

"Can you tell me the names of any of the famous athletes or entertainers?" Gabriela asked.

"You would easily recognize many of their names, but I can't reveal them because before I started work, I signed a confidentiality agreement."

'That makes sense."

"Many of the whales thought I was one of the perks. I regularly received tips and offers to spend the night and have sex with one or more of them. I avoided that by telling them the casino owners were my uncles. But I accepted their gifts and entertainment, went to events, and gambled with them in their private high roller villas."

"During the day, I was fine reading a book while lounging around the pool, but at night I was bored stiff, and I was lonely. I started to go to clubs. Some of the clubs would not let a single woman enter. In others, if I was not drinking an alcoholic beverage, men assumed I was an escort.

If I was drinking, they assumed I was someone who would jump in the sack with them. I think I heard more pick-up lines in one week in Las Vegas than I had ever heard in Texas."

"That's one reason I've never been interested in Las Vegas."

"I decided to take up gambling myself. After all, I was not gambling with my own money. While I couldn't gamble in any of my uncles' casinos, I could gamble in any of the other casinos.

"After a show one night, I walked into one of the downtown casinos. After a while I was overwhelmed and could not breathe from all the cigarette smoke in the air, so I went from there to one of the top line hotels and casinos on the strip, known among other things for its ventilation. I played blackjack for a while and then took my winnings to the craps table, where I lost it all in about 10 minutes. When I left the craps table, I was determined to either learn how to play or never play again. I decided to play poker. I quickly learned that the first rule for being a successful poker player is to sit at the right table."

"What is the right table?"

"The table occupied by rich men at least half-drunk who pay more attention to an attractive woman to winning at poker."

Gabriela laughed.

I wanted to tell her the rest of the story, but I froze.

"What does any of this have to do with your work for Burke and you not testifying?

I had to come up with an answer. I took a breath. "I know you won't like my answer," I said to warn her. "It has to do with how I was able to negotiate a better deal on the Cross-Town contract than even Randall Burke expected."

"How so?" Gabriela asked.

"Austin Harrington was at the right table. He needed the Cross-Town project to launch his Presidential run and I could tell he was interested in me."

"Did you seduce him?"

"No, no. That wasn't necessary. I just led him to believe there was a possibility. All I did was make eye contact and smiled."

"So, you got him to agree to tolls on the expressway during construction because you made eye contact and smiled?"

"And told him, 'Texas Roads to Destiny' was his ticket to the White House."

Gabriela turned from me in disgust. I decided I would end the story right then and there.

Gabriela had appeared before Judge Jennifer Rose, but I knew Rose only by reputation. She had been a trial lawyer in the Dallas City Prosecutor's office. Her husband Harold owned a prosperous tech company and was a major Democratic donor. With his help, in 2008, Jennifer Rose had been elected to the Court of Appeals, 5th District of Texas in Dallas. In 2012, Jennifer Rose was elected to a 6-year term on the Texas Supreme Court, where she had caught the attention of liberal legal scholars. In March of 2014, the President appointed Rose to the Federal Court for the Northern District of Texas. Since the Democratic senate had decided to confirm judges with only 51 votes, she had been narrowly confirmed after one of the more controversial and confrontational hearings.

Gabriela had told me Jennifer Rose was the most liberal-leaning federal judge in Texas. That was after Chief Justice Roberts had called out the President for referring to a judge as an "Obama judge." So much for the independent judiciary.

Rose's political views sharply differed from Austin Harrington's. She certainly would not want to see him on the Supreme Court of the United States. She had been through the gauntlet at the Senate hearings and presiding over this case would give her a chance for payback.

The claim that the case against me was an open and shut case was arguable. A federal judge ordered me to testify. I had refused. My refusal was textbook obstruction of justice. Our only chance of winning was a jury nullification strategy. It had worked in the O. J. Simpson trial, and Gabriela Sanchez was convinced we could use it in my trial.

I was skeptical. We wouldn't cross-exam a witness like Mark Fuhrman. Gabriela Sanchez was no Johnny Cochran, and I would not be trying on gloves that didn't fit. Gabriela insisted that the early morning raid on my house would tilt the jury in my favor.

My father had once told me that jury selection is vital in any trial, but it is especially important in a high-profile trial, and my trial was most certainly high profile. I suspect it is even more crucial in a high-profile trial with a defense strategy of jury nullification. We needed to select jurors who would hear the evidence, realize the government had proved their case, and then find me not guilty for other reasons.

One hundred potential jurors had been summoned, and they sat in the jury box and in seats behind the rail. Gabriela didn't hire a jury consultant, as she instinctively knew which jurors she wanted to decide my fate. She asked dozens of questions on their education, what TV shows they watch, and what books they read, then she turned to more specific questions.

"Do any of you on the jury believe that the Cross-Town Tollway project was a bad deal for Texas?"

A few jurors raised their hands.

Gabriela moved to excuse those jurors for cause.

"Ms. Sanchez, I'm going to deny your motion to excuse those jurors for cause."

"Do any of you believe your doctor should keep secret what you tell him about your health?"

Most of the potential jurors raised their hands. I thought that was a good sign.

"Would you want your doctor to keep your health questions secret even if a judge ordered the doctor to disclose what you told him?"

Fewer hands were raised, but still a majority.

"Are any of you Catholic?"

A few hands were raised.

"For those of you who are Catholic, do you believe what you tell your priest in the confession booth should be kept private by your priest? Do you think your priest should keep what you confessed secret - even if a judge ordered him to disclose what you told him?"

All of the same jurors raised their hands.

"Suppose an innocent man is accused of murder and another lawyer's client confesses to him that he murdered the victim, not the accused person. Do you believe the lawyer should keep his client's confession secret?"

This time only a few potential jurors raised their hands.

"Are you familiar with the Special Counsel's investigation on this matter?"

Almost every juror raised a hand.

"Do any of you believe the special counsel has gone beyond what he was tasked to investigate?"

Several potential jurors raised their hands.

First and foremost, potential jurors who believed in the right to keep private what they told their doctor, or their priest were ideal jurors.

Next, we wanted jurors who had voted for the President. Beyond that, Gabriela wanted blue-collar, high school educated men.

After four hours of questioning, the jury had been selected. Four of the jurors were white men who had not graduated from college. There were three white women, one Hispanic man, two African American men, and two African American women.

At 2:00 p.m., Judge Rose looked down from the bench and said, "Mr. Daniels, you may give the jury your opening statement."

Jason Daniels rose and walked to the lectern with a legal pad. He looked like the elite Ivy League arrogant prick Gabriela had described to me in great detail. She was certain several of the jurors would not like him. I hoped she was right.

"Ladies and gentlemen of the jury, my name is Jason Daniels. I am the government prosecutor in this case. You might be wondering, why are we here? What has Gina Rossi done that causes her to be sitting in that chair?"

Daniels turned and pointed at me.

"Austin Harrington is the former governor of Texas. He personally decided the state should build the $2 billion Cross-Town Tollway project. Gina Rossi's client, Burke Construction Company, submitted the only proposal to construct the Cross-Town Tollway, and at the governor's insistence, the Texas Department of Transportation accepted that proposal and entered into a contract with Burke Construction Company. The government is investigating why that happened."

I sat as still as I could, a smile plastered on my face, and wishing I was invisible. Gabriela's eyes were on the jury, even as she scribbled a note or two on a pad.

"Before he became governor," Daniels continued. "Austin Harrington and his wife became business partners with Randall Burke and his wife in the Hill Country Estates development. When he was running for governor, Harrington and his wife sold their share of that partnership to Burke and his wife at an inflated price. The government has been investigating whether Randall Burke gave Governor Harrington and his wife the opportunity to earn millions of dollars in return for the governor's pushing the Texas Department of Transportation to enter into the $2 billion Cross-Town Tollway contract with Burke Construction.

"Both the former Governor Harrington, and Randall Burke were smart enough not to leave a paper trail evidencing their scheme. So, the government was forced to dig deeper to find out what happened. Who other than the two men would know whether a bribe had occurred? None other than Gina Rossi, the Burke company lawyer who was deeply involved in both transactions. We subpoenaed Gina Rossi to testify before the grand jury. She refused, claiming she would be violating the lawyer-client privilege."

I looked at the jurors. A few seemed bored already. Apparently, Jason Daniels couldn't see it because he was continually looking down at his legal pad on the lectern.

"We went before a judge who ordered the defendant to testify because the lawyer-client privilege does not apply when a lawyer like the defendant helps her client commit fraud."

"After questioning the defendant, the judge agreed with the government. Gina Rossi, the defendant, had helped her client bribe the former governor, and he ordered her to testify."

Gabriela Sanchez shot to her feet. "Your Honor, Mr. Daniels has purposely misled the jury. Judge Parsons did *not* decide that Gina Rossi had helped her client bribe the former governor. He simply concluded that she should be required to testify."

"Ms. Sanchez, I'll let you make that point in your opening statement. Continue Mr. Daniels."

"Thank you, Your Honor. Ladies and gentlemen, as a Special Counsel, my job is to seek justice and to ensure that no one, including a potential Supreme Court Justice, is above the law. Our justice system is built on the premise of searching for the truth.

"The defendant, Gina Rossi, could have helped fulfill that promise, but instead she chose to obstruct justice. At the end of what will be a relatively short trial, we will ask you to send a message to future witnesses. Send a message that says the rich and powerful in our country must adhere to the law just the same as you, and you and you. Send a message that the rich and powerful in this country cannot hide behind their lawyers, and their lawyers can't obstruct an investigation. Find Gina Rossi guilty of criminal contempt and obstruction of justice."

I looked over at Gabriela Sanchez and whispered. "Go, girl!"

CHAPTER 32

Gabriela Sanchez

"**M**s. Sanchez, you may address the jury now."

The one question the press had asked repeatedly when Gina and I walked toward the courtroom was, "Gabriela, do you plan on calling Gina as a witness?"

I had not decided yet. I knew Gina wanted to tell her story, but Randall Burke had not given her permission to testify. I worried how she would handle cross-examination. Based on our work together, I worried she would be offended, become emotional and lose her temper. Worse yet, I was worried she would lie and that would put me in an ethical crisis. I had experience representing a defendant who was unable to control himself during cross-examination, and the jury had hated him.

We had spent hours going over what Jason Daniels might ask, and I was still not sure how Gina would handle the questions. I was even more worried that he knew something Gina had not told me.

I walked to the lectern with no notes. I didn't need notes and I wanted to create rapport with the jury.

I had started work on my opening statement the day I took Gina Rossi home from the prison in Fort Worth. I knew that in spite of instructions from judges to keep an open mind, the vast majority of jurors make up their minds by the end of opening statements. I had to persuade them before I sat back down.

Like I had done in the Duval trial, I had practiced in front of the mirror, traveled to the Rio Grande Valley to get feedback from my father, Roberto, and had one of my associates shoot video. I practiced my pacing, my tone, and my body language. Everything had to click this morning.

Knowing that Jason Daniels would be dressed in a dark suit, I had decided to wear a white suit: a tailored fit single-buttoned jacket, a solid white pencil skirt, and a black silk blouse with a round neckline. I hoped the subtle white versus dark contrast would not be lost on the jury.

"Ladies and gentlemen, a woman I know received a summons for jury duty in federal court. Even though she is retired, she was busy in her community and gone for weeks at a time traveling with her retired husband. She called me and asked if I could help her be excused from serving on the jury. I shared with her that our entire system of justice is based on people like her, people like you serving on a jury. All of us here are grateful for your service.

I told them I had grown up in the Rio Grande Valley, in South Texas along the border and that my father, Roberto, is a lawyer, and that he had tried to convince me not to follow in his footsteps.

I paused. Several jurors smiled. I stood back from the lectern and put my arms out. "As you can see, he was unsuccessful." The same jurors smiled again, and I made a note in my mind which ones were with me.

"When my father finally gave up on convincing me to find another career, he started talking to me about what it means to be a lawyer. He told me that the lawyer-client privilege is sacred in our legal system. It is the fundamental cornerstone of the American legal system. He told me that wives cannot be compelled to testify against their husbands, priests cannot be forced to disclose what they learn in confessional, and lawyers are ethically bound not to disclose what they learn in their work for their clients."

I could see that the same jurors were nodding in agreement-a good sign.

"When you speak to your lawyer, you can count on that communication being kept confidential. Why is it so important? It's deeply rooted in the concept of trust and the idea that a client confronting a legal issue should be able to fully and completely trust the lawyer whose advice they are seeking. The lawyer-client privilege means that whatever you share privately with your lawyer while seeking legal advice, you share in confidence. Because the information you disclose to your lawyer is secret, you can fully disclose the facts and seek your lawyer's best advice. The privilege is held by you, the client, not a lawyer like Gina Rossi - and only you, the client, can waive the privilege, not your lawyer."

I paused for a moment and looked at each juror. The same jurors nodded their heads again. They understood.

"So, what happened here? Gina Rossi represented Randall Burke and the Burke Construction Company. She represented Mr. Burke and his wife when they entered into a partnership called Hill Country Estates, with his lifelong friend, Austin Harrington and his wife. At the time, Austin Harrington was a judge on the Texas Supreme Court."

I heard Jason Daniels coughing behind me. I waited until he finished.

"Shortly before Austin Harrington decided to run for governor, Gina Rossi again represented Randall Burke and his wife when they purchased the Harringtons' interest in the Hill Country Estates partnership. Over a year later, Austin Harrington was elected governor. I'm sure all of you know who Austin Harrington is. Many of you saw him on TV when he was Governor. Some of you may have even voted for him."

I paused for a moment and then continued. "Several months after he was elected Governor, Austin Harrington launched the Texas Roads to Destiny program. You are probably familiar with that program."

I paused again and looked at the jurors. Eight of the twelve jurors were nodding their heads affirmatively.

I continued. "After Governor Harrington launched the Texas Roads to Destiny program, he asked the Texas Department of Transportation to request proposals to build the Cross-Town Tollway here in Dallas. Gina Rossi represented Burke Construction Company and found the financing for the project. She helped prepare the proposal. After it was submitted, she met with the Texas Department of Transportation attorney and explained the proposal. She met with Governor Harrington and explained the proposal to him, including the necessity for putting tolls on the old expressway during construction of the new tollway to make the project financially viable.

"Everything I told you was not confidential. But Gina Rossi's discussions with Randall Burke about the Hill Country Estates partnership and about the Cross-Town Tollway contract were confidential. Those were the conversations that were privileged. Those were the conversations that Mr. Daniels sought to force Ms. Rossi to disclose to the grand jury. Those were the conversations that Randall Burke believed would forever be confidential. And, those were the conversations that Gina Rossi courageously refused to disclose."

I paused for a moment. Then, I stood up as straight as possible and leaned toward the jurors.

"Ladies and gentlemen, Mr. Daniels is from Washington, D.C. He is part of the Special Counsel team in Washington. They have been investigating the President and others for a long time. How did this investigation start? I find it hard to believe, but it started when someone still unknown sent an anonymous tip to the Special Counsel's office after the President had shared with the public a list of potential Supreme Court nominees, and Austin Harrington was on the list. An anonymous tip, ladies and gentlemen.

I turned for a moment.

"Do you suppose the anonymous tip might have come from someone who didn't like the President and wanted to make sure that Austin Harrington would never be named to the Supreme Court?"

I paused again. *Let them think that one over.*

"What did the Special Counsel's team do? They didn't call Austin Harrington or Randall Burke and ask to meet with them. Instead, they issued Grand Jury subpoenas, including one to Gina Rossi, demanding that she break the vow she had made to her client to keep their conversations secret. The same vow your lawyer would make to you.

"Mr. Daniels is right about one thing. Judge Parsons directed Gina Rossi to testify in spite of the lawyer-client privilege. Gina Rossi is loyal to her client. Gina Rossi is an ethical lawyer who had worked hard, who did her best to give her client legal advice. The Special Counsel's team demanded to learn what advice Gina had given her client, and convinced Judge Parsons to order her to testify. Gina thought Judge Parsons' ruling was wrong. I strongly believed his ruling was wrong. When I was unable to convince him to change his mind, we appealed his decision to the Fifth Circuit Court of Appeals. At that point I asked Judge Parsons to stay, meaning not enforce, his order holding Gina Rossi in contempt so she could stay home with her son until the Fifth Circuit ruled on the appeal. He refused. So, Ladies and gentlemen, on the second day of

January this year, Gina Rossi kissed her husband and young son goodbye and checked into the Federal Prison for Women in Fort Worth.

"To be able to appeal Judge Parsons' ruling to the Fifth Circuit, Gina Rossi had no choice. She had to continue to refuse to testify until the Fifth Court decided. Had she testified and the court agreed with us that the conversations were indeed privileged, it would have been too late to put the genie back in the bottle, meaning Randall Burke's right to have those conversations remain confidential would have been lost.

"What the Special Counsel's office did next is even more egregious." I looked over at Jason Daniels and paused for about two seconds and then continued.

"Ladies and gentlemen, before the Fifth Circuit ruled, and as a pre-emptive strike, Mr. Daniels convinced a grand jury to indict Gina Rossi for obstruction of justice, and criminal contempt. Mr. Daniels was afraid that the Fifth Circuit would find that Gina Rossi could not be compelled to testify, and Mr. Daniels investigation of our former governor based on an anonymous tip would be derailed."

I looked back again at Jason Daniels.

"I want to emphasize what the evidence will show. Mr. Daniels didn't allow the Fifth Circuit to rule on Gina Rossi's appeal. Mr. Daniels did not indict former Governor Harrington, Mr. Daniels did not indict Randall Burke. Instead, after trying to use Gina Rossi as a pawn in an attempt to destroy our former governor, Mr. Daniels hoodwinked a grand jury to indict Gina.

"But it gets worse. When the Special Counsel's office dismissed the grand jury investigating former Governor Harrington and Randall Burke, they released Gina Rossi from the Fort Worth Women's Federal Prison. The next morning, she took a run outside and then fixed breakfast for her son and husband. While they were sitting at the breakfast table, they heard a knock. When Gina opened the door, a dozen FBI agents entered in protective vests with drawn automatic weapons and pushed their way into her house with news media outside shooting video of her arrest. They terrorized Gina's son and took all of the family hard drives, tablets, phones and other electronic devices, including her son's iPad."

Two women covered their mouths. A couple of the men shook their heads. I knew Daniels wanted to object, but he couldn't. I'm sure he wished now that he had called me and asked for Gina to turn herself in voluntarily.

"Gina Rossi did not obstruct justice. Instead, Mr. Daniels and his Washington, D.C. special prosecution team terrorized Gina and her family while trying to obstruct Ms. Rossi from keeping the promise she made when she took the oath to become a lawyer. That promise was to keep secret her communications with her clients. I am confident you will find her not guilty."

When I sat down, I felt Gina grab my forearm. When I looked over, she nodded and whispered, "well done."

"Ladies and gentlemen," Judge Rose said looking at the jury. "You've heard the opening statements from the prosecution and the defense. When we reconvene tomorrow at 10:00 a.m., Mr. Daniels will begin presenting witnesses. Remember, do not discuss what you have heard with anyone and do not discuss what you have heard with each other."

CHAPTER 33

──── ❧ ────

Gabriela Sanchez

A s we left the crowded courtroom, Gina and I were joined by Leo Baretti, Tony, and a throng of reporters.

"What do you think so far, Gabriela?"

"You likely know that Judge Rose has directed us not to discuss the case with the media. I'll leave it to you to reach your own conclusions on how it has gone so far."

"Will Gina Rossi testify?"

We kept walking.

"Do you really think the Department of Justice was out to derail Harrington's chances of being nominated to the Supreme Court?"

I didn't need to answer that question. Obviously, the President would not nominate Austin Harrington if he had an opportunity to fill a third Supreme Court vacancy.

I wanted to make our case for the press, but under the gag order, I would be held in contempt.

"Gabriela, have you talked to the President about a pardon for Gina?"

I had not, and I hoped she wouldn't need one.

When we returned to my office conference room, I asked Gina, "Has Burke given you permission to testify?"

"We've talked about it, and he is consulting with his lawyer."

"If he did nothing wrong, or you have no knowledge of anything he did wrong, he shouldn't care if you testify."

"I understand, but as you know, it's not that simple."

Leo Baretti set his briefcase on the table. "I'll call Ken Sanders and find out if Burke will waive the lawyer-client privilege."

I spent most of the night sharpening my cross-examination of Special Agent, Dylan Forkum, whom I anticipated would be Jason Daniels' first witness.

I had never heard the surname Forkum, and when I did some research, I discovered that the name was thought to be an altered form of the Irish name Forkin. Dylan Forkum had grown up in Sevierville, Tennessee, and had graduated from Middle-Tennessee University and University of Tennessee Law School.

After law school, Forkum started his law practice in a small East Tennessee town, and later he ran as a Democrat in a heavily Republican county and was elected District Attorney. After serving four years, he became an FBI agent and moved to the Washington, D. C. headquarters where he was assigned to the fraud unit. As a fraud and bribery investigator, Forkum was known for following the money.

I discovered that Forkum had donated money to the Democratic Party throughout his career, including in the last Presidential election in 2016. He was definitely a partisan.

When my phone rang, Leo Baretti's caller ID flashed on the screen.

"Ken Sanders says Randall Burke will not waive the privilege."

"Even if his refusal will make it likely Gina will be convicted?"

"Yes. But he gave permission for you to talk directly to Burke."

"I will talk to him right away."

"Hopefully you can find out what Burke's hiding."

I suspected Burke and Gina were indeed hiding something.

Leo Baretti thought so too. He said, "Gabriela, the problem is Burke isn't the only one. Whatever Burke is hiding, Gina is also hiding. I don't believe her refusal to testify has anything to do with standing up for the lawyer-client privilege. I think she knows something that if it became public would be a big problem for Harrington."

Did Leo Baretti know something I didn't know? I asked, "what makes you think Gina knows something Harrington does not want to be public?"

Leo replied, "It's the only way I can explain how she negotiated a deal with Harrington that TxDOT didn't want, John Randolph didn't want, and Randall Burke wasn't expecting."

"You think Gina's secret is what she used to negotiate charging tolls on the old expressway during the construction of the new Cross-Town Tollway?"

"Maybe. Gina bragged about her *coup d'état* and told me Randall Burke wasn't even aware she would ask for it. Why did she go for more and what made her believe Austin Harrington would accept her request?"

"Leo, Gina is a top-notch negotiator and was clearly willing to take a risk in her negotiations with Harrington and Burke."

"You better be prepared for Jason Daniels to bring up something that Gina hasn't told you. Have you asked her what she is hiding?"

"I've asked her more times than you can imagine. Gina believes her best work and her loyalty are being questioned."

"Her best work and loyalty *are* being questioned. And, that will impact her judgment, and she will be prone to say things she later regrets."

"I know. She didn't think before addressing Judge Parsons. I've spent hours and days working with her on testimony. The only chance we have to win this case is for Randall Burke to allow Gina to testify and for her to be cool and calm while she is grilled by Jason Daniels."

"Tony knows Gina. He keeps her grounded. I'll talk to him."

I wasn't sure it was a good idea to get Tony involved at this point, so I told Leo, "I doubt Tony knows what Gina is hiding."

"I'll ask Jim Hardy, but if Harrington does not want something made public, Hardy won't tell me either. One final question. Does the Special Counsel's office know what Gina had as leverage?"

"I don't know."

CHAPTER 34

Gabriela Sanchez

As soon as we hung up, I called Randall Burke. I asked if I could come by his office. At first, he hesitated. When I told him that Gina's future depended on my talking with him, Burke finally gave in.

Thirty minutes later I was sitting in his office overlooking Dallas.

"Mr. Burke, Gina will be convicted if she doesn't testify. She has been loyal to you to the end. She needs for you to waive the lawyer-client privilege now."

I looked into his face and held my hands out, palms upward.

"Did you expect Governor Harrington to award you the Cross-Town Tollway Contract when you bought the Harringtons' interest in the Hill Country Estates partnership?"

"No, I never thought the Cross-Town project would be resurrected."

"Then, you can't let Gina go to prison simply because she won't have a chance to tell her story."

I looked into his face again.

"We've spent the last two months going over what she might say if given the chance to testify. She has told me nothing that would incriminate you or Austin Harrington. She has been loyal to you, and she needs you to return the favor now."

Finally, Randall Burke started to speak.

"Okay, okay, I will waive the lawyer-client privilege. But, has Gina told you about her relationship with Austin Harrington?"

I was puzzled. "What about her relationship with Austin Harrington?"

"You better have her tell you before she testifies. Daniels and the DOJ may know and believe she used it to obtain an advantage in her negotiations on the Cross-Town Tollway Contract."

What relationship? "I will discuss it with Gina."

"And by the way. I believe the whistleblower wasn't some random Democrat who wanted to derail Austin Harrington's Supreme Court nomination. I strongly believe David Coleman was the whistleblower."

"Why would he want to put you, a firm client, in jail?"

"He's sanctimonious, vindictive and a liberal democrat. He believes he should be our lawyer, not Gina. He also believes that Austin had an affair with Gina Rossi. He wasn't out to get me. He was out to expose the affair and keep Austin off the Supreme Court. I'm just collateral damage. Gina needs to be prepared for questions about her relationship with Austin Harrington. Daniels plans to paint a sleazy picture of the two of them."

"May I ask you a couple more questions, and will you honestly answer them?"

"You can ask the questions, but I cannot guarantee I will give you an honest answer."

"Okay. Did you have Mario spy on Gina after she received the grand jury subpoena?"

"You said you wanted an honest answer, right?"

"Yes."

"Mario has worked for me his entire adult life. Gina may have forgotten that. I wouldn't say I asked him to spy on her. I'd say I asked him to keep an eye on her and protect her because I was aware Gina had received death threats from the protestors who demanded she testify against Harrington. He reported to me several times a day while he was protecting her."

"But Gina believes Mario was reporting to you from the first day she received the subpoena. That was before the death threats."

"As I told you, Mario has worked for me his entire adult life. While he is driving Gina or anyone else, he keeps me informed. What is your other question?"

"Did you have someone threaten Gina as a way to convince her not to testify?"

"That wasn't me. I didn't need to do anything like that, and I never would anyway. I simply told her that if she testified without my permission, she would never have another client in Texas. That was all I needed to say."

I stood to go, and Randall Burke grabbed my arm. "I have a question for you, Ms. Sanchez."

"What?"

"How do you plan to win a case the government thinks is a sure conviction?"

As soon as I started my car, I called Gina.

"Gina, Randall Burke has agreed to waive the lawyer-client privilege. That might save you. Burke also told me Daniels plans to attack you for having an affair with Harrington."

For a few seconds, there was no response.

"I need for you to come by my office right away. We need to talk, and I need to know what you have been keeping from me."

"I'll be right there," she stammered.

I drove to the office, stewing on the idea that whether she'd had an affair with Harrington or not. David Coleman and Randall Burke thought she had. If Coleman was the whistle blower, he undoubtedly shared what he thought with Jason Daniels. While I was waiting for Gina, I was pacing in our conference room. I was angry. I had suspected all along that she'd been involved with Harrington. She had better tell me all about it before I put her on the witness stand.

When she arrived, Gina sat down, but I remained standing.

"Okay, Gina, the gig is up. If you are going to testify, I need to know right now what you have been hiding from me."

"Okay, okay. Please sit. I don't want to feel like you are cross-examining me."

She stared at me with those cold brown eyes. Finally, she started talking.

"What I am about to tell you, I have never told anyone, including Tony. If it comes out at the trial, it will be a disaster."

"Is what you are about to tell me the reason you refused to testify?"

"Yes."

I picked up a pen to take notes.

"Please don't take notes. Take my word, you will have no problem remembering what I am about to tell you."

"Okay."

"Remember I told you about being a flight attendant for my uncle's corporate jet, and gambling when I was off?"

"Yes."

"I didn't tell you the whole story."

She sat up straight in her chair and continued.

"One night, after some gambling I went to the bar at the casino. While I was there an attractive woman sat down next to me. We started talking about Las Vegas, and she told me her name was Carrie Collins. We talked for the next couple of hours and exchanged phone numbers.

"The next day Carrie called me and asked if I wanted to meet her at Monique Club, one of the top singles clubs in Las Vegas. I decided I would join her. That night since I wasn't alone, I had a great time. Carrie knew the bartenders, the bouncers and many of the customers who were there."

Gina took a deep breath.

"I started going to other clubs with Carrie, and she introduced me to her friends, most of whom were men with lots of money. I thought it was odd, but she always introduced me as Jordan Jamison rather than using my real name."

Right then, it dawned on me where Gina's story might be going. I let her continue.

"After one night of the men buying us drinks, Carrie introduced me to a man named Tom. He was also a good-looking guy in his 40s. Tom told me he was a real estate developer from Los Angeles. When we were in the ladies' room, Carrie asked me if I wanted to have sex with Tom. I told her I didn't know him, so I wasn't sure. That was when she asked me the question that would change my college life."

I thought I knew what the question was, but I asked her, "What was Carrie's question?"

"She asked if I would have sex with him if he paid me $1000 for the experience. I had been offered that, and more, by the whales I met on my uncles' private jet. This was the first time I wasn't worried that my uncles would find out and tell my father."

I was right about where Gina was going with her story, but I knew there must be more to it. I was sure she agreed to the proposition, but I let her continue.

"I easily get aroused and excited, and I thought I might enjoy having sex with Tom, but I had never thought I might be paid $1000 for an hour with him. That seemed like the best of both worlds at the time for a college girl. Carrie told me that escorting was safer than dating in Las Vegas -and - she was probably right."

"You agreed?"

"Yes. And the next night I agreed again. I discovered that Carrie ran an escort service and Jordan Jamison became a highly compensated Las Vegas escort. At that point, I quit gambling for hours at a time. Over time, I became one of the top-rated escorts in Las Vegas. Thankfully, none of the photos of Jordan Jamison that were on the website showed my face."

"But during law school, you told Tony you were acting as a flight attendant for your uncles in Las Vegas and gambling?"

"I did. I was still a flight attendant, so that part was true. I visited my uncles when I returned from trips with the whales. For my cover on the gambling, I always played poker or blackjack for a few hours."

"How did Tony respond?"

"He kept trying to convince me to quit gambling. When I continued the flight attendant work during law school, he thought I was addicted to gambling and not paying attention to my studies. The truth was I had far more time to study when I was escorting in Las Vegas than when I was gambling."

"Did your uncles ever ask what you were doing in Las Vegas between flights?"

"Sure. I told my uncles I was gambling. They didn't approve of it, but they believed me."

"So, did you refuse to testify because you were concerned someone would out you and then Tony would find out you were not gambling when you returned to Las Vegas on flights?"

"Yes, but there's more to the story."

"Go ahead and tell me."

"One night, Carrie introduced me to a lawyer she said was from Texas."

"No way. Austin Harrington?"

"Yes, but he told me his name was Travis Harris."

"So, Travis Harris became a client of Jordan Jamison?"

"Yes, Travis Harris became a regular client and offered to pay for me to fly to Houston and to Dallas. I declined and told him I would only see him in Las Vegas. Thankfully, we never ran into each other on the streets of Austin."

"So, when did you quit your escort life?"

"When Tony and I got engaged. I told Carrie I was retiring. At that point I told Tony I was quitting gambling cold turkey. Carrie was not happy with my decision, since I had made a lot of money for her. Travis Harris told me he was also disappointed."

"You continued while you were a young lawyer?"

"Yes, but only on weekends. It's only a two-hour flight from Dallas to Las Vegas and two hours back. In one night, I could make more money than I made in a week practicing law."

"When did you next see Austin Harrington, aka Travis Harris?"

"Shortly after Randall Burke hired me. He invited Tony and me to sit in his suite at a Cowboys game, and when we arrived, he introduced me to Austin Harrington and his wife, Laura Ray."

"That must have been awkward."

"That's an understatement. But to be honest, I thought it was amusing. I was at least single during our escapades. Harrington was married. I wasn't expecting that Austin Harrington would help me make it in my daddy's world, but as you know, he did with the Cross-Town Tollway contract."

"I understand. Did you tell Randall Burke the story?"

"No. I assume Harrington told him. I believe Harrington was the one he was trying to protect when he refused to waive the lawyer-client privilege."

"I suspect you're right. It had nothing to do with any advice or help you gave Burke on the Hill Country partnership or the Cross-Town Tollway contract."

"You know most of the rest of the story. Let's get ready to kick some ass in court, and make sure Jordan Jamison and Travis Harris do not come up in the trial."

"That sounds like a great plan, but I need to talk to Carrie Collins right away to find out if anyone from the DOJ or Special Counsel's office has called her to ask about Jordan Jamison or Gina Rossi."

"Good point. What if Daniels or the FBI has talked to Carrie?"

"Then, they would know you are Jordan Jamison."

"True."

"You have a big decision to make. If you don't testify, you will most likely be found guilty and go to prison. If you testify, there is a chance your secret might come out and destroy your marriage. I have only one more question."

"What's that?"

"Is there anything at all about Jordan Jamison, Travis Harris, or Carrie's escort business on your computer or electronic devices that the FBI has now?"

"No way. That was all before I owned this computer or any of the electronic devices. I was probably using a BlackBerry in those days."

I may have made a big mistake learning about Jordan Jamison and Travis Harris. It would have been easier to argue Gina Rossi's desire to protect the lawyer-client privilege defense had I not known about Jordan and Travis. But at least Daniels wouldn't be able to blindside me.

CHAPTER 35

Gabriela Sanchez

At 10:00 a.m., Judge Rose walked from behind the bench into the courtroom, and the U.S. Marshal shouted, "All rise."

"You may be seated. Mr. Daniels, you may call your first witness."

"We call FBI Agent, Dylan Forkum."

A couple of the jurors snickered at the sound of Forkum. I made a note of those jurors and decided that every question I asked would include the name Forkum.

As he walked to the witness stand, I thought Forkum didn't look like he was dressed to be on the cover of *GQ Magazine*, and I was surprised that Jason Daniels didn't suggest a better-looking wardrobe.

Forkum wore a light gray suit with brown loafers that looked like they had never been shined. He wore a white shirt that was at least an inch too small in the neck. His neck was wrinkled, and it looked like Forkum was choking.

When he was sitting down in the witness chair, Forkum unbuttoned his suit jacket button, putting on full view the black paisley tie with a tie clip that likely had gone out of style several years ago. I grinned. I had found photos of Forkum when his hair was curly and much longer. But that morning he wore his hair in a flat top with curly hairs in the back standing out rather than standing up.

Jason Daniels ambled up to the lectern with a legal pad.

"Special Agent Forkum, would you state your full name for the record, please?"

"Special Agent, Dylan Connor Forkum."

I looked at the jury. Three jurors were still smiling.

Must be real hell growing up with the last name Forkum.

"Special Agent, tell the Jury what your position is with the FBI."

"I work in the Criminal Investigation Division, and I focus on fraud and corruption of government officials."

"How long have you investigated fraud and bribery cases?"

"About 10 years. I was assigned to a task force after the real estate meltdown in 2008."

"What did you do before you began investigating government corruption cases?"

"I was part of the Enron Task Force that investigated and convicted high ranking Enron officials in Houston."

"First, please tell the Jury what public officials' corruption is?"

"Sure. In its most simple terms, public corruption in any form is the misuse of a public or government office for private gain. An example would be taking money in return for doing something to benefit the donor. Another example would be using public power unlawfully."

"Please tell the Jury about your experience investigating public officials in government fraud and bribery cases."

"Okay. I was the lead agent case in a case involving state public officials."

"What was that case about?"

"Former governor appointees were convicted of political retaliation against a local mayor."

"Tell us about some other cases you investigated."

"I was the lead investigator in the bribery case against a former state assembly speaker."

"What was that case about?"

"The state assembly speaker was twice found guilty of taking nearly $4 million in return for legislative favors he performed for some real estate and union cronies."

I took note that Forkum never mentioned the states where these crimes had occurred. They were not in Texas.

"When did you get involved in the investigation of Governor Harrington and Randall Burke?"

"It was after a Senator sent our office a letter from a constituent outlining what the constituent contended was a pay-to-play bribe by Randall Burke to Governor Harrington."

"Can you be more specific?"

"The constituent alleged that Randall Burke and his wife gave Governor Harrington and his wife a sweetheart deal in what was called the Hill Country Estates partnership and then acquired their interest back at a premium price to secure Governor Harrington's direction to the Texas Department of Transportation to award a $2 billion contract called the Cross-Town Tollway Contract without any competition."

"What were you trying to determine?"

"Whether Harrington committed (or agreed to commit) an official act - namely directing the award of a $2 billion contract in exchange for the loans and gifts from Randall Burke. We wanted to determine what if anything former Governor Harrington did in the award of the contract and whether what he did was done as a result of loans and gifts by Randall Burke."

"What did you do after first receiving the constituent's allegation?"

"We first checked on what the constituent alleged and discovered that Randall Burke and his wife, Jenna had purchased land. Then they transferred the land to a partnership, the Hill Country Estates partnership and Austin Harrington and his wife, Laura Ray Harrington, became 50-50 partners with the Burkes. When Harrington decided to run for governor, he and his wife sold their interest to the Burkes."

"What happened after that?"

"Harrington was elected governor. In his first year in office, he created a program he called 'Texas Roads to Destiny.' In his second year in office, the Texas Department of Transportation awarded a $2 billion contract to Burke Construction Company without any competition. Since many people thought it was odd to award the largest contract in Texas history with no competition, we decided to investigate whether there was any connection between the Hill Country Estates investment and the Cross-Town Tollway contract."

"What did you do?"

"We subpoenaed documents from Burke Construction, the Burkes, the Harringtons and sent them target letters."

"What is a target letter?"

"It advises the recipient that he or she is a target of a grand jury investigation for a major financial crime."

"What else did you do?"

"We issued a subpoena to Ms. Rossi, seeking her Burke Construction Company and Randall Burke files, and her testimony before the grand jury."

"Why did you subpoena Ms. Rossi?"

"We didn't expect to find a smoking gun in either the former governor's files or in Randall Burke's and Burke Construction Company's files, and we expected that neither Austin Harrington nor Randall Burke would testify. Ms. Rossi was deeply involved in all Burke Construction and Randall Burke deals and transactions. We expected her to have firsthand knowledge of whether Burke had bribed Harrington to win the contract."

"Was there anything unusual about the Cross-Town Tollway contract?"

I stood up. "Your Honor, I object. Mr. Forkum has no knowledge of what is usual or unusual in the Texas Department of Transportation contracts."

Jason Daniels responded. "Your Honor, I am simply asking the special agent the question to provide a framework for the government's next steps in the investigation."

"Okay, Mr. Daniels, I expect you to get right to the next steps. Agent Forkum is not an expert on Texas Department of Transportation contracting."

Jason Daniels repeated the question, and Agent Forkum responded.

"There were several things. First, it was unusual to have a project that years before the Austin Harrington was governor, the Texas Department of Transportation received three proposals from contractors before Harrington was elected, and just one proposal after he was elected."

"Did you interview the other two contractors?"

"Yes. Both contractors believed Burke Construction Company had a lock on winning the contract."

"Did they say why?"

"They said Randall Burke was connected with Governor Harrington."

"What else did you find unusual?"

"It was highly unusual that Harrington was involved in the negotiation and the award of the contract. As best we were able to determine, no governor before or since has played a role in the negotiation of a state contract."

"What else was unusual?"

I stood quickly.

"Your Honor, I object again. As I argued before, Agent Forkum is not an expert and clearly is not qualified to testify what is normal or usual in Texas contracting."

Jason Daniels replied. "Your Honor, I asked this question as a prelude for discussing why Gina Rossi was an important witness."

"I agree with Ms. Sanchez, but I am going to allow it based on Mr. Daniels' representation. I will also let the jury decide what, if any, weight to give the answer. And, you may test Agent Forkum's knowledge in your cross-examination. Agent Forkum, you may answer the question."

"It was unusual for a contractor's lawyer to negotiate a contract first with the Texas Department of Transportation lawyer, and then directly with Governor Harrington."

"What would be normal?"

"It is normal for either the contractor to negotiate the contract with the Texas Department of Transportation or the contractor's lawyer to negotiate the contract with the Texas Department of Transportation's lawyer. This was quite unusual. The contractor's lawyer negotiated directly with Governor Harrington."

"How did you determine that Ms. Rossi negotiated the Cross-Town Tollway contract with former Governor Harrington?"

"First, we reviewed news interviews Ms. Rossi gave after the contract was signed. She was on TV and interviewed by newspapers and magazines. In the interviews, she took credit for convincing former Governor Harrington to initiate the project and she took credit for negotiating the deal that the current Texas Governor calls …"

I stood again. "Your Honor, I object. What the current Texas Governor calls the Cross-Town Tollway Contract is irrelevant."

"Mr. Daniels, I agree with Ms. Sanchez. Agent Forkum, you answered Mr. Daniels' question when you told the jury you reviewed interviews of Ms. Rossi. Mr. Daniels, ask your next question."

"Yes, Your Honor. Special Agent, what happened after you subpoenaed Ms. Rossi?"

"Her client, Randall Burke, filed a motion to quash the subpoena, meaning he wanted the judge not to permit Ms. Rossi to testify."

"What happened next?"

"Your office filed a response, and Judge Parsons ordered Ms. Rossi to appear before him and answer questions so he could decide whether she should be compelled to testify. Judge Parsons ruled…"

I jumped to my feet. "Your Honor, I object to Mr. Forkum's characterizing what Judge Parsons ruled."

"Your Honor," Daniels responded, "we can easily remedy that problem. We offer Judge Parsons' order as an exhibit."

"Any objection, Ms. Sanchez?"

"No, Your Honor."

"Special Agent, please read Judge Parson's opinion to the jury.

"It's a Memorandum Opinion, Judge Parsons wrote:

'The Special Counsel Office (SCO) seeks to compel the Witness to testify before a grand jury regarding limited aspects of her legal representation of the Target, Burke Construction and Randall Burke, which testimony the SCO believes will reveal whether the Targets provided gifts, loans, and benefits to former Governor Austin Harrington and his wife, Laura Ray Harrington.

'The Witness has refused to testify unless directed by a court order, due to professional ethical obligations, because the Targets have invoked their attorney-client and work-product privileges.

'The SCO asserts that the crime-fraud exception to both privileges and those privileges are overcome by a showing of adequate reasons to compel the Witness's testimony.

'The Court recognizes the importance of the lawyer-client privilege and the work-product privilege in the American legal system.

'However, there is an exception to the privileges. When a person uses the attorney-client relationship to further a criminal scheme, the law is well established that a claim of attorney-client or work-product privilege must yield to the grand jury's investigatory needs.

'Based on consideration of the factual proffers made by the SCO, as well as the arguments articulated by the SCO, the privilege holders and the Witness over multiple filings and a hearing, the Court finds that the SCO has made a sufficient *prima facie* showing that the crime-fraud exception to the attorney-client and work-product privileges applies.

'Finally, the SCO overcomes any work-product privilege by showing that the testimony sought from the Witness is necessary to uncover criminal conduct and cannot be obtained through other means. Thus, the SCO may compel the Witness to testify as to the specific matters related to her representation of Burke Construction Company and Randall Burke related to the Hill Country Estates partnership and any other business dealings between Randall Burke and Austin Harrington and the Cross-Town Tollway Contract.'

"And, what happened after Judge Parsons issued the order?"

"Ms. Rossi refused to testify."

"Did Ms. Rossi assert her Fifth Amendment rights?"

"No, but if she had, we would have granted her immunity."

"Explain to the jury what immunity is."

"With immunity, we would not use any of her testimony in a case against her."

"What happened after Ms. Rossi refused to testify?"

"Judge Parsons found her in contempt and sent her to the federal women's prison in Fort Worth."

"What happened to your investigation of Austin Harrington and Randall Burke?"

"It's stalled because of Ms. Rossi's refusal to testify."

"Did you ever tell Ms. Rossi or her lawyer what you wanted Ms. Rossi to say to the grand jury?"

"No. We wanted her to tell us what happened. We wanted her to testify truthfully. She had the opportunity to clear her client and Governor Harrington."

"Thank you, Special Agent. I have nothing further, Your Honor."

Judge Rose looked at her watch. "Ladies and gentlemen, this is a good time for us to break for lunch. When we return at 2:00 p.m., Ms. Sanchez will cross-examine Special Agent Forkum."

As we walked out of the courtroom, Gina Rossi leaned closed and murmured at my shoulder. "You need to bury this guy this afternoon."

CHAPTER 36

Gabriela Sanchez

"**M**s. Sanchez, you may question Agent Forkum now," Judge Rose said looking down at me.

"Thank you, Your Honor. Mr. Forkum, isn't it true that you made a contribution to the Democratic party during the Presidential Campaign in 2016?"

As I expected, Jason Daniels lept to his feet. "Your Honor, I object. The agent's political contributions are irrelevant."

"Your Honor, I am entitled to show that Mr. Forkum is prejudiced against the President and any potential Supreme Court nominee he has identified."

"Ms. Sanchez. Just because a government investigator has made a political contribution to a candidate does not make the investigator biased in his investigation."

"Your Honor, text messages and emails between an FBI official and his Justice Department mistress show they were out to destroy the President. I should be entitled to show the jury that Mr. Forkum is part of the group in the Justice Department hell-bent on destroying the President."

"Ms. Sanchez, stop and stop now. I have ruled that you are not entitled to pursue this line of questioning. Stop now."

I shook my head and looked at the jury. I was convinced several jurors understood my point. I decided to continue with the political components of the investigation.

"Mr. Forkum, isn't it true that Senator Schmidt received the anonymous tip from a constituent on the same day as the Senate vote confirming the last Supreme Court nominee?"

"I'm not sure of the exact date."

"Isn't it true that the Special Counsel's office received the anonymous tip on the same day that the new Supreme Court Justice was sworn in?"

"I'm not sure of the date, I wasn't the first person in our office to review the letter."

"Did anyone in your office, to your knowledge, question whether the anonymous tip was politically motivated, like the dossier that was used to get a FISA warrant and investigate the President's campaign?"

"Your Honor, you've instructed Ms. Sanchez to stop this line of questioning."

"Ms. Sanchez, I've warned you once. This is the second warning. You don't want me to warn you again."

"I will re-word my question. Mr. Forkum, did anyone from your office question whether the anonymous tip was politically motivated?"

"Not to my knowledge. There were questions raised about the Cross-Town Tollway contract before we received the anonymous tip."

"Did your office receive any other anonymous accusations against other judges on the President's list of potential Supreme Court nominees?"

"I'm not sure."

"Come on, Mr. Forkum, even the *Washington Post* has acknowledged your office received accusations against other potential Supreme Court nominees."

Jason Daniels stood. "Your Honor, I didn't hear a question."

Before Judge Rose could speak, I said, "Let me rephrase. "Mr. Forkum, isn't it true as reported in the *Washington Post*, that your office received several anonymous tips about wrongdoing by judges on the President's Supreme Court nominees list?"

"I don't know if it was several."

I looked over at the jury, and I think several jurors got the point.

"Mr. Forkum, the Cross-Town Tollway project was a P3 project, is that correct?"

Forkum looked a little confused. "Yes, I understand that it was."

"Mr. Forkum, can you explain to the jury what P3 means?"

Forkum looked over at Jason Daniels. To make the point to the jury, I too looked back at Daniels, He sat there stone-faced.

"Mr. Forkum, it looks like Mr. Daniels is not going to be able to help you. Can you answer…"

As I expected, Daniels rose to his feet. "Your Honor," he said, "I object to Ms. Sanchez's characterization."

To my surprise, Judge Rose responded, "Mr. Daniels, are you telling us that Agent Forkum did not look at you for help with his answer?"

Several jurors laughed as Jason Daniels sat down.

"You may continue, Ms. Sanchez."

"Mr. Forkum, help the jury understand what a P3 project is."

"It's a toll road where the public will be paying for the construction with tolls."

"Mr. Forkum, P3 stands for Public-Private partnership. In this case, the Texas Department of Transportation is the public partner, correct?"

"Yes."

"And Burke Construction was the private partner, correct?"

"Yes."

"What was Burke Construction responsible for providing?"

"Construction of the project."

"Anything else?"

"Collection of tolls for 70 years."

"Anything else?"

Forkum looked confused. Before he could answer, I went on. "Isn't it true that Burke construction was responsible for financing the $2 billion contract?"

"Oh, yes. Burke Construction was responsible for financing the project."

"To submit a proposal, a contractor had to provide financing, correct?"

"Yes."

"When you interviewed other contractors in Texas, did you ask any of them if they had been able to provide financing for the Cross-Town Tollway project?"

Forkum looked down, then he raised his head. "I didn't ask."

"So instead of what you told the jury when Mr. Daniels questioned you, it is normal in Texas that the contractor provides financing for P3 projects, correct?"

"Yes."

I went back to counsel's desk and picked up a legal pad.

"Mr. Forkum, when you served Ms. Rossi with the subpoena on December 21, you spoke with her, correct?"

"I'm not sure of the date, but I served the subpoena and spoke with Ms. Rossi in December."

I looked at my legal pad. "Mr. Forkum, isn't it true that you told Ms. Rossi, 'You know what the investigation is about, and you know what we want from you?'"

"Yes, I said that. I wanted Ms. Rossi to know that we thought she could clear her client and Governor Harrington."

"But you didn't say that to her, did you?"

His face was red, and he shifted in the witness chair. "No. I expected her to understand."

I hoped jurors would find his explanation not believable. I looked at them and thought at least four of the jurors looked like they weren't buying his explanation.

"Mr. Forkum, in a nutshell, this investigation all started because the FBI received an anonymous tip, right?"

"Yes."

"And the FBI never determined who sent the anonymous tip?"

"That's correct."

"For all you know, it could have easily come from a political enemy of the President's or of Governor Harrington?"

"I don't know."

"But you commenced an investigation, a witch hunt, without knowing whether it was a politically motivated tip?"

Jason Daniels stood. "Your Honor, this is no witch hunt investigation. I object to that characterization."

"Sustained. Ms. Sanchez, that's three strikes, and you're out. I will deal with you after the trial."

"Your Honor, I'm trying to represent Ms. Rossi to the best of my ability. You are making it more difficult."

"Ms. Sanchez."

I looked at the jury and decided the damage I hoped to create had been accomplished. I decided to just move on.

Mr. Forkum, were you part of the morning raid of Ms. Rossi's home?"

"I wasn't there if that's what you mean."

"Then you were in charge of it?"

"Yes."

"Do you know Assistant U. S. Attorney, Brian Renfro?"

"Sure."

"Were you aware that Brian Renfro had assured me that if a grand jury indicted Gina Rossi I would be able to bring her in to surrender voluntarily?"

"I may have been told that."

"In spite of the promise Brian Renfro made to me, you directed that the FBI make a morning raid on Ms. Rossi's home."

"Yes. This investigation was being conducted out of the Special Counsel's office in Washington, D.C., not the Dallas U. S. Attorney's office."

"How did you feel, knowing that your fellow agents were about to terrorize a young boy?"

"Your Honor, I object to the characterization," Daniels said while getting out of his seat.

Before Judge Rose could rule, I responded, "Your Honor, how would Mr. Daniels characterize the feelings of a young boy when a dozen FBI agents with protective vests and drawn automatic weapons marched through his house and hauled his mother away in handcuffs?"

"The objection is sustained. Move on, Ms. Sanchez.

"Your Honor, that's all I have."

"Any redirect, Mr. Daniels?"

"No, Your Honor."

CHAPTER 37

Gabriela Sanchez

"**M**r. Daniels, you can call your next witness."

"We call Susan Gross to testify."

I knew Daniels planned to call grand jurors, and Susan Gross was the first of those witnesses. I had done a Google search of Susan Gross and discovered she was in her 50s, lived in Richardson, Texas, and taught middle-school history. Her husband, Stanley, was a computer engineer with a technology firm there in Richardson.

After Susan Gross was sworn in, Daniels started.

"Ms. Gross, were you a member of the grand jury investigating former Governor Harrington and Randall Burke?"

"Yes Sir, I was."

"Tell the jury how you and the other grand jurors were treated by the government lawyers."

"They showed us consideration and treated us well."

"Did they call witnesses to testify about the case?"

"Yes."

"Was John Randolph one of the witnesses?"

"Yes."

"Tell the jury who John Randolph is."

"He told us he is a lawyer and he is the Texas Department of Transportation lawyer."

"Was he asked about the Cross-Town Tollway project?"

"Yes."

I stood. "Your Honor, I object. Mr. Daniels should call John Randolph as a witness if he wants the jurors to hear his testimony."

Daniels responded, "Your Honor, we have called Ms. Gross to discuss what took place during the Grand Jury sessions, how the grand jurors were treated and why the grand jurors wanted to hear from Gina Rossi."

"I'm going to allow this line of testimony. You may proceed, Mr. Daniels."

"What did John Randolph tell the grand jury about the project?"

"He told us it was the centerpiece of Governor Harrington's 'Texas Roads to Destiny' campaign. He said it was a project that had been a top priority for many years, and that previously three contractors had submitted proposals to build the tollway."

"What did he tell the Grand Jury happened next?"

"He told us there was not enough money to build the project at that time and the project was pretty much forgotten until Governor Harrington was elected."

"What did John Randolph tell you happened next?"

"He told us he was hired by Governor Harrington, who directed him to prepare a request for proposals to build the Cross-Town Tollway. He testified he prepared the request for proposals and the Texas Department of Transportation sent them to the three contractors who had previously submitted proposals."

"What did John Randolph tell the grand jury who submitted proposals?"

"Mr. Randolph told us Burke Construction Company submitted the only proposal and that he suggested to Governor Harrington that the state not accept the proposal and instead ask again for proposals."

"Did Mr. Randolph tell you how Governor Harrington responded?"

"Yes, he said Governor Harrington told him that he had talked to the other two contractors and they told him they did not intend to submit proposals for the project."

"Did representatives of the other two contractors testify?"

"Yes."

"Did they tell the grand jury why they did not submit a proposal?"

"Each contractor representative testified they didn't believe they could compete with Burke Construction."

"What were you hoping to learn from Gina Rossi?"

"We were informed that Gina Rossi had represented Randall Burke and his wife in the Hill Country Estates partnership with Austin Harrington and his wife. We were told that before Harrington ran for governor, Mr. Burke and his wife purchased the Harrington's interest. We wanted to learn if Governor Harrington directed the Texas Department of Transportation to award the Cross-Town Tollway Project to Burke Construction with no competition in return for including the governor and his wife in the Hill Country Estates partnership."

"And why did you want to hear from Gina Rossi?"

"She was Burke's lawyer in both the Hill Country Estates partnership and the Cross-Town Tollway Contract and we believed she could enlighten us on whether there was a connection."

That sounded like a carefully rehearsed question and answer.

"Did any of the prosecutors tell your Grand Jury how to vote?"

"No, to the contrary, they told us the final decision was up to us and they were providing the information, so we could make an informed judgment."

"Thank you, Ms. Gross. That's all I have, Your Honor."

"Let's take a 15 minutes recess. When we return, Ms. Sanchez may cross-examine the witness."

When we were alone, Gina asked me my strategy for dealing with Susan Gross, since she was obviously a sympathetic witness.

"You're right. She is a sympathetic witness. I won't make her look bad in front of the jury."

Twenty minutes later, I walked up to the lectern.

"Thank you for being here, Ms. Gross, and thank you for your service as a grand juror. I'm sure you have been inconvenienced."

Susan Gross smiled, nodded and thanked me.

"Ms. Gross, did the Office of Special Counsel inform grand jurors that Mr. Burke and Mr. Harrington had been best friends since childhood?"

"No, not that I recall."

"Did the Office of Special Counsel inform grand jurors that for many years, long before Austin Harrington was elected governor, he and Randall Burke attended University of Texas and Dallas Cowboys games together and sat in Randall Burke's suite?"

"No."

"Did the Office of Special Counsel inform grand jurors that the Burkes and Harringtons entered into the Hill Country Estates partnership years before Austin Harrington ran for governor?"

"We were told it was before he became governor because the Burkes purchased the Harringtons' interest in the partnership right before Austin Harrington announced he was running for governor."

Then I asked, "Did the Office of Special Counsel inform grand jurors that Randall Burke had asserted that his conversations with Gina Rossi were protected by the lawyer-client privilege?"

Susan Gross replied, "No, but we were told that a judge had ordered Ms. Rossi to testify."

"Did the Office of Special Counsel inform you that leaders in the FBI and the Justice Department talked about creating an 'insurance policy' just in case…"

"Object, Your Honor!" Jason Daniels shouted.

I didn't stop. "…in case the President was elected in 2016."

"Ms. Sanchez, I have warned you about asking that kind of question. Stop doing it. Objection sustained."

"Ms. Gross, did you meet with anyone from the Office of Special Counsel before you testified here?"

She looked at Jason Daniels and stammered. "No."

"Ms. Gross, no one from the government sat down with you before you testified and went over what they wanted you to say?"

She looked again at Jason Daniels, who nodded. "They didn't tell me what they wanted me to say. They asked me questions, and I responded."

"Did they offer any suggestions on changing the wording of your answers?"

"Yes, but I can't remember the specifics."

"Did anyone from the government tell you the reasons they wanted Ms. Rossi to testify?"

"Yes."

"So, when you testified about the reasons you wanted Ms. Rossi to testify, you were simply recited what they had told you to say, right?"

"No, I had my own reasons also."

"I have nothing further, Your Honor."

"Mr. Daniels, any redirect?"

"Just a couple of questions, Your Honor. Ms. Gross, did we tell you to tell the truth when you testified?"

"Yes."

"And did you tell the jury the truth, as we had instructed?"

"Yes."

"Your Honor, that's all I have for this witness."

"Ok, Mr. Daniels, call your next witness."

CHAPTER 38

Gina Rossi

As I expected, Daniels called Anna Lang as his next witness. After asking her name and her occupation Daniels got to the meat of the matter.

"Miss Lang, do you work for any particular lawyer at Roberson Grant?"

"Yes, I work for Gina Rossi."

"Is she in the courtroom?"

"Yes," Lang replied pointing to me."

"How long have you worked for Ms. Rossi?" Daniels asked.

"Since I joined the law firm as a first-year associate six years ago."

"Did you help Mrs. Rossi on the Hill Country Estates Partnership?'

"Yes. I drafted the partnership documents and Gina reviewed and edited them."

"Did she give you any specific instructions?"

"She said it was important that Mr. and Mrs. Harrington contribute their share at the beginning and continue to pay their share during the duration of the partnership."

"Was there anything unusual about the partnership?"

"The Burkes owned the land. They didn't need the Harringtons to be their partners. It seemed to me the Burkes were making a gift to the Harringtons."

Gabriela rose. "Your Honor, I object. Ms. Lang's opinion is irrelevant."

"I agree. The jury will disregard Ms. Lang's opinion."

Her opinion was not only irrelevant, but also naïve. But the jury was not likely to disregard what she said.

"Did you help Ms. Rossi when the partnership dissolved?"

"Yes, I drafted the dissolution papers for her."

"Was any evaluation made of the value of the Harringtons' share?"

"No. Ms. Rossi told Mr. Burke an evaluation should be done, but he ignored her advice."

"Were you privy to any conversations between the two of them?"

"No. I was copied on an email Ms. Rossi sent advising Mr. Burke to get an evaluation but I was not privy to any private conversations."

"Did you help Ms. Rossi on the Cross-Town Tollway contract?"

"Yes. I helped draft the proposal."

"Did you see any connection between the buyout of the Hill Country Estates partnership and the Cross-Town Tollway contract."

"Your Honor, I object," Gina said while leaping to her feet.

"Mr. Daniels, perhaps you can re-phrase your question."

"Yes, Your Honor," Daniels replied as if laying the foundation for what he really wanted to ask.

"Ms. Lang. Did you voice any concern to Ms. Rossi about a connection between the Hill Country Estates partnership buyout and the Cross-Town Tollway contract?"

"Yes, Lang answered. "I asked Ms. Rossi if someone might think Governor Harrington awarded the Cross-Town Tollway contract in return for receiving an inflated price for the Harringtons' share of the Hill Country Estates partnership."

I wrote "LIE" and pushed it in front of Gabriela.

"What did Ms. Rossi say?"

"She said my job was to draft documents not to question a connection between the two contracts. Essentially she told me to mind my own business and do only the work she asked me to do."

"Did you receive a subpoena to testify before the grand jury investigating Randall Burke and Austin Harrington?"

"I received a subpoena the same day Ms. Rossi received a subpoena."

"And did you agree to testify?"

"Yes. The firm hired a lawyer for me and with his advice I agreed to testify."

"Did Ms. Rossi do anything to discourage you from testifying?"

"We never talked about it, but she left a Code of Ethics book on my desk with a Post-It on the page discussing lawyer-client privilege."

"Did she tell you not to testify?"

"No, but she started ignoring me and giving what should have been my work to other lawyers."

"Did you testify on the second of January?"

"I did."

"Have you talked to Ms. Rossi any time since that day?"

"No."

"I have no further questions," Daniels said.

"Ms. Sanchez, you may cross-examine."

"Your Honor, give me a moment to confer with my client."

Gabriela wrote, "she really hasn't hurt us. I will ask a few questions."

I shook my head in agreement.

"Ms. Lang, you mentioned that Ms. Rossi left the Code of Ethics on your desk, are you sure she was the one who left it."

"I believe it was."

"But, you don't know for sure. You didn't see her leave it, right?"

"Yes,"

"The section on lawyer-client privilege didn't really even apply to you, did it?"

Anna Lang sat up in the witness chair.

"Sure, it applied," she responded.

"Ms. Lang, you never had a privileged communication with Mr. Burke, isn't that true?"

She stammered then answered, "I guess that is true."

"You've never even had any conversation with Mr. Burke?"

"That's true," Lang answered.

"So, you had no reason not to testify before the grand jury, did you?"

"That's correct."

"So, Ms, Rossi did nothing to discourage you from testifying before the grand jury, did she?"

"She quit assigning any work to me."

"Don't you suppose, Ms. Lang, that the firm asked Ms. Rossi to minimize any contact with you, so there would be no appearance that the firm or Ms. Rossi was trying to keep you from testifying?"

"I suppose that could be true."

"Thank you. Your Honor, I have no further questions."

"Let's take a break."

CHAPTER 39

Gabriela Sanchez

I knew Judge Rose would never direct a verdict of not guilty, but after the jury was excused, I made the motion anyway. As expected, she denied my motion and told me to call my first witness when we returned from the lunch break.

Gina and I had spent hours and days preparing. I had explained at length that her credibility was the key to a favorable verdict and that meant the jury had to believe her reasons for not wanting to testify. I told her to speak slowly, look at the jury, and whatever Jason Daniels asked, she could *not* lose her temper, even if her secret life came up in cross-examination. But I knew she had still not told me everything I needed to know.

One hour later we were back in the courtroom.

"Ms. Sanchez, you may call your first witness."

"The defense calls Gina Rossi."

I looked over at Jason Daniels. He was scrambling to find his notes. I took that to mean he had not expected Gina to testify.

After she was sworn in, I began. "State your full name for the jury."

As we had prepared, Gina looked over at the jury and responded, "My name is Gina Sophia Rossi."

Gina told me her father named her after the two most famous Italian actresses, knowing that Grandma Mary would be forever upset by the Italian names.

We spent the next hour going over what she had shared with me about her early career with the Roberson Grant law firm. Gina then told a shortened and less critical version of how Burke Construction Company had become a client, and the work she had done for the company and Randall and Jenna Burke.

We then turned to the partnership.

"Were you the lawyer who handled the Hill Country Estates partnership?"

"Yes, I was."

"Please tell the jury about the partnership."

"Randall and Jenna Burke owned more than 5,000 acres in the Texas Hill Country. Mr. Burke told me he wanted to be in a partnership with his boyhood friend, Austin Harrington and his wife, Laura Ray. In 2008, Mr. Burke asked me to draft partnership documents, and the two couples were moving forward, and when they were ready to sign the papers, the real estate meltdown of 2008 occurred."

"What happened then?"

"Randall Burke was always loyal to his friends and looking out for their interest, and Austin Harrington was his best friend. Randall Burke did not want his friend to lose money, so he put the partnership on hold. Mr. Burke began developing the property in 2010. By 2012, the real estate market had come back, and Mr. Burke asked me to redraft the partnership documents. I did, and the two families entered into the Hill Country Estates partnership."

"To the best of your knowledge, did Austin and Laura Ray Harrington contribute their share to purchase their interest in the partnership?"

"Yes, I handled the closing and the Harringtons wrote a check for half of the value of the land."

"Did they continue to write checks as the property was developed?"

"I was not part of those dealings, but I had advised Mr. Burke to make sure the Harringtons paid their share."

"What other work were you asked to do on the Hill Country Estates partnership?"

"In 2014, Randall Burke asked for my legal advice and asked me to draft the buyout papers."

"Did Mr. Burke tell you why he wanted to purchase the Harrington's share of the partnership?"

"He did. For over a year, Laura Ray Harrington had been asking for distributions while Mr. Burke wanted to plow the money back into the development. That created a lot of friction. He wanted to buy the Harringtons' interest to eliminate the problem."

"Did he know that Austin Harrington planned to run for governor?"

"No, but as I worked on the buyout, Austin Harrington told Mr. Burke he planned to run for governor."

"What if any advice did you give Mr. Burke when you learned his friend and partner planned to run for governor?"

"I told him it was important to pay the Harringtons the fair market value for their share of the partnership, so no one would question the amount paid if Austin Harrington was elected governor. I suggested he retain an expert appraiser to determine the value."

"What was Mr. Burke's response?"

"He said he could determine the fair market value and he was willing to pay the Harringtons more to get rid of Laura Ray Harrington as a partner."

"How much did the Burke pays the Harringtons for their share?"

"It was $7.5 million."

I looked at the jury, and several of the jurors perked up when they heard that amount. I decided to turn to the "Texas Roads to Destiny" program.

"After Austin Harrington was elected governor, did you have conversations with him about transportation in Texas?"

"Yes. I knew Governor Harrington wanted to ultimately launch a campaign for President. And, corporations were moving from California, New York, and other high-tax states to Texas, so our freeways and tollways were almost outdated as soon as they were completed or widened. I told Austin Harrington he could make the biggest difference for Texas if he created an expansive highway construction program that he might call 'Texas Roads to Destiny.'"

"What was his response?"

"He was all for it."

"Did you see any problem, given that more highway construction would benefit your client, Burke Construction?"

"No, anyone who lived in Dallas, Houston, Austin, or San Antonio knows we desperately needed new roads and expansion of existing roads."

I looked over at the jury, and several of their heads were nodding up and down.

"What happened after Governor Harrington launched the 'Texas Roads to Destiny' program?"

"I discovered that years ago the Texas Department of Transportation, we call it TxDOT, had asked for proposals to build what was called the Cross-Town Expressway."

"Did you find out why it was not built?"

"TxDOT could not finance the project, so it was abandoned at the time."

"What happened?"

"When Governor Harrington was elected, TxDOT told contractors that it would be seeking proposals for the Cross-Town project as a tollway, meaning the contractors would have to provide the financing for the project."

"What happened then?"

"I started looking for a finance partner for Burke Construction and found an Australian Finance company called Merit that was seeking to finance toll roads in the United States, so Burke Construction Company was ready to submit a proposal as soon as TxDOT sought proposals."

"Did the contractors who had previously submitted proposals also submit proposals?"

"No, Governor Harrington personally asked the two contractors and other large contractors to submit proposals, but they didn't."

"To your knowledge, did Randall Burke or Burke Construction Company offer anything to Governor Harrington to persuade him to encourage TxDOT to award the contract to Burke Construction Company?"

"No."

"Did you offer anything on behalf of Burke Construction Company to persuade Governor Harrington to encourage the TxDOT to award the contract to Burke Construction Company?"

"No. Everyone in Texas knew the Cross-Town Tollway was much needed in Dallas and when Burke Construction found a way to finance the project, TxDOT wanted to award the contract."

Jason Daniels stood. "Your Honor, Ms. Rossi has no idea whether the TxDOT wanted to award the contract."

Before Judge Rose could rule, Gina blurted, "They said so in the newspaper."

"Ms. Rossi, if Mr. Daniels objects, I want you to give me time to make a ruling, okay?"

I looked over and saw a few jurors grinning.

"Yes, Your Honor. I will," Gina said.

"Mr. Daniels, I'll let the answer stand. You can clarify if you wish on cross-examination."

I continued.

"Gina, shortly before Christmas last year, were you served with a subpoena to testify before a grand jury investigating Governor Harrington and Randall Burke?'

"Yes, it was December 19, when I was served with the subpoena."

"What happened then?"

"Well, first off, my law firm hired you to help me deal with this problem."

"Then what happened?"

"My client, Randall Burke, filed a motion saying that our communications were protected by the lawyer-client privilege. I agreed with him."

"Then what happened?"

"Mr. Daniels," she said pointing at him, "refused to recognize the lawyer-client communications privilege and asked the judge to rule that I must break the privilege, which is one of the most sacred and important of any of our ethics requirements."

"What happened?"

"Mr. Daniels wrongly persuaded a judge to interrogate me, and after the judge did, he ordered me to testify before the grand jury."

Jason Daniels rose. "I object, Your Honor."

"Ms. Rossi, please keep your opinions to yourself and just tell the jury what happened."

"What happened then?"

"I asked Mr. Burke if he would waive the privilege and let me testify since he had done nothing wrong."

As expected, Jason Daniels leapt to his feet. "Your Honor, Ms. Rossi can't testify that Mr. Burke did nothing wrong."

Judge Rose looked at Gina. "Ms. Rossi, you know you can't testify that Mr. Burke did nothing wrong. Jurors, disregard what Ms. Rossi said. Continue, Ms. Sanchez."

"Okay, Your Honor. What happened after the judge ordered you to testify?"

Gina looked at the jury. "We asked Judge Parsons to stay his order and allow us to appeal to the higher court, but he refused and put me in the women's prison in Fort Worth."

Two of the jurors gasped. Probably the only two who hadn't followed this in the news.

"Please explain to the jury what you mean by 'stay his order.'"

"Judge Parsons had ordered I be held in civil contempt. That was meant to punish me. He could have let me stay free and be home with my son and husband while our appeal was heard and decided. Instead, he ordered that I go to prison."

"Why didn't you testify after Judge Parsons ordered you to testify?"

"Because I believed – and I - still believe that he was wrong and the only way we could get a ruling was to appeal while I sat in the Women's prison in Fort Worth."

"How did you happen to leave prison?"

"The grand jury's term of service expired. At that point, Daniels and his team had to release me."

"What happened after you were released?"

"Mr. Daniels hoodwinked a new grand jury into indicting me."

Jason Daniels shot to his feet and loudly said, "Your Honor! How many times do you need to direct the witness not to offer her derogatory opinions?"

Before I could continue, Gina turned to Judge Rose. "Your Honor, the jurors need to know that the Grand Jury, in this case, did exactly what Mr. Daniels wanted them to do. You and I both know that, but the jury needs to know it."

"Ms. Rossi, you are trying my patience. No more opinions or disparaging remarks. Do you understand?'

"I do, Your Honor, but my integrity is being questioned. My future and the future of my family are at stake. It's hard not to offer my opinions."

"Then I suggest you think before you speak. You may continue asking questions, Ms. Sanchez, but I am telling you to control your client."

"Yes, Your Honor. "Ms. Rossi, did anything happen after you were indicted and before the trial?"

"Yes, indeed."

"What happened?'

"The morning after I was released from prison I went for a run. At about 7:00 a.m.I sat down to eat breakfast with my husband and my son. I heard a loud knock on my door. When I got closer, I heard someone announce it was the FBI and then he yelled at me to open my door immediately."

"Your Honor, I object, interjected Daniels. "The manner of Ms. Rossi's arrest has nothing to do with whether she obstructed justice and committed criminal contempt."

"Ms. Sanchez, do you have a response?"

"Yes, Your Honor. The FBI's terrorizing of Gina Rossi, her husband, and even her son, is indeed relevant in considering why she didn't testify in the first place."

"Ms. Sanchez, that seems to be a bit of a stretch, but I'm going to allow it."

Daniels was still unhappy. "Your Honor, this is extremely prejudicial."

"Mr. Daniels, I'm sure that is exactly what Ms. Sanchez has in mind. The FBI treated Ms. Rossi like she was a dangerous criminal, not like she was nothing more than a grand jury witness. I'm going to allow the questions."

"What happened next?'

"Before I could tell my husband to take my son into his bedroom, a dozen or so FBI agents in vests with drawn automatic weapons pushed past me, announcing that I was under arrest and that they had a search warrant for our electronic devices. As they handcuffed on me, a cluster of video cameras with spotlights recorded my arrest."

"Do you or your husband own any weapons?"

"No."

"Were you planning to flee the country?"

Gina smiled. "No."

"Were you planning to destroy evidence?'

"There was no damaging evidence to destroy, and even if there were, as a lawyer and officer of the court, I would never destroy evidence."

"What happened while they were in the house?"

"I couldn't see everything, but while I was in handcuffs, the FBI agents made a mess of our house looking for our electronic computers and devices. They carried out my laptop, Tony's laptop, our iPads, our iPhones and even my son's iPad. My son was terrified. He thought they were going to kill me."

As expected, Daniels was on his feet again. Your Honor, Ms. Rossi can't testify about what her son was thinking."

"Mr. Daniels, she can testify what he told her."

"Thank you, Your Honor. Later that day when I returned home, my son was crying and told me he thought the bad men were going to kill me."

"Did you know they were coming?"

"No. The lead FBI agent showed me an arrest warrant and a search warrant as the rest of the agents were going through our house. They didn't need to draw their guns and terrify my son. If they had simply asked, even though we thought they had no right to our computers, tablets, and phones, we would have voluntarily given them to the agents."

"Ms. Rossi, does your home have an outside video security system?"

"Yes."

"Did your home security video record the FBI raid?"

"Yes."

I could see Jason Daniels out of the corner of my eye. His hands were on the table ready to push him out of his seat to object.

"Your Honor, I request permission to play the video for the jury."

Daniels leapt to his feet. "I object, Your Honor. The FBI's arrest of Ms. Rossi is irrelevant to whether she is guilty of obstruction of justice and criminal contempt."

"Your Honor, it's extremely relevant. Ms. Rossi has testified the FBI tried to coerce her to testify only to support their attempted wrongful prosecution of Governor Harrington and Randall Burke. The video shows the tactics used by the government and supports why Ms. Rossi refused to testify."

"Mr. Daniels, I'm going to allow the jury to see the video."

Jason Daniels shook his head, sat back down, and put his face in his hands.

We started the video. It showed a TV van arriving in front of the Rossi home and setting up cameras. A couple of minutes later several SUVs pulled up in front of the Rossi home and 10 men with drawn automatic assault weapons piled out and headed toward the door. One of the men has an automatic assault weapon in one hand and a battering ram in the other. As the men reached the door, they held their weapons in the shooting position. The man in front pounded on the Rossi's front door and then returned his hand to the trigger of his weapon. Thirty seconds later, Gina Rossi opened the front door. The lead FBI agent turned her around, and another agent placed her in handcuffs. Then they all entered the Rossi home with their automatic weapons still drawn.

"Ms. Rossi, does the video we just played accurately reflect what happened that morning?"

"Yes, but we don't have a video showing the terror in my son's eyes when he saw 10 men with automatic assault weapons drawn and one man pushing me in handcuffs back into the house."

"Do you know how the news media became aware of the raid before you or I knew about it?"

"No, I only know the video they shot was soon on the local and national news, and further terrorized my son when he went to school."

I looked at the jurors. Several of them were shifting in their seats. A couple of jurors' arms were folded over their chests. Two jurors were shaking their heads in disapproval. Every juror was frowning. I was satisfied we had accomplished our mission on the raid.

"Did you try to impede the government's investigation of your client, Randall Burke?"

"No, I tried to uphold the most important and oldest confidential privilege in law. It's as sacred as the privileged communications with a priest."

I looked over at each Catholic on the jury and they each nodded, a good sign.

"Did you intend to be in contempt of the court?"

"No, as I said, the only way I could get the higher court to rule in Mr. Burke's favor was not to testify and appeal Judge Parsons' ruling. I had no choice."

"And, why are you testifying now, in this trial?"

"Because Mr. Burke gave me permission so I could defend myself." She looked over at the jury again.

I tried not to smile. "Your Honor, I have no further questions."

"Mr. Daniels, let's take a 15-minute break, then you may cross-examine."

As we walked out of the courtroom, I was worried sick about what might come up during cross-examination and what I would do if Gina Rossi lied while testifying.

CHAPTER 40

⤬

Gina Rossi

G abriela had told me I couldn't lie on the stand and if I did, she was ethically bound to notify Judge Rose. She had offered to find another lawyer for me, but I didn't plan to lie, even if it meant disclosing my deepest secrets in front of Tony, who was sitting in the front row of the spectator area.

Gabriela also told me to pay close attention to each question Daniels asked and answer only the question asked. She reminded me of the famous line, "it depends on what the definition of 'is' is."

We practiced my answers to questions she expected Daniels to ask, and as I walked to the witness chair, I felt more confident than I had when I testified before Judge Parsons.

I sat down and Judge Rose said, "You may cross-examine the witness, Mr. Daniels."

"Thank you, Your Honor. Ms. Rossi, when Judge Parsons ordered you to testify before the grand jury, you knew you were in criminal contempt of court, right?"

"No, Mr. Daniels, I believed Judge Parsons' ruling was wrong and I had appealed his ruling to the Fifth Circuit Court of Appeals, fully expecting the Court to overturn his ruling. Mr. Daniels, since you are from Washington, D. C. I'm not sure you know that the attorney-client privilege is sacred in Texas and the United States, and you were demanding that I testify about conversations that my client, Mr. Burke, expected to remain confidential."

As Gabriela had suggested, I had annoyed Jason Daniels in less than one minute.

"Your Honor, would you instruct the witness to simply answer the question and not give a speech to the jury?"

"Mr. Daniels, given the nature of the charges against Ms. Rossi, I believe she should have the opportunity to explain. Maybe you should make your questions more precise."

I looked at Gabriela, who was smiling. *Score one for the good guys.*

Jason Daniels frowned and continued.

"Let's start from the beginning, Ms. Rossi. When did you first meet Governor Harrington?"

"I met Governor Harrington at his inaugural, the day he became Governor."

Daniels looked puzzled by my answer.

"Isn't it true that you had met Governor Harrington when you represented Mr. and Ms. Burke in the Hill Country Estates partnership?"

"Yes, but he was not governor then. You asked when I first met Governor Harrington."

"Don't play games with me, Ms. Rossi."

Gabriela jumped to her feet. "Your Honor, Mr. Daniels knows better than to make such an accusation against Ms. Rossi. She answered the question he asked her. It was no game."

"Mr. Daniels, maybe you should rephrase your question."

"Ms. Rossi, when did you first meet Austin Harrington?"

Gabriela and I had anticipated this question and prepared my answer.

"Mr. Daniels, my client Randall Burke, introduced me to Austin Harrington in the Burke Construction Company suite at a Cowboys game. I believe it was in the fall of 2007, but I am not sure."

Gabriela and I had pondered how that was an honest answer. In Las Vegas, I had met a man named Travis Harris, not Austin Harrington.

"You were the Burkes' lawyer when they entered into the Hill Country Estates partnership with the Harringtons, right?"

My first thought when Daniels asked this question was that he was not aware of Travis Harris, otherwise he would have pursued my trysts with Harris at this point. I hoped I was right.

"Yes."

"And the Burkes owned the land before they invited the Harringtons to become partners, isn't that true?"

"Yes. And, Randall Burke and Austin Harrington were lifelong friends before they became partners."

"Your Honor, please instruct the defendant to just answer the question."

"Ms. Rossi, Mr. Daniels is right, and I don't like what you are trying to do in my courtroom." She looked over at the jury. "Ladies and gentlemen, please disregard what Ms. Rossi said about Randall Burke and Austin Harrington. You may continue, Mr. Daniels."

"Did Mr. Burke tell you why he invited the Harringtons to become partners?"

"Yes, he reminded me that they had been friends going back to their childhood. Then Mr. Burke said that Mr. Harrington was making a lot of money as a lawyer and had asked him if he and his wife could become partners in the real estate development."

"Isn't it true that at the time, Mr. Burke knew that Austin Harrington intended to run for Governor of Texas?"

"Mr. Daniels, the opposite is true. Mrs. Harrington actually told the Burkes that she and her husband were happy, and he never wanted to serve the public again."

"You are not positive that Austin and Laura Ray Harrington contributed their share to the partnership, isn't that true?"

"Austin Harrington handed me a check. It was drawn on a joint checking account with his and Ms. Harrington's names on the check, and his signature on the check. That is what I know."

"For all you know, the Burkes could have given the money to the Harringtons, isn't that true?"

"That is not true. I have never known Randall Burke to give a business partner money to simply be returned to buy his share of a partnership with Mr. Burke."

Jason Daniels looked annoyed again.

"The Burkes purchased the Harringtons' share of the partnership when Austin Harrington decided to run for governor, isn't that true?"

"It was about that time, but Mr. Burke had told me months before that he wanted to purchase the Harringtons' interest because Mrs. Harrington wanted distributions of money rather than reinvesting it to develop more of the property."

"And you advised Randall Burke to hire an expert appraiser to set a value on the property so no one could later claim he gave the Harringtons more for their interest to get favors if Austin Harrington became Governor, isn't that true?"

"Yes, and Mr. Burke told me he was an expert at the determining the value and he was willing to pay more to get Mrs. Harrington out of the partnership."

"And, he did pay the Harringtons more than their share was worth isn't that true?"

I had been waiting and planning to answer one of his questions with the famous 'it depends the definition' response. I grinned to myself and then answered slowly.

"Mr. Daniels, I guess that depends on what your definition of the word 'worth' is. The Harringtons owned 50 percent of the partnership, and their ability to stop the Burkes from expanding the development made their share worth more than it would have been otherwise."

I looked over at the jury and some nodded, which I took to mean they understood my point.

"Mr. Burke paid more than fair market value for the Harringtons' share and he knew Austin Harrington planned to run for governor of Texas, isn't that true?"

"Mr. Daniels, you imply in your question that the two things are connected. Mr. Burke was willing to pay more than fair market value for the Harringtons' interest in the partnership to rid himself of Mrs. Harrington's demands for money. It had nothing to do with Austin Harrington running for governor."

"Ms. Rossi, isn't it true that you never personally negotiated a contract with a Texas governor before the Cross-Town Tollway contract?"

"Yes, that is true."

"Isn't it true you never negotiated a Burke Construction contract with the governor of any other state?"

"Yes, that is also true."

"Why was Governor Harrington involved in the negotiation of the Cross-Town Tollway contract negotiations?"

"You would have to ask him that question. I know he viewed the Cross-Town Tollway contract as the linchpin of his 'Texas Roads to Destiny' program."

"Governor Harrington wasn't involved in the negotiation of any other Burke Construction Company contract, right?"

"You asked that question a minute ago, Mr. Daniels, and my answer is the same, that is right."

Daniels frowned - a good sign.

"Isn't it true that Burke Construction Company submitted the only proposal to build the Cross-Town Tollway contract?"

"Yes, Mr. Daniels, that was because Burke Construction Company was the only company to find a partner to finance the project."

"And, your brother Samuel helped you find the Merit Financial for the Cross-Town Tollway project, right?"

"Yes, that's right, Mr. Daniels."

"How did your brother even know about the project?"

"I told him. The project first surfaced several years ago, and it had sat on the shelf because of the economic meltdown."

"Isn't it true the other Texas contractors believed they had no chance to win the contract given Mr. Burke's friendship with Governor Harrington?"

Gabriela stood. "Your Honor, I object. Ms. Rossi has no way of knowing what other Texas contractors believed."

"Ms. Rossi, isn't it true that Mr. Burke directed you in an email to do whatever was necessary to convince the TxDOT to award the Cross-Town Tollway contract to Burke Construction Company?"

"Yes, Mr. Daniels. You have the email and I believe that is what he said in it. He said do whatever was necessary to me on almost every major project on which I offered legal advice."

"Did you do what was necessary to win the contract for Burke Construction Company?"

"I must have, since the TxDOT awarded the contract."

"What did you do?"

"I pointed out that the only way to finance the project was to put tolls on the freeway during construction."

"Your client didn't ask you to negotiate that concession by the state, isn't that true?"

"Burke Construction did not request it, but the Merit Financial threatened to pull the financing."

"How did you know that?"

"My brother Samuel told me."

"How did Samuel know the finance partner had threatened to pull the financing?"

"You would have to ask him."

"Didn't Samuel tell you?"

"He told me the Australians weren't sure the deal would cover all the costs."

"Who came up with the idea to put tolls on the freeway while the tollway was being constructed?"

I sat up as straight as I could, and I looked over at the jury. Then I proudly responded, "I did."

Jason Daniels stared at me, stood still and slowly asked, "Ms. Rossi, isn't it true that you had a secret sexual relationship with Austin Harrington, and that was the real reason you refused to testify?"

I was stunned. *Damn, damn, damn.*

I looked at Gabriela Sanchez for help, but she didn't stand up to object. I still believed I could honestly answer that I did not have a sexual relationship with Austin Harrington, since at the time he called himself, Travis Harris. I was at least arguably sort of telling the truth.

"Mr. Daniels, I never had a sexual relationship secret, or otherwise, with Austin Harrington, and the reason I refused to testify was because my clients, Burke Construction Company and Randall Burke, invoked the lawyer-client privilege. I was following their request that I keep our conversations confidential."

Judge Rose interrupted. "Mr. Daniels, let's take a 15-minute break."

Jason Daniels looked at me. "Judge Rose, I have a video I want to show the witness and play for the jury when we return, I will set it up during the break."

Good God. Does he have video of Jordan Jamison from Las Vegas?

CHAPTER 41

— ✢ —

Gabriela Sanchez

During the next 15 minutes, Gina was in a near panic.

"What video does Daniels have?"

"I don't know."

"You should know. Didn't Daniels have to disclose it to you before the trial?"

"No. Anything he plans to use to discredit your testimony does not have to be disclosed."

"He must think it is a big deal, to have created such drama about it."

"Pay attention to what he asks you and make sure you recognize the video."

Ten minutes later, Judge Rose was on the bench, the jury was seated, and Gina was in the witness chair, and Jason Daniels was poised at the lectern.

"Ms. Rossi, I want you to look at this video taken in the elevator and hallway at the historic Diamond Hotel in Austin."

A video started playing on the big screen in the courtroom. It was of Austin Harrington and Gina.

"Isn't that you on the video with Governor Harrington?"

Gina took a deep breath. The video was shot in Austin, not Las Vegas.

"Yes, that's Governor Harrington and me."

"Ms. Rossi, where is Governor Harrington's hand?"

"It's on my behind."

"And as you are walking down the hall, where is Governor Harrington's hand?"

"It's on my waist."

"And doesn't the video show the two of you entering Governor Harrington's hotel room?"

"Yes."

"So, isn't it true that you had a secret sexual relationship with Governor Harrington and that was the real reason you did not want to testify?"

"Mr. Daniels, that is not true. I did not have sex with Governor Harrington in his hotel room."

"Then, how do you explain his hand being on your behind and later around your waist?"

"Mr. Daniels, if I had a dollar for every man who has touched my behind or put his arm around my waist, I would be a very wealthy woman. But it doesn't mean I let any of those men have sex with me."

"Then why did you go with Governor Harrington to his hotel room in the Diamond Hotel?"

"Because it was extremely noisy in the Diamond Hotel lobby, bar, and restaurant. The Governor thought we could more easily talk about the Cross-Town Tollway contract in his hotel room."

"Isn't it true that you seduced Governor Harrington, and that is why he agreed to Burke Construction receiving tolls on the freeway while the tollway was being built?"

"Mr. Daniels, I play golf. Men, like you negotiate on the golf course, or sometimes in a gentleman's club. I understand you frequently visit the strip clubs here in Dallas. Is that right?"

"Your Honor! Please direct the defendant to answer the question asked."

"Ms. Rossi, don't be smart and don't answer a question with a question."

"Yes, Your Honor. While I enjoy golf, I'm competitive, and I hate to lose, so I rarely play golf with a client or a man with whom I am negotiating a deal. I made a connection with the governor long before the video you just showed. He likes me, and I may have flirted with him. I doubt he would say I seduced him, and I wouldn't say I did either, since there was no sex in his room."

I looked at the jury. She may have pulled it off. I wasn't sure the jurors were buying what Gina had said, but I thought a couple of the women may have been offended by Daniels' implication that Gina had seduced the governor. Daniels was on the right track, but he made stupid assumptions that enabled Gina to answer his questions truthfully.

"Ms. Rossi, let's summarize. You were served with a subpoena to testify before the grand jury, right?"

"Yes."

"You refused to testify, right?"

"Yes, I refused to testify until my client agreed I could testify."

"Judge Parsons ordered you to testify, is that correct?"

"That's correct, but I believed his decision was wrong and I appealed his decision to a higher court. You refused to let the court rule, and instead indicted me and that's why I am here today."

"You ignored Judge Parsons' order, and refused to provide testimony that may have exonerated your client and Governor Harrington, isn't that true?"

"I followed my conscience and my understanding of my ethical obligations to my client. I did not testify until he gave me permission to in this trial."

"And, Judge Parsons held you in contempt of court, isn't that true?"

"Only because he would not let me appeal his decision, first."

Jason Daniels looked like a debate moderator who asked questions that were never fully answered. Gina and I had practiced "bridging," which means she used his questions to bridge into what she wanted to convey to the jury. I wasn't sure she had succeeded, but I was sure Daniels was pissed off. More important, Daniels so far had not asked Gina about her escort experience in Las Vegas.

"Ms. Rossi, I have just one more area to cover."

Gina looked at me. She looked like she was holding her breath.

Breathe Gina. Breathe.

"Ms. Rossi, are you a member of the Ashley Madison adultery dating website?"

"I immediately objected. "May we approach the bench?'

"Yes, counsel."

When we stood in front of Judge Rose, I whispered.

"Your Honor. Ms. Rossi's membership on the Ashley Madison website is irrelevant and extremely prejudicial. May we continue this argument in your chambers, so the jurors and audience don't hear it?"

"Yes, Ms. Sanchez, all right."

Ten minutes later we were in Judge Rose's chambers.

"Your Honor, are you aware of Ashley Madison?"

"Is that the website for adults that was hacked a couple of years ago?"

"Yes. Ms. Rossi's membership has nothing to do with the charges against her and Mr. Daniels is seeking to question her about it to prejudice the jurors against her. She is entitled to her privacy."

"Mr. Daniels, how does Ms. Rossi's membership with this Ashley Madison site have anything to do with her refusal to testify before your grand jury?"

"Your Honor, we believe the real reason Ms. Rossi did not want to testify is because she did not want her secret Ashley Madison life to become public. We are entitled to explore that."

"Your Honor, we both know that is a bogus argument. Ms. Rossi is testifying in this trial. If she had been afraid of her Ashley Madison membership becoming public, she would have declined to testify. Since the breach Ashley Madison has beefed up its privacy protection. You might ask Mr. Daniels, whether the government hacked Ms. Rossi's computer and discovered her membership, or if not, how does Mr. Daniels know about her membership."

"Mr. Daniels, did the government hack into Ms. Rossi's computer?"

Daniels looked away. The man was getting ready to lie to Judge Rose.

"Your Honor, I received the information as an anonymous tip. I have no idea who told us about Ms. Rossi's participation on the Ashley Madison website."

"Mr. Daniels, based on Ms. Rossi's expectation of privacy, and your lack of knowledge of who provided you with the information, I am going to sustain Ms. Sanchez's objection. I do not want to hear the words Ashley Madison again in this trial, nor do I want any further questions about Ms. Rossi's sex life. Do you understand?"

"Yes, Your Honor."

"Let's go back in the courtroom and call the jury back in."

As we walked back into the courtroom, I looked where Tony Rossi had been sitting. He was gone.

Jason Daniels asked two more questions. When he finished his cross-examination of Gina, I looked at the jury to determine whether they disliked Daniels or Gina more. I decided they disliked Daniels more, and when Judge Rose asked if I had any redirect examination, I decided to leave well enough alone.

"Ms. Sanchez, you may call your next witness."

"Your Honor, that's all we have. The Defense rests."

"Mr. Daniels, do you have any additional evidence you want to present?'

I held my breath as I waited to hear his answer. If he advised Judge Rose he wanted to present additional evidence, I was afraid he would bring up Gina's secret life in Las Vegas.

So, I was relieved when Jason Daniels said, "Your Honor, we have no further evidence to present." I seriously felt like we had dodged a bullet.

"Ladies and gentlemen, both the Government and the Defense rest. We will take a break now to go over instructions I will give you. We'll reconvene in the morning and Mr. Daniels will make the Government's final argument followed by Ms. Sanchez and then finally, Mr. Daniels will have a chance to make a final argument. Remember, do not discuss the case with each other or with anyone outside of the courtroom."

As we walked out of the courtroom, the reporters gathered and pushed microphones at both of us.

"Gina, are you a member of Ashley Madison?"

"Are you cheating on your husband?"

"What do you think the jury will do?" a reporter yelled while being pushed into me.

I pushed forward without answering. I didn't want my opinions aired on news that night.

"Gina, were you just trying to be a martyr?"

To my surprise, she stopped to respond. I reached for her arm, but she pulled away.

"Sir, that is an insult not just to me, but to the legal profession in the United States. You most clearly don't have a clue about ethics in our profession, and you must be stupid to think I would want to go through this ordeal with the chance of being sent to prison just to be a martyr. Ask me a question that doesn't demonstrate your total ignorance."

"Okay, why don't you tell us about your affair with Governor Harrison and how you were able to manipulate him into making the worst financial deal in Texas history?"

Gina turned to reply. This time I grabbed her arm and held on tight while she tried to get away from me.

"Keep walking Gina."

She turned back, and I grabbed her arm even tighter while forgetting what we might look like on TV that night.

"Gina, things are going well for us. You don't want to do anything to change that."

"But I didn't have an affair with Governor Harrington, and we can't let the press report that I did."

"Nothing you can say will change what they report. The media have people right now looking for your dating profile. The last thing you want the media to do is to investigate you any further."

"My Ashley Madison profile has been deleted."

"Don't count on that being sufficient."

When I got home and turned on the TV, sure enough, the trial was the lead story, and our walk through the reporters was a large part of the video. Over the evening, I flipped through the national cable news stations I knew were following the trial. Two of them featured so-called legal experts who had not sat in the courtroom but still offered the opinion, based on what they had heard, that Gina had been deceptive, and Judge Rose should have allowed Jason Daniels to question Gina on her Ashley Madison membership. The third cable news network featured a lawyer who believed the special counsel had no business prosecuting Gina in the first place, and that she had demonstrated through her testimony that she had good reason to refuse to testify.

I had prepared my final argument months ago, so I decided to go to bed early. But first, I called Gina Rossi.

"How is it going with Tony?"

"I asked him to make no judgments until the trial is over. Then we can talk about what happened."

"Was he willing to wait?"

"He reluctantly agreed we could talk about it after the trial. I am sure he will be hearing from his mother. I can only imagine what she will say about me."

"Will he come to court for the final arguments?"

"I don't know."

After hanging up, I got into bed. Going to bed was one thing; going to sleep was quite another.

CHAPTER 42

—— ◈ ——

Gabriela Sanchez

The FBI raid was terrible, but Jason Daniels had purposely attempted to destroy Gina's marriage, knowing his question about Ashley Madison was improper. I was seriously angry, and I shifted my priorities from just successfully defending Gina Rossi, and attacking the morning raid of her house, to persuading the jury to hate Jason Daniels. And I was pretty sure I could do it.

The next morning, Mario dropped us off in front of the courthouse. Once again there were video cameras, microphones, and reporters shouting questions, along with protestors whose signs featured Gina's photo and Ashley Madison. I pushed ahead and pulled Gina along behind me, while protestors screamed at her. Once we went through security, we entered the courtroom together. Gina stared for a moment at a woman sitting quietly in the audience.

"Excuse me, Gabriela," she said. "I helped Gloria Ramirez when I was in prison. Let me introduce you."

I walked with Gina to the third row.

"Gloria, ¿*Cómo está?*"

She stood and hugged Gina. *"Muy bien gracias."*

Gina looked at me. "*Le presento a Gabriela Sanchez. Es mi abogada.*"
"*Mucho gusto, Señorita.*"

Gloria hugged Gina again,. Tears ran down her cheeks.

I looked around the courtroom. Leo Baretti and Sam sat in the first row, but Tony was not in the front row seat he had occupied throughout the trial.

Will any jurors wonder why Tony is not here? Do any jurors know what Ashley Madison is?

"Ladies and gentlemen, Mr. Daniels will make a presentation to you. Then Ms. Sanchez will respond, and Mr. Daniels will get one final chance to rebut what Ms. Sanchez has told you. Before you retire to the jury room, I will explain the law governing this case to you."

Judge Rose had instructed the jury that to convict Gina Rossi of contempt, they must conclude that she willfully intended to violate the order that she testify, and that the crime was committed willfully if it was done voluntarily and intentionally, and not by "accident, mistake, or other innocent reason."

She hurt us with that instruction. I would not be allowed to argue that Gina's refusal to testify was because of any wrongdoing by Daniels, the Special Counsel's office, or the FBI. I was not happy, but I also realized that during the 60-plus minutes she would spend explaining the law to the jury, most, if not all the jurors would have their minds on something else.

When I had defended Sparks Duval, my father, Roberto, gave me a crash course on the attention span of jurors. He told me when he grew up, TV commercials were typically one minute long. Later, they became 30 seconds long, and now usually just 15 seconds long. His point was that our attention spans had been shrinking for years.

He showed me the transcript of a brilliant Clarence Darrow final argument in the Sweet trial. Darrow stood and argued for seven hours. I could hardly imagine that.

My father told me to speak for no longer than 20 minutes, about the length of a TED Talk, then hope Jason Daniels would drone on forever. My argument would not be any longer than 20 minutes.

"Mr. Daniels, you may address the jury now."

Jason Daniels rose to speak. As I expected, he was wearing the same dark charcoal gray suit he had worn for the final argument in the Duval case. He wore a white shirt and a red tie.

"Thank you, Your Honor. Ladies and gentlemen, Judge Rose has given us each three hours to present what we believe the evidence shows. As she explained. I have two opportunities to use my three hours, and Ms. Sanchez will speak to you in between my time.

"I noticed some of you grimaced when I mentioned three hours. I understand. I normally glance at my watch several times keeping track of my time, but this case is simple. It's easy to understand. I won't take nearly three hours to explain why you must convict the defendant, Gina Rossi.

"Before I get to that, I want to thank you for your service. Our system of justice in the United States depends on people, like you sacrificing to serve on a jury. So, thank you.

"But our system of justice in the United States also depends on people, like the defendant, Gina Rossi, who testify when they receive a subpoena, people testifying when the court orders them to, testifying to help determine the guilt or innocence of people under investigation.

"If there ever was a cut and dried case, this is the one. Gina Rossi was ordered by a federal judge to testify before a grand jury, she refused.

That's the end of the story. No more needs to be told to prove she is guilty of criminal contempt."

I thought he might stop there since he had made his point, but Daniels continued.

"The defendant, Gina Rossi, refused to testify even after she had been ordered by a federal judge to do so, not because she was concerned about the lawyer-client privilege, but rather because she wanted to help her client and the former governor get away with something secret that she knew about because of the legal work she did for Burke Construction and Randall Burke.

"When Ms. Sanchez and I are finished, you will hear from Judge Rose about the law. One thing she will instruct you is you can disregard all of a witness's testimony if you find any part of it untruthful. You don't have to pick out the defendant's lies and consider the rest."

I was waiting for Daniels to explain what he considered to be Gina's lie, but he never did.

"Ladies and gentlemen, Gina Rossi was a smart-aleck witness. She didn't take this proceeding seriously, and more important, she didn't take you seriously. You can disregard everything she said because of her flippant responses to my questions."

That was it. I stood up. "Your Honor, Mr. Daniels is stretching the instruction. There is nothing in your jury instruction about a smart-aleck witness or flippant responses, and I assert that you advised Mr. Daniels to improve his questions if he wanted better answers."

"Mr. Daniels, I agree with Ms. Sanchez. If you want to use the instruction, you must assert what you believe Ms. Rossi testified that was a lie."

I smiled. Daniels was always overreaching, and this was a clear overreach.

"Ladies and gentlemen of the Jury. You saw the video. Governor Harrington's hands were all over Ms. Rossi. Isn't it reasonable to conclude they were having an affair?"

I stood again. "Your Honor, there is zero evidence that Governor Harrington and Gina Rossi were having an affair. It's as reasonable to conclude that the former governor was sexually harassing Gina Rossi as it is to conclude they were having an affair."

I had made my point, and at the least the women jurors got it. A few minutes later, Daniels finally concluded.

"Ladies and gentlemen, Gina Rossi has denied us the opportunity to determine what happened in the Hill Country Estates partnership and in the Cross-Town Tollway contract. She must now pay the price. You must find her guilty. Our system of justice in the United States depends on it."

CHAPTER 43

Gabriela Sanchez

I had begun preparing for my final argument the day Gina was arrested. I had typed and retyped every word as I added, deleted, and edited. I had gone over what I wanted to say, how I wanted to say it, and what I wanted to emphasize over and over again. I had practiced giving the final argument in front of a mirror. I had practiced in front of a video camera. I was prepared to deliver the argument that would convince the jury to find Gina Rossi not guilty.

If I could avoid it, I would have no notes, not even my iPad at the lectern while delivering my final argument. I once heard a famous trial lawyer say that lawyers who are not prepared need notes.

I thought about what Judge Comstock had told me back when I was his clerk. After a lawyer had given a final argument, he said the lawyer had looked and sounded like he was giving a lecture to the jury. I agreed. Judge Comstock told, "speak to the jurors as if you are having a conversation. If you have been authentic throughout the trial, and demonstrated that you genuinely care about your client, you will succeed."

I thought back to my conversation with my father back when he took me to the airport that first day I met with Gina Rossi. I had told him that based on what I'd heard, I wasn't sure I liked her. I thought about his response. "You don't need to like her. If liking a client was important, I would have had very few clients over the years."

I was still not sure whether I liked Gina Rossi, but I genuinely cared about her. In spite of terrible instruction Judge Rose would be giving the jury, I believed what the government had done to her was wrong, and I hoped that the judge would not stop me from bringing up the FBI raid and I hoped the jury would trust me and decide what the government had done from the beginning to this very day was wrong.

As I walked to the lectern, I looked back. Gloria Ramirez sat quietly in the third row, and her eyes met mine. I turned again and caught my father's eye. He nodded from the last row of the benches. He must have flown up from McAllen early that morning. Tony Rossi was seated in the front row just behind Gina. I nodded and Gina turned toward her husband.

I took a deep breath and began. "Ladies and gentlemen, I want you to use your imagination for a moment. You and your spouse and your children are sitting at your table eating breakfast. Suddenly, without any warning, there is a knock on your door. When you answer, a dozen FBI agents with drawn automatic assault weapons barge into your house with a search warrant, terrifying you, your husband or wife, and worst of all your children, who will forever see that image in their nightmares."

As expected, Jason Daniels was on his feet. "Your Honor, I object. The execution of the search warrant has nothing to do with whether the defendant is guilty or innocent of obstruction of justice and criminal contempt. Ms. Sanchez is trying to get around the instruction you will give the jury on the law of this case."

"Mr. Daniels, I'm going to allow it. You may continue, Ms. Sanchez."

"I know that all of you remember in May of 2011, when the SEAL Team Six killed Osama Bin Laden. There were fewer SEALs on the mission to capture or kill the world's leading terrorist than the number of FBI agents sent to terrorize Gina Rossi, her husband and son."

I wasn't 100 percent sure that was true, but I had made my point.

"Mr. Daniels and his team of automatic assault weapon toting FBI agents weren't seeking the truth. They wanted to intimidate Gina Rossi to the point where she would tell them what they wanted to indict our former Governor Harrington and his friend, Randall Burke.

"Judge Rose will tell you that to convict Ms. Rossi of contempt, you must conclude that she willfully intended to violate the court order that she testify. The crucial word is willfully. Judge Rose will tell you that a crime is committed willfully if it is done voluntarily and intentionally, and not by accident, mistake or other innocent reason.

"Let's explore "other innocent reason," and what that means.

"I once watched a TV police show a few years ago. I think it was the one starring Tom Selleck. I'm trying to think of the name of the show."

One of the jurors spoke up, "It's *Blue Bloods*."

"Yes, that's it, *Bluebloods*. In the episode, I remember that a man had raced into a Catholic church, found a priest and made a confession. When the police confronted the priest during their investigation, the conflicted priest refused to break the seal of confession that might have helped the police find a missing boy.

"Well, under our law, a spouse cannot be compelled to testify against a husband or wife. Communications between a husband and wife are presumed to be confidential, and for that reason they are privileged.

"Ladies and gentlemen, the attorney-client privilege is as sacred in our judicial system as the priest's seal of confession or the spousal communication privilege. The attorney-client privilege affords an invaluable and vital right to a client to have his communications with his lawyer protected from compelled disclosure to any third party, including a grand jury. Gina Rossi upheld that lawyer-client privilege - and that was her innocent reason referred to in law. Judge Parsons and Jason Daniels put Gina between a rock and a hard place. They refused to allow her to appeal Judge Parsons' ruling that she would be required to testify. The only way she could appeal was to be held in contempt of court."

I paused for a moment and looked at each juror.

"Then, before her appeal could be heard, Jason Daniels persuaded a grand jury to indict Gina. Then, Jason Daniels sent the FBI in protective vests, with drawn, loaded, automatic assault weapons and night-vision equipment to terrorize the Rossi family."

I expected Jason Daniels to jump to his feet objecting. When he didn't, I paused again to make sure the jurors were following me.

"When her client, Randall Burke, waived the privilege so she could tell you what happened, Gina testified, and I'm sure you noticed that Mr. Daniels was unable to lay a glove on her. So, he showed you a video of Governor Harrington placing his hand on her and tried to convince you that Gina was having an affair with him.

"Ladies and gentlemen, instead of sitting here as a defendant," I turned and looked back at Gina. "Gina Rossi should be applauded for upholding the lawyer-client privilege. You and I would want our lawyer to represent us and keep our conversations private.

"You've heard the evidence. Now it's your turn. This is a countdown to justice. You won't be able to take the fear away from Gina Rossi's son. But, you are able to send his mother home to him. Gina Rossi and her family have been waiting for you to do justice and send a message to Washington."

I turned and walked back to the counsel table. My father nodded at me and clapped silently. When I sat down, Gina Rossi grabbed my hand.

Jason Daniels delivered his rebuttal in a short time. After he finished and Judge Rose spent two hours explaining the law to the jury, we were finally able to walk out of the courtroom.

CHAPTER 44

━━━━━ ✌ ━━━━━

Gina Rossi

Tony didn't say one word all the way home. When we arrived back home, Mateo was still in school. I opened up the conversation.

"I'm sorry."

"Are you sorry for what you did, or are you sorry you got caught?"

I knew what I should say, but I didn't regret what I had done.

"I'm sorry that you had to learn about it, and I embarrassed you."

"I knew you were doing something."

"How did you know?"

"Because you stopped pestering me for more. I figured you found another way to deal with your urges."

"Why didn't you say something to me?"

"Because I was okay with it as long as it was private."

"Why were you okay with it?"

"Because I love you and I know you do not manage your impulses."

"I don't have impulses. I can stop anything."

"Gina, how many times have you sat at a poker or blackjack table and played for more 12 hours, or 18 hours, all night without sleep?"

"I don't know, but I haven't done that in years. I have gambling under control."

"And you believe you have drinking under control?"

"I can stop any time. I have stopped many times."

"Gina, I don't want to argue with you."

"Then stop arguing and acting like I have all kinds of problems."

"I love you, and I want you to control your urges. You need to see a doctor and find out what is going on in your brain."

"I visited a doctor shortly after my mother died. The doctor said I was hyperactive and gave me pills that made me drowsy. I quit taking them."

"You are not driven to have sex, gamble and drink alcohol because you are hyperactive. There's more to it. Mateo may be hyperactive, but something more is influencing his behavior. I talked to a friend who is both a lawyer and a psychologist. She recommended a doctor who is the leading specialist in Dallas. I want you to see him. I want Mateo to see him."

"The jury must declare I am not guilty first."

"Even if the jury finds you guilty, you need to see him before Judge Rose sentences you."

"Have you talked to your mother?"

"She's called me several times. I haven't answered because I know what she will say."

"Okay."

"Will you promise to see the doctor?"

"I promise, but I don't need his help."

The jury was out the rest of the day and the next day. Gabriela said the jury may be wrestling with whether I refused to testify for an innocent reason. We proved my refusal to testify was for an innocent reason - because Randall Burke asserted the lawyer-client privilege"

On the third day, Gabriela called. "Judge Rose called me. The jury has reached a verdict on one count, and they are unable to reach a unanimous verdict on the other."

"What do you think that means?" I asked.

"If the jury can't reach a unanimous verdict on the obstruction count, we are in trouble. If the jury can't reach a unanimous verdict on the contempt count, we won."

"Gabriela, please explain."

"Jason Daniels believes the contempt count is a slam dunk. Judge Parsons ordered you to testify, and you refused. Daniels believes the obstruction count was more difficult to prove. So, if the jury can't reach a verdict on the contempt count, that would mean they found you not guilty on the obstruction count."

"What would happen if that is the case?"

"They could re-try you for contempt. I don't believe they will do that given the public outrage over your arrest and the trial."

One hour later we were sitting in court.

Judge Rose addressed the jury. "Ladies and gentlemen, you have informed me that you have reached a verdict on one count and cannot reach a verdict on the second. Is that correct?"

A middle-aged woman rose from the first seat. "Yes, Your Honor, that is correct."

"Are you the foreperson of the jury?"

"Yes, Your Honor."

"Are you certain you cannot reach a verdict on one of the two counts?"

"Yes, Your Honor."

Gabriela grabbed my hand signaling that was a good sign.

"Please hand the verdict you have reached to the Deputy Marshal. I want to see it."

The Deputy Marshal took the verdict form from the juror and handed it to Judge Rose. She looked it over for what seemed like too long a time, then handed it down and said, "The Clerk will read the verdict, and the defendant will rise."

I could barely get to my feet. I couldn't breathe.

"United States versus Gina Rossi, Verdict: We the Jury find the defendant, Gina Rossi, not guilty as to Count II of the indictment, Obstruction of Justice, dated March 29, 2019, signed Louise Lancaster, foreperson."

I gasped.

"Ladies and gentlemen, you are excused. Thank you for your service."

I hugged Gabriela. I turned and hugged Tony too, and then my father. He smiled. We all smiled. I looked over at Jason Daniels. He was shaking his hand. I wanted to tell him he had kept his perfect record because he was now zero and three in his Texas trials.

Gabriela walked over and extended her hand to him, but he turned away and gathered his materials off the desk.

When I had first learned Gabriela Sanchez was my lawyer, I had questioned whether she was smart enough, experienced enough, and tough enough to defend me. Gabriela had proven to be smart, experienced, tough – and more.

CHAPTER 45

❧

Gina Rossi

After the trial, local and cable newscasters asked me to appear for interviews. They asked me questions about Ashley Madison. I spent my 15 minutes of fame advocating for prison reform. To make that the point of the interview I asked Gloria Ramirez to appear with me.

I was even invited to testify before Congress. The Senate Judiciary Committee wanted to hear my views on prison reform. The House Judiciary Committee wanted to grill me on what I knew about Austin Harrington and why I had refused to testify.

Four weeks later, I was sitting in Dr. Ken Rosenburg's waiting area. It was my second visit. At 10:00 a.m. His assistant escorted into an office. After I'd waited several minutes, Dr. Rosenburg came in and said, "Ms. Rossi, I think I understand why you were driven to succeed, while at the same time you were driven to engage in risky behavior."

I wasn't buying it. "Doctor, I'm not looking for an excuse for any of my so-called risky behavior."

"I'm not trying to give you an excuse. I'm simply helping you to understand yourself. When you were a child, a doctor diagnosed you as hyperactive. Today we call it ADHD. A doctor has diagnosed Mateo diagnosed as having ADHD. Your diagnosis was wrong, and your son's diagnosis may also be wrong."

"Then, what is your diagnosis, Doctor?"

"I believe you are hypomanic, and that is different."

"Hypomanic, what is that?"

"Hypomania is a mild form of mania, but it is not an illness. Instead, it is a temperament. Hypomanics have the "ups" of manic depression, but not the "downs." You've told me that it's not unusual for you to feel abnormally upbeat and jumpy for days at a time. If you felt depressed after the upbeat days, you'd be bipolar. People with your condition are ultra-confident and believe nothing is impossible. They love life and are full of energy. They require little sleep, they are uninhibited, and they think they can conquer the world."

"Is that a bad thing?"

"It can be, but some of the most successful people in America are hypomanic."

"Really?"

"Think about the immigrants who risked everything to come to America. Think about the inventors, the visionaries, the entrepreneurs who see something others miss and throw all their energy into achieving it."

I started feeling better about myself.

"There's a downside to being hypomanic. Just as it drives people like you to achieve great things, it also drives them to take risks, and even do foolish or dangerous things without thinking about the consequences. When you were young, you likely got in trouble at school because you were full of energy, impulsive, and easily bored. Does that describe you?"

"Yes. Teachers bored me in school, and I could never settle down. How did I get this condition?"

"I'm certain you inherited it."

"You think my mother was hypomanic?"

"I don't know. If your mother had some of the traits I described, she might have been."

For the first time, I understood why some of my behavior was out of control, and why Tony had nagged me to not act on snap decisions and on impulse. When I was young, I knew I was different. I thought it was because I was being raised by a widowed father and a stern grandmother who didn't get along with each other.

My hypomanic condition had both driven me to succeed in law, and also led me to think I was invincible and that the rules didn't apply to me. I'm sure this contributed to my successful negotiation of the Cross-Town Tollway contract, and my later incarceration and trial for refusing to testify.

"Is there any treatment we can implement that will help me avoid compulsions but not cause me to be lethargic?"

"We can treat your mania with mood stabilizers that will reduce the symptoms of mania. You also need to get eight hours of sleep a night."

As I left the doctor's office, I became certain I had inherited hypomania from my mother. Even though I never had the chance to talk to her, I understood her and myself better than ever before.

I wanted, I should say needed, to learn more about myself, if for no other reason so I could help Mateo navigate his future. I would start on the mood stabilizer medicine, but only if it didn't change my energy and drive.

When I got home, I told Tony about Doctor Rosenburg's findings and his recommendations. And after I put Mateo to bed, I called Grandma Mary.

"Grandma did my mother get in trouble in school?"

"No, I didn't let her get in trouble. She was smart as a whip and, like you, she was full of energy. I kept her focused on her schoolwork and tennis."

"Did she thrive on only a few hours of sleep?"

"Yes, she slept only four or five hours a night."

When the trial was over, I decided to leave the Roberson Grant law firm. Allen O'Grady smiled and looked me in the eye for the first time in years. I joined my father's firm, with the express condition that I would be fighting for women in prison.

Over the last several months I have been on the lecture tour. I make presentations at universities, law schools, and on YouTube. I speak about the difference between success and fulfillment. I believe about one-half of what I say. I tell students that I spent several years trying to prove I was a top-notch lawyer. I wanted recognition and attention. *I still do.*

I may have achieved at least some of that, but I was never satisfied – never content. I needed more. Now, I am less focused on what I want to achieve, or at least I'm less stressed out about it. I still want more.

Tony and I went through a tough time after the trial. His mother harassed him to leave me. He told me he had known about my Ashley Madison account. When I pressed him, he refused to tell me how he had found out. One good thing about Silva's harassment is that at least for the foreseeable future, I am not invited to the Rossi home in League City. That may be awkward, but so far, I'm not complaining.

We sold our house. It was bigger than we needed, and I hated paying for the pool service. After months of dealing with protests in front of our house I assumed the neighbors were happy to see us go. We didn't know many of them, in part because people came home entered their garage from an alley in the back and rarely spent time in the front yard.

We moved into a smaller home now in a neighborhood where the children are outside playing, and parents meet for coffee. I'm happy with my new life and forever grateful that Gabriela Sanchez fought for me.

I always feared I would be forever under my father's giant shadow if I joined his law firm. That may have been true in the past, but no more-he's easing toward retirement and now I'm taking over. It's my turn and I'm jumping right on it.

CPSIA information can be obtained
at www.ICGtesting.com
Printed in the USA
BVHW071012170521
607542BV00002B/129